Praise for *Gajarah*

"Somia Sadiq has written not just a book, but a *banquet*; not just a story, but a *feast*, filled with delicious language, tasting love and pain, seared in the fire of war and loss, and softened in the water of peace and forgiveness. When we are surrounded by so much hatred and hostility toward immigrants, Sadiq reminds us of what travelers bring—the gift of cultures that are different from our own, and stories that connect us, and make us human."

—Kenneth Cloke, author of *The Dance of Opposites* and *The Magic in Mediation*

"*Gajarah* by Somia Sadiq is a lush, rich, and sometimes dark descent into the life of its heroine, Emahn. Through intoxicating poetry, prose, and lyrical passages, Sadiq guides readers across continents and through the many iterations of Emahn's life—each marked by trauma, healing, and the quiet, difficult work of forgiveness.

This novel is both a psychological and emotional gut punch, inviting readers to relate, connect, and reflect—regardless of background. *Gajarah* reveals the universal threads that allow us to heal: the need for persistence, the power of connection, and the deep, often overlooked healing that emerges through a reconnection with culture.

More than a novel, *Gajarah* is a journey through survival and softness, grief and grace. It's a testament to the quiet strength of Emahn and the enduring power of story, memory, and identity. This is a book that lingers—haunting and healing in equal measure—long after the final page."

—Dr. R. Abdulrehman, clinical psychologist and author of *Developing Anti-Racist Cultural Competence*, *Jinn in the Family* (forthcoming), and *The Poetry of Angry Black and Brown People* (forthcoming)

"*Gajarah* is a fierce and tender ode to the strength of women and the power of community. With raw honesty, Sadiq weaves vibrant storytelling with lyrical grace to create a story that settles deep in your bones—haunted by sorrow and pain, lit by identity and survival, and held together by a shared humanity that binds us all."
—Sara Davidson, registered psychotherapist and author of *Any Body Can Heal*

"In Somia Sadiq's rich literary novel, *Gajarah*, a Pakistani woman reclaims her story after violence . . . Objects assume a powerful role in the story throughout, becoming focal points for Emahn's memories. Sumptuous fabrics, dishware, and bangle bracelets are featured, used to convey both longing for home and Emahn's feelings of displacement in Canada. When she turns toward humanitarian work in her adulthood, it prompts her to muse on the meaning of forgiveness and who holds the power to bestow it."
—*Foreword* Clarion Reviews

"Somia Sadiq takes the reader on a wonderfully intertwined journey of emotions and memories, full of colours and smells that bring these memories alive. It is a powerful telling of the cultural, social, and psychological roots of her choice to heal and, through that healing, make a positive difference in the world."
—Susan Hartley, PhD, psychologist and editor *of Global Voices for Peace: An Introduction to Peacebuilders and the Hope They Bring*

"Fascinating and worthy of book club discussion . . . Thoroughly engrossing and hard to put down, *Gajarah* depicts a journey well worth the time taken to walk in this woman's shoes and navigate her life."
—Midwest Book Review

GAJARAH

GAJARAH

a novel

SOMIA SADIQ

This is a work of fiction. Names, characters, organizations, places, events, and incidents are either products of the author's imagination or are used fictitiously.

Copyright © 2025 by Somia Sadiq

All rights reserved.

No part of this book may be reproduced, or stored in a retrieval system, or transmitted in any form or by any means, electronic, mechanical, photocopying, recording, or otherwise, without express written permission of the publisher.

Published by GFB™, Seattle
www.girlfridayproductions.com

Produced by Girl Friday Productions

Design: Paul Barrett
Development & editorial: Diana Rico
Production editorial: Reshma Kooner
Project management: Kristin Duran

Image credits: cover © iStock/kool99 (cloth), Narratives (illustration)

ISBN (paperback): 978-1-964721-88-0
ISBN (ebook): 978-1-964721-89-7

Library of Congress Control Number: 2025908003

First edition

*To the little girl
who ran before she walked,
steps defying the rhythm of the world,
singing before she talked,
her voice a melody
strung from the threads of resilience.*

*To the little girl
ripped from home yet clinging to the dirt,
learning to survive before she could live,
the weight of absence, held in her tiny hands
like a fragile ember, nurturing it,
feeding it, moulding it, taming it
into a flame despite the shadows.*

*To the little girl, my little girl,
your strength, your song,
your laughter, your beauty,
your big, big heart,
broken, and mended a million times.*

*To the little girl, my little girl,
may your journey remind us
it is in the hardest of soils,
that wildflowers bloom.
It's in the darkest of depths, the loneliest of nooks
when the world goes silent,
chatter, questions, hurts and all,
that you find yourself.*

*To the little girl, my little girl,
know that I carry you, all of you,
in love, in care, in admiration,
in adoration, in awe,
in power.*

Humans in this book survive rape, sexual abuse, domestic violence, misogyny, bigotry, racism, sexism, lateral violence, Islamophobia, terrorism, internalized oppression, gender-based violence, self-harm, loss of a child, disconnection from land and culture, war, and poverty.

The Becoming

Survival is easy,
instinctual,
from deep within,
uninvited, unwelcome even.
Rising in our bones,
muscles, souls,
no matter how tired or weary.

Survival is easy.
To channel it, though,
all of it,
that rage, that agony,
that scraping, raw, soul-scratching pain,
into beauty,
into love, acceptance,
believing.
That, that, that
is the mountain I stand at the feet of.

Prologue

I get on all fours and crawl inside. Elder Mayra has explained the sacredness of the rocks, what it means to be in the sweat lodge, that it'll be as if we're all floating in our mothers' wombs. That thought comforts me, warms me, hugs me. Instinctually, my hand goes to my belly, and I silently honour my little one, my Zoya, now resting in the spirit world.

Elder Mayra tells us there will be four rounds in the ceremony. In the first round, we will all introduce ourselves and prepare ourselves physically, mentally, and spiritually for the ceremony. She looks at me and says I can introduce myself in my language if I feel comfortable. Her smile is ever so kind. I nod but also know that I'm not brave enough to speak my language in front of those who don't know it, understand it, or feel it.

Language is powerful that way, carrying a life of its own.

I adore Elder Mayra. When I'm feeling brave, I even call her Mama Mayra, and it always makes her smile. Her daughter Jane is my good friend. Mama Mayra reminds me of Naano jaan, my maternal grandmother. My heart warms at the fleeting thought of Naano jaan and Mama Mayra meeting each other someday. They would have so much to laugh about.

The second round, Mama Mayra explains, will be about expressing gratitude and seeking healing. The third round will allow us, encourage us, nudge us to reflect more deeply, and continue to express gratitude. The fourth round will be to seek guidance and clarity, and express gratitude for the opportunity to heal.

I appreciate the intentional expression of gratitude in each round. Naano jaan always used to say that we must learn to not just *be* thankful, but to also express it so we can hear it, not just in our hearts but in our voices. And that to do so is to heal.

I understand that now. I didn't back then.

To practise gratitude, we must accept that we are not complete, we are not perfect, that we are like one thread that requires other threads, other colours, textures, feels, voices to become a piece of fabric.

Acknowledging everything else that makes us whole is gratitude.

Once inside the sweat lodge, I make my way around, starting on the left, moving clockwise so others can enter and we can complete the circle.

Elder Mayra's helper brings the rocks in and closes the door, and I feel my anxiety rising. I can't quite explain why. Confined spaces, perhaps?

Fffff: I pull a deep breath in through my nose, trying to calm my nerves. *Pffff:* I slowly exhale through my lips.

Mama Mayra said that when we enter the lodge, we invite our ancestors to join us. And I know my ancestors have always walked with me, watched over me. Could they be here? Would I sense them?

Sigh.

Before my mind gets ahead of me, I take another deep breath in, close my eyes, and tell myself to stay with it. That it will be okay.

Elder Mayra pours water over the hot rocks. The hiss, the sizzle, the crackle, the rising steam, the ever-so-slight echo in the dome shape of the sweat lodge come together in an invitation to breathe, to acknowledge where we are, and to be present.

So, I do. I breathe. Deeply.

Ffff. Pfff.

As we begin the first round, Elder Mayra invites us to introduce ourselves and share why we enter the ceremony today. When it is my turn, Elder Mayra holds my gaze as if urging me to speak in my language, but I can't muster the courage. I look down, embarrassed at having disappointed her, and quietly say my name, and acknowledge the names of my ancestors. Lowering my voice further, I whisper, "I . . .

um... don't have an intention... but. Naano jaan, Daada jaani, Daado jaan, please watch over me?" And more quietly yet, I add, "I want to be in reverence of this ceremony Mama Mayra has invited me to, so help me, okay?"

Elder Mayra picks up her hand drum. The first strike feels like a bold call to wake up and embrace the sacredness of the ritual, the sacredness of the lodge. As she starts singing, her voice courses through me in all its beauty. It is strength, resilience, power, humility, curiosity, plea, permission, all beautifully wrapped into one melody. My heart finds the beat of the drum, grabs it quietly, pulls it into my being, and soon my heart and Mama Mayra's drum seem to become one.

Elder Mayra sings two more songs, each lifting me higher, making me feel lighter. In between songs, she adds a little bit of sage to the rocks, followed by a little bit of water.

The round ends several minutes later, and we all step outside.

Mama Mayra grabs a chair by the opening of the lodge and gestures to me to come sit on the ground beside her chair.

"Thank you, Mama Mayra, for inviting me...."

She reaches out and touches my hair. And as if she didn't even hear me, she says, "You know, my girl, someone tells me your hair was too short to braid. It seems long now. I'm going to braid it; come."

She nudges me to sit in front of her as she braids. I don't know how to respond or what to do. No one has touched my hair with such tenderness since I was eleven. Suddenly, I am transported back to Naano jaan's rooftop, asking her, begging her, to braid it, begging her to put little jasmine flowers in it, and Naano jaan is saying I need to stop going to Baba jaani's barber to get my hair cut like a boy if I want braids.

I feel Naano jaan's laughter. The laughter of my aunties.

Oh, such beautiful laughter.

"All done, my girl." Mama Mayra turns me around and admires her work, smiling broadly. She has taken a small piece of red string from somewhere and tied the bottom of the braid, which she now flips over my shoulder, and it quietly lands on my chest. It's such a beautiful braid, and how can it not be? Anything created with love and tenderness is beautiful. I touch it, admiring the loosely woven strands brought together, binding my wild waves and curls into place, some wisps still rogue, of course, and smile.

"Thank you, Mama Mayra," I try to squeak out, holding back what feels like a mountain of emotions.

"Now, now, keep smiling that big smile, my girl, and let's go back inside," she urges.

We do another two rounds and I'm feeling lighter, somehow empowered by this braid. I tell myself that if I knew braids could make me feel this amazing, I would have stuck to braiding my hair all the time instead of letting it run wild. Or maybe it's the braid woven with Elder Mayra's magical voice, the medicines softly dancing on the rocks, that makes it all so special.

As we enter the lodge for the fourth round of the ceremony, Elder Mayra reminds us of the purpose of the round. This is about renewal, about emerging from the ceremony with purpose. I haven't really identified a question to seek clarity on other than to open my heart, open my mind, be present, honour the ceremony, honour my friends in the sweat, and honour Mama Mayra for all the teachings she has shared with us.

Mama Mayra adds the last of the stones, covers them in cedar, sage, tobacco, and sweetgrass, and pours water over it all. The aroma of all four medicines together encompasses me, quietly lifting me off the ground.

Suddenly I am walking through a field of daisies, delicate white petals with bright-yellow centres, and soft green stems. Something about the white, the yellow, and the green in harmony reminds me of home—the careful coming together of not very bold colours to start preparing us for bolder, more dramatic pairings every spring; the fuchsias, stunning deep purples, bright greens, and marigolds. My heart smiles, swaying with the light breeze that seems to kiss each of the flowers, inviting them to join in the dance of the wind.

They all seem to move as one, right to left to right to left.

And I find myself wanting to sway with them, but I must keep walking.

As I carefully move through the field, my eyes rest on a weeping willow. Its sturdy, gnarly trunk stands tall, resilient, having survived perhaps one too many storms, each one having left a mark in its textured bark.

They've always been my favourite trees, these willows; a symbol of grace, elegance, long thin branches draping down as if being pulled, being hugged closer to mother earth. I tell myself this is because mother earth wants to know what new stories the blowing wind has brought the willows, so she asks them to come closer so the willows can quietly whisper the stories to her.

As I step to the willow, I realise it is getting darker around me. The birds quiet down as if wanting to hear what is happening in the field. The sound of a critter or two reaches my ears at first, but then that disappears too.

My heart starts racing. I pick up my pace. I should get to the willow. Quickly.

The light keeps fading. I open my eyes wider, hoping they'll take in whatever light there is left . . . and suddenly there is complete silence. And then complete darkness.

I stop.

I can't see my hands.

"Hello?" Nothing. I take a step forward. If I keep walking, I'll reach the willow.

So, I walk.

And then I'm there. As my fingers touch the gnarly trunk, suddenly I hear, "Laachiye?"

Naano jaan? I hold my breath. It can't be. I don't blink.

"Laachiye? Idhar aa, puttar," she says softly. *"Come here, my little one."*

Carefully, I take another step.

"Naano jaan?"

And then I see her, the willow casting a graceful glow on her.

My eyes well up, and I run to her. I don't say a word. I want to, but nothing comes to me. I just cling to her, and my heart spills open like the skies after rumbling thunder. All those times I asked Naano jaan to help me cry seem to converge in this one moment as I weep.

She just holds me.

And then I'm laughing at the absurdity of her being there. I look up, wondering if this was all just an illusion. But it is indeed her. Before I can speak, she smiles the warm smile of hers that pulls every part of my being into her old soulful eyes.

"Laachiye, I'm here to ask you for something."

Anything. I would do anything for her. I nod, beaming.

"Remember how you used to find me spices and would drop them in the pot for me?"

I nod excitedly. Those were the best times of my life.

"Find me your happiest memories, Laachiye, and put them in a basket for me."

"But there are so many, Naano jaan! It will take me days!"

"You better start soon, then." She smiles.

I gather a bunch of random happy memories that come to mind and toss them in the basket. The basket fills right up, so I stop. There are so many more memories, but this will do. I look up.

"Merbaani, puttar. *Thank you, little one.*" Smiling, she nods approvingly. "Now, bring me your dreams, your visions for your life."

I frown, puzzled by this. There were so many, I don't know which one to pick. The one where I wanted to be an army doctor, the one where I wanted to be a pilot? Or maybe the one where I wanted to be an astronaut, or the one where I wanted to be a cardiologist? Oh, a singer, a poet? A writer? A surgeon, a chef? A zookeeper, an elephant keeper, a shepherd! I'm taking too long, and I worry Naano jaan will be disappointed, so I gather whatever comes to me and toss them in the second basket. It fills right up. I look up.

She is smiling. And her smile makes my heart dance on its tiptoes.

She looks at me deeply, trying to hold my excited gaze.

"Merbaani, puttar. Now, bring me your darkest memories."

My heart sinks.

I don't want Naano jaan to know my darkest memories. What if they hurt her? They're mine to keep tucked away where no one can find them. Ever.

I shake my head.

"You trust me, Laachiye?"

"Mmhmm."

"Chal fer," she urges. *"Go on, then."*

Reluctantly, I gather them, at least the ones I can remember, and I carefully put them in the third basket. The basket fills up. Worried it'll spill over, I stop. She gestures to me to keep going. As I gather more of my darkest memories and place them in the basket, it grows. I appreciate this. I wouldn't want them falling on the ground. I don't want to hurt anything their darkness may touch. When I think I have placed them all in, I stop.

I look up. Naano jaan's eyes are locked on mine. She walks over to me, holds my face in her hands, and tenderly kisses my forehead.

"Merbaani, puttar," she says, with the softness of a cool breeze on a hot summer day. *"Thank you, little one."*

"Now I have a gift for you. Your favourite thing in the whole world."

What is she talking about? *She* is my favourite thing in the whole world. There can't possibly be . . . And just as I am thinking about it, she holds out a gajarah, a flower bracelet, and my whole world lights up. It is the most beautiful gajarah I have ever seen in my life. It has white jasmine intertwined with three deep-crimson roses, little green leaves peeking out here and there. It is as if the flowers are all holding each other, protecting each other in a perfect little circle.

As Naano jaan slides the gajarah on my wrist, its touch is like that of a beautiful poem—mysterious, and inquisitive. Suddenly the daisies are back, the breeze is back, the birds are singing again, the little critters are chirping, and the sun is beaming down on us.

As I admire the gajarah on my wrist, feeling its strength, its beauty, its complicated yet simple construction—a beautiful harmony of jasmines, roses, and a thread binding it all together, I realise I am alone again. Naano jaan has left. But I know she is a part of me, in my tears and my laughter, in my mischief and my songs, and in this gajarah.

"Merbaani, Naano jaan."

As I emerge from the sweat lodge in my braid, I know the name of the book.

Gajarah.

I was taught that paradise lies at the feet of our mothers.

I walk over to Mama Mayra, touch both her feet, kiss her cheeks, and hold my hands together in gratitude. Between Mama Mayra and Naano jaan, they have gifted me with the strength to honour my daughter in my way—in the ways of my people, people who dwell in the fields of Punjab and the valleys of Kashmir. They have gifted me the strength to honour my daughter in story.

In songs.

In poems.

In power.

PART 1—MOTIA

Jasmine

The Threads Touching My Motia

Woven in my gajarah,
resting softly against my skin,
its scent rising with every breath I take,
a silent echo of another place.

Each petal, small and white,
carries the memory of my homeland,
its fragrance familiar,
like the soils once beneath my bare feet.

The flowers hold stories
of mornings filled with dew,
of hands that once gathered them
in courtyards far away.

Now, they circle my wrist,
binding my past and my present
in a connection I cannot undo,
a path I cannot return on.

Its scent journeys with the winds,
staying close to me,
carrying the essence of my home,
memories of distant fields,
sounds of soft rain on the rooftops,
the laughter of my aunties,
the banter of my baby cousins.

Though my journey is long,
the beauty of the motia remains.
An invisible thread pulling me back
to where the homeland blooms,
where the sun shines warmly.
To the land of stories,
songs and poems,
legends and folklore.

Motia

Jasmine

I imagine what it would be like if you ever came to the dahleez, the entrance, of my home.

I wouldn't know the intentions, the reasons, the callings that brought you there. Perhaps this is something we will discover together. But until I know, I'd honour you in the ways of my people, those that dwell in the fields of Punjab and in the valleys of Kashmir.

I'd show you with pride my red-brick home, a magical place, a place where time would sometimes stand still. A place of beauty in little things, beauty in little moments, gentle glimmers, beauty in colours, in smells, in sounds, in touch, in musical instruments, in words, in songs, in poetry, in dances. A place where the stars shine brighter in the sky, inviting you to dance with them, where the moonlight is warmer, where the sun is gentler, wrapping you in its glow so you can bask in its beauty.

You see, though, beauty is not beauty without darkness. As you enter my home, I'd also tell you, just so you know, just so you're prepared, that my home is also a place where there can sometimes be frightening firestorms and dark howling winds that bring bitter tastes; gnawing, agonising discomfort; suffocating truths that rise from deep within, churning you inside out; unacceptable realities; and unexplainable complexity.

I hope you'd see in my home a place where all these live together, sometimes in harmony, other times in confusion, but always in acceptance of each other.

In my home, every red brick and the gentle grey mortar in between, every quiet little nook, every curtain that hangs and sways in the breeze that flows through its hallways, every little ornate figurine, every clay pot—painted, unpainted, broken, and put back together—is a carrier of stories. My home is a place where stories are told, heard, held, and celebrated. I would show you around. It may take us days, months, years, or many lives to get through.

We'd enter my home together. At the arched wooden door, a deep, weathered espresso with intricate carvings like the designs of henna on the palms of a bride. As it opens, the door would creak, like a grandmother's achy bones as they settle into a new movement. Through the door, we'd walk into a courtyard bathing in soft morning light, warmed by the deep-red bricks, the red of our soils. Stunning fuchsias; rich yellow marigolds; deep greens of the forest; joyful, playful purples; striking blues of happy skies; gleaming golds and silvers tucked in fabrics, flowers, and lanterns would all welcome you.

These are, after all, my happy colours.

Story time in my home, though, would always be by the motia—the jasmine bush, lush and vibrant, rich with deep-green leaves and delicate white flowers, petals soft and star shaped, each one a tiny marvel. This motia would be a special place, a place I'd visit every morning at Fajr, with my tasbih, my prayer beads. Each time I'd roll a bead between my thumb and index finger, I'd convey my gratitude for the beauty in the world around me. Most days, the gratitude would be for the motia itself, its calming presence. Some days, it would be for the morning. Some days, it would be for the little birds that welcome the sun. Other days, it would be for the darkness of the night prior, for without it, the motia wouldn't attract the little pollinators it needs to bloom.

Motia has always been so mysterious to me. She lies awake as the rest of us sleep. In the darkness of the night, while some of us twist and turn with nightmares, she blooms, singing the melodies of her fragrance, inviting the little critters to her so they may share her pollen with others, so she may bear more flowers for us.

And we pluck these flowers with the rising sun, lovingly, with gratitude, braiding them in our hair, in our gajaray, in our teas, in our medicines, in our rituals, and in our stories.

It is magic, this motia.

We'd sit by the motia as I tell you a story. A story of a little girl born in a land far away. A story somewhere between truth and fiction, reality and imagination. A story with a king and a queen, a story where the two-spirited beings and the winds, the rivers, the stars and moons live in harmony. A story somewhere between the core of the earth and the depths of the cosmos.

Memories

As I touch them,
dissolving slowly,
the ink, the colours,
the tastes, the smells fading.
The depth wearing out,
textures flattening,
blurring, spreading.

Mixing like the sands of time,
playfully like the smells of spices
in a pot stirred lovingly,
patiently,
for hours, days, months, and years.

The memories that fill my stories are odd,
somewhere in between
what happened and what could have been,
what was said and unsaid,
felt and forgotten,
held, then let go,
remembered and told.

Pedaysh

Birth

It is 1983, a scorching summer afternoon in Sharjah, United Arab Emirates. The sun blazes fiercely, casting a stunningly deep marigold light over the bustling city. The streets hum with the sounds of life, cars moving steadily under the sweltering heat. The Asr Azaan echoes from a nearby mosque. Inside a hospital along the coast of the Arabian Gulf, cool air offers respite from the outside heat. Within the walls of the delivery room, a new chapter is about to begin for a young man from Punjab and his beautiful green-eyed bride from Kashmir, both far from the homeland that birthed them.

The delivery room is filled with a quiet hum, the occasional beeping of machines, and the gentle rustle of nurses moving efficiently and lightly on their feet.

As the spirits of the bride's matriarchal ancestors gather around her, preparing her, the moment finally arrives. A fiercely loud, strong, insistent cry breaks the stillness, announcing the arrival of a tiny brown person.

Stepping outside moments later to the father and the other men waiting outside the delivery room, the nurse announces, "Allah has gifted you a beautiful baby girl, my brother, and even better, she emerged with a smile on her face. It is like she has been here before. Your bride is doing well too. Please give us a few moments; we will bring you inside. Mabrouk!" *"Congratulations."*

Gratitude, relief, and joy erupt, as the man falls to the floor to perform a sajdah.

Inside, the mother, despite the weariness of labour, reaches out to hold her little one close. Feeling the warmth of her daughter's small body against her own, her being fills with a beautifully silent, sacred connection. Smiling through her tears, the mother admires what she has made. Her baby has a full head of thick dark hair framing her tiny face, already curling in soft, wild waves. Her skin is warm, golden brown, and glistens under the bright hospital lights, still damp with the traces of her first moments outside her mother's warm belly.

The baby's little hands wave in the air, her fingers curling instinctively as if reaching out to grasp this new world around her. Her cries have turned to murmurs, as she opens her eyes to the world, blinking against the lights, her brown eyes wide, curious, and exploring. Her eyes land on her mother's, and a curious expression covers her face. As they look into each other's eyes, the mother wishes the baby had her green eyes, but brown will do. At least they are a tad lighter than her husband's dark-brown ones, she notices.

She accepts. As they gaze through each other, they become one, the mother and her little one.

Moments pass, and finally the mother looks up, nodding at the only nurse left in the room, waiting by the door. She gestures that it is okay to let her husband into the room now.

Her husband enters, walks over to his bride, kisses her forehead, and whispers, "Merbaani, Zooni," eyes glowing with pride at the labour she has endured, at the beautiful gift she has given him. *"Thank you."*

His eyes land then on the gift she has given him, and he starts laughing through his tears of joy. "She is so tiny, and just look at those big brown eyes! Those are definitely my eyes." He beams.

"Not entirely, but yes, she has your brown eyes," the mother offers with a tired smile.

Taking a deep breath in as if to capture this moment in his memory, he looks at his tired bride and nods, and she nods back.

It is time.

It is time for the rituals. Rituals that would typically be performed by their elders in the safety of their courtyard, in the care of the neem tree, in the nurturing fragrance of the motia bush, as they would all gather on the mud floor, comforted by the red soils of their homeland. But here they are, two birds far away from the nests they know, nests they flew from years prior, his in Punjab, and hers in Kashmir.

And today they have brought a little life into the world.

He walks across the room and pulls out a deep-ferozi, or deep turquoise, shawl with mirrors, a gold surme daani, a little jar of honey, and his intricately embroidered white prayer cap. These are things they had carefully packed for this moment to make sure they welcomed their child properly into this world.

He passes the shawl to her, settling beside her on the hospital bed. For the next few moments, he watches in awe as she wraps their baby in the shawl in motions that seem tender, tentative, yet knowing, as if she always knew how to nurture a little one. His heart smiles. They are going to be okay.

Satisfied that the baby is safely tucked, she looks up at him, nudging him to come closer as she nestles the baby tightly between them both. The baby looks content as the turquoise of the shawl and the sunlight reflected by the sparkling mirrors creates a little private celebration of three souls.

He twists open the surme daani and hands it over to his bride. He takes hold of the baby. With a practised hand, she dips the salai into the fine dark-black surma inside, ensuring just the right amount clings to it. The motion is fluid and familiar, a ritual passed down to her through generations. She raises the salai to her eye, carefully pulling down her lower eyelid with one finger to create a little gap. With a steady hand, she slides the salai along the inner rim of her eyelid, a smooth and confident motion that deposits a thin line of the rich, dark surma. She then adds surma to the other eye. Blinking a few times to make sure the surma is evenly distributed, she is ready. Reaching over to her baby in her husband's arms, holding back tears, she does the same for her little one, who lies still for it, as if knowing this is something sacred.

"May you see the world in ways no one can," the mother says as she smiles at the baby, now adorned with thick kohl around her large brown eyes.

With the salai, the mother then deposits a little dot on the baby's cheek.

"In the beauty you radiate, may there always be an imperfection, so you may be protected from the evil eye," she whispers softly, still holding back tears. She looks up at her husband, who nods knowingly.

She watches him as he adjusts the prayer cap on his head. Bringing the baby's right ear up to him, he recites the Azaan as the baby's eyes widen with the melody. They were familiar, these words and their melody. The baby had heard them as she floated in her mother's womb.

He then recites the Azaan in the baby's left ear.

"Jeeyondi ray," he says, tears rolling from his eyes. *"Live well."* He concludes his ritual.

He reaches for the jar of honey for the final birth ritual, the goorti. Taking a bit of honey on his little finger, he smiles at his bride, gesturing his head in a nudge for her to take some too. She hesitates briefly, knowing goorti is usually meant to be done by one person, not two, but then obliges.

They bring their little fingers to the baby's mouth together then, the honey-dipped tips lightly placed on the baby's rosy lips. In a knowing urgency, the baby sucks and licks their fingers hungrily, as they laugh.

"May you carry the determination and humour of your father," he starts. "The playfulness, stubbornness, and love to feed others of your mother"—the mother clicks her tongue and laughs—"and the patience, courage, and tenacity of all your elders."

The mother nods in agreement, beaming with pride.

They both giggle again, knowing in their hearts that they have done the best they can, perhaps modified a few rituals, but it is what it is. The baby smiles again, as if joining in on the secret.

"I can't believe she knows how to smile," the mother says.

"It is odd, yes, but maybe that is how it is meant to be. Maybe she will be an odd one," he replies.

"Tsk, tsk! Changiyan galan karo; kee karday o tussi?" the mother says, laughter spilling out of her. *"Say good things; why do you do this?"*

Getting up from the hospital bed, he turns his gaze to the heavens. "Merbaani, Rabba! Hun himmat dayeen menon main apni tee nu puttaran akan paal sakan," he says, raising his hands up in prayer. *"Thank you, Creator! Now give me courage so I may raise my daughter as I would raise any sons."*

And so, I became.

Over the week that followed my arrival into this world, my parents fussed over who would get to name me. It is curious to me that they didn't have this conversation leading up to my birth. Perhaps they wanted to see what awaited them.

Naming ceremonies are a big deal in our world. For the most part, the parents choose who gets to name their child. In doing so, a few promises are made. Unspoken ones. Promises that have been honoured for generations. The person who names the child becomes responsible for making important decisions for them, should anything ever happen to the parents. This is different from caring for or raising a child. Raising a child is a family responsibility, a responsibility carried by all—the aunties, the uncles, the older siblings, the cousins, the community. The person who names the child carries a little extra, becoming, through the course of the parents' lives, the main advisor on all matters pertaining to the child. To reciprocate for having played this important part in their lives, the child carries the responsibility to care for this person in their most vulnerable times.

Often, the parents choose multiple relatives to name their children and, in doing so, spread the responsibility—both the responsibility of the family to their child, and of their child to their family. I, for example, have had the honour of naming six children in our family—which also provides a solid insurance policy as the years go by and I walk towards times when I would undoubtedly need care.

After much discussion, the person who got to name me was my maternal grandmother, whom I grew up to call Naano jaan. The word "naano" is endearingly derived from the word "naani" in Punjabi, as was her relation to me as my mother's mother. And "jaan" means life. Naano was, is, and always will be my life in all its beauty, meaning, richness, and complexity.

The name she gave me is Emahn, which means trust, confidence, inner strength, hope, and belief in something despite uncertainty.

I often wondered if the name given to me was what Naano jaan saw in the newborn me.

Turns out, it wasn't. In giving me the name Emahn, she was passing on a basket of magical powers I would need to do life.

Trust.

Confidence.

Inner strength.

Hope.

Belief in something despite uncertainty.

Barkat—A Blessing

May you be the reason
the world ends wars.
May you be the reason
we find the power of courage.
May you be the reason
we love deeper than we know.
May you be the reason
to live, to laugh, to be, to become.

Ik Si Raja

There Once Was a King

Over the days and weeks and months and years that followed my entry into the world, much happened. Everyone who came to visit me looked at me from this way and that way and pronounced who I looked like, who I behaved like. Father's eyes, Mother's nose, my daado jaan's hair, Daada jaani's cheekbones, Khaala jaani's attitude, Phupho jaan's frown.

I wonder sometimes that if all parts of me were like others, what parts were me? Or maybe I carried parts of me with parts of many of my people. Perhaps.

My early days were in a work camp in Sharjah. The trailer assigned to us didn't have much room for a baby, so my little cot got shuffled outside when Baba jaani needed to lay his prayer mat to pray. Mama jaan claims this was what really got him into the habit of going to the mosque to pray.

In raising me, Mama jaan and Baba jaani didn't have the support Mama jaan would have had back home, so they had to figure a lot of things out themselves. Baba worked long hours to earn enough to sustain us and to send back home for the family. So, really, it was mostly Mama jaan and me. And we got to do a lot together.

This is also where I first started learning about the power of stories.

Ik si raja, ik si rani. *There was once a king and a queen.*
This is how Mama jaan's stories would always begin, and later mine.

The raja was a handsome ruler and loved by all the beings in his kingdom. He was kind, fair, and very protective of all his beings. People would come to his court from all corners of his kingdom to ask him to decide on disputes for them. Sometimes, the raja would pass them on to his advisors in the lower court to address. Some matters, the raja would handle himself.

The raja's people could never figure out why he would handle some conflicts himself and why he would send other conflicts to the lower court to settle. Some in his court speculated that when it came to matters of the land where one of the parties was much stronger than the other, the raja felt it was his duty to resolve. Others speculated it was usually matters where someone's daughter or sister had been wronged that pulled on the raja. Yet sometimes the raja would say yes to the simplest of matters that others thought might not be the best use of his precious time.

The raja would listen carefully, sometimes for hours, to those who needed a resolution. He would listen to everyone in the conflict. The young, the old, the men, the women. He would then call upon others from the community to ask about those in conflict. He would ask the two-spirited beings, whom he knew were the keepers of the power of insight. He would ask the animals, both big and small, for he knew the animals carried the magic of observation. He would ask the rivers, both shallow and deep, for he knew they carried the power of listening. He would ask the skies, both the night and the day, star-filled and starless, for he knew they had the ancient power of wisdom. Finally, he would ask the winds, both the gentle and the howling, for he knew they carried all our memories. He would ask them all if the people in conflict had been honest in their dealings. Were they fair? Were they respected? Were they kind? Had they wronged anyone?

As they spoke, the raja's shahi darzi, the royal tailors, would be busily embroidering all the stories into the black shahi razai, the royal quilt, made of the finest black velvet in all the kingdoms, woven especially for the raja. Every account was documented meticulously in beautiful silk threads of silver and turquoise, some words carrying sequins, and others little mirrors. With every story told in the raja's court, the shahi razai would grow bigger and bigger with even more words and sequins and mirrors.

It is said that the shahi razai sits in the first of the seven skies, and when we see the stars, they are the sequins and mirrors from stories told in the raja's court many lives ago.

Once the raja had listened to all the beings, he would summon them to return again.

He would then turn to the rani, his confidante, his beautiful advisor, and together they would walk across the sky, across the shahi razai, recounting what everyone had said so they could offer a resolution that would be fair and kind and keep the community together.

"Waaaah, Mama jaan. Are all those stars from the razai, then?" I point to the stars outside the bedroom window.

"Sure are, meri jaan," says Mama jaan with a smile.

"But the sky is so big. That's so many stories. They're all there? Forever?!" My eyes are filled with awe and wonder at the vastness of what I have just learned.

"Sure are, meri jaan," says Mama jaan, laughing. "And you can float amongst the stars to listen to them."

"Can I?" I ask excitedly. "But, Mama jaan, how did they know which words to put mirrors and sequins on?"

"All the words said with kindness, love, compassion, and care got mirrors, Laachiye."

"Waaaah. That's so many words."

"Mmhmm." She nods. And before I can ask her more questions, she reaches over to kiss my forehead and says in the softest of whispers, "Shub-a-kher, meri jaan. *Good night, my life.* See you in the skies."

"Shub-a-kher," I mumble, letting sleep take over me as I float to touch the stories in the skies.

Baantna Batwaana

To Share and Be Shared

When I turn six, I learn my first tough lesson. Sharing my parents with my little twin brothers.

The two came from Mama jaan's belly. Now, while I arrived in this world with a smile, my brothers arrived with screeching cries and the tenacity of a thousand warriors. They were very little, looked the same, were very hairy and a real pain in the ass. They both cried all night, and given our small living quarters, it meant most people in the flat stirred every time they wailed.

On the way back from the hospital, I asked Mama jaan if I came with someone too. Was I missing a sister somewhere my parents hadn't told me about?

"Naah, pagliye. *No, you silly one.* I don't think I could have managed two of you," Mama jaan said with a tired smile as she held one brother on one side, and the other on the other side. "Eh jurwa praa nay teray. *These are your twin brothers,*" she said. "Tay ay teri zimaydaari nay. *And they are your responsibility,*" she added.

I nodded dutifully, knowingly. I would just have to learn how to take care of them with Mama jaan. She would show me, I'm sure.

By then, we had moved from the trailer to a small three-bedroom flat that we shared with two other families. One family was from Sri Lanka: Sanjay Uncle and Ranjini Auntie, and their three little daughters. Dilini, the oldest of the three, was my age, and we got along famously. Her name means one who is soft-hearted. And she really was. She and I shared our toys, did crafts together, laughed together, and eventually took care of our little siblings together.

The bedroom that Mama jaan, Baba jaani, my brothers, and I now stayed in was still modest but had enough space for a large cot for my twin brothers, and a mattress on the floor for me, right next to my parents' bed. All families shared the living room, so my study table was nestled in a corner in the living room along with the study tables of the other children in the flat.

As months passed after my brothers' arrival, I noticed a shift in Mama jaan. She was always busy with them. It was either time to feed one, change one, rock one for a nap, cook, clean, or make a list for me to grab groceries from Agha Uncle's little supermarket downstairs.

With my brothers' arrival in this world, Mama jaan didn't play with me as much as she used to. Story time was less frequent too. She was more tired. Sometimes, when Mama jaan was helping me with homework, one of the brothers would start crying and I'd ask Mama jaan to just leave them and see if my homework was good. She would just smile and say I need to learn to share better.

Share. I wondered what that meant.

I figure I should ask Naano jaan when I see her next.

It had been so long since I had seen Naano jaan, and I missed her. I told her as much every two weeks or so when Mama jaan let me speak to her on the phone. I always loved listening to Naano jaan's voice. It was sweet like honey, and it always made me feel like she was holding me when she talked.

Every morning, as the first light of dawn peeks through the curtains in our small bedroom, casting a soft, golden glow on everything, I watch as Baba jaani moves quietly around the room. I love these early mornings, even if I am supposed to be asleep. Our little room feels so peaceful at this time, just before the morning sounds take flight, as if the world is just taking a deep breath to gather its thoughts, process its dreams from the night, before the day can begin.

I usually lie still, peeking from under my blanket. I can hear the gentle sound of water splashing in the bathroom as Baba jaani performs his wudu. This meant he was getting ready to go to the masjid. Baba jaani did this every morning, always so quietly, so he wouldn't wake us up, especially knowing Mama jaan always had a long night with my brothers. Listening to him every morning, I knew the sounds by heart—the turning of the tap, the quiet swish of water, the gentle splashes of his motions as he went through the ten-step ritual to prepare himself. Baba jaani explained the wudu to me several times, and though I would sometimes get the order wrong, I'd usually cover all ten steps.

"First, we declare our intention," he would say.

"I am performing wudu," I'd say loudly.

"Tsk. Oye, you can say this quietly in your head, puttar." He'd click his tongue and laugh.

"Oh," I'd whisper, "I am performing wudu."

"We then say, 'Bismillah ar rahman ar Raheem,'" he'd continue, with a big smile on his face.

"Bismillah ar rahman ar Raheem," I'd repeat.

"Then we wash our hands." I'd follow.

And then we'd rinse our mouths, then rinse our nose, which was still a bit of a tricky one for me, but I was getting better. Then we'd wash our faces, wash our arms up to our elbows, wipe our heads, wipe our ears, and finally wash our feet. Because the sink was too high for me, Baba jaani would usually pour a little bit of water on my feet with a plastic cup so I could wipe them myself.

And then we'd be ready. When Baba jaani prayed at home, I would join him. But not at the masjid.

Maybe when I was older, he'd let me join him.

Lying under the sheets, listening to Baba jaani performing his wudu, I hold my breath and listen for the soft shuffle of his feet as Baba jaani moves around the flat, ready to head out. I hear him grabbing his white kurta from the hook by the door, pulling it on over his pyjamas, reaching for his prayer cap from the shelf, slipping on his shoes at the main entrance, and then leaving the flat.

I imagine what it would be like outside, the air cool and fresh. Baba would pass Security Uncle downstairs, who always smiles at us when we walk by together. I like Security Uncle. He once showed Baba jaani and me photos that his beautiful wife had sent him of their children. He had teared up, saying he really misses them and hopes they'll remember him when he is finally able to return home. Baba had put his hand on Security Uncle's shoulder and said, "Our kids never forget our sacrifices, my friend. Of course they will remember you."

Heading up to our flat in the elevator, I asked Baba jaani what sacrifices were.

He smiled and said, "It's when we give up our comfort or our wants for someone else. Security Uncle has been giving up being close to his wife and his children so that he can support his whole family. That is a sacrifice."

I nodded and asked, "Will I have to sacrifice, Baba jaani?"

"You already are sacrificing, puttar," he said, pinching my nose. "You share your mama jaan and baba jaani with your pesky brothers, even though you want to have us all to yourself." He gave me a curious sideways glance then.

I spent a few seconds considering this, and then scrunching my face, folding my arms, said, "It's true. And I don't like that too much. They better not forget that, Baba jaani!"

"They won't, puttar," he said, his voice soft and packed with such tenderness.

"But how will we know?" I asked, with a deep frown.

"Hmmm . . . they'll show it in their love for you, puttar. They'll be the first ones to be there should you ever need anything. They'll fight for you. They'll protect you. They'll adore you more than all the stars in the sky. That's how."

"Waaaah," I said, letting the beauty of the thought sink in.

As I lay on the mattress, I breathe deeply, acknowledging the beauty of that thought. By now Baba jaani would have passed Security Uncle and arrived at the masjid, where the jamaat, the ritual of praying together, was already beginning, echoing between the tall buildings. The masjid was connected to Qari Uncle's home, where I spent two hours each afternoon after school learning how to recite the Quran.

I imagine Baba jaani standing in a line with the other uncles, all of them praying together in quiet whispers, shoulder to shoulder, bowing together, performing sajdah together.

With that thought, a smile on my face, I drift back to sleep, knowing that when I wake up, it would be time to get ready for school.

That morning, I'm woken up by the familiar sounds of Ranjini Auntie singing the gayatri mantra as part of her morning pooja for her lord Ganesha. For her, there were many Gods. Ranjini Auntie had explained this to me one day when I had asked her why she prayed to this God instead of to Allah, like Baba jaani and I did.

"Ganesha is the remover of obstacles, little one," she said. "And in this foreign land so far from our homes, there are so many obstacles."

"What are obstacles?" I asked.

"Difficulties. Troubles. Things we must figure out that take longer, like a puzzle, you curious child. Now go help your mom make breakfast so we don't run late for school," she said.

Some days, if breakfast wasn't ready yet, I'd sit next to Ranjini Auntie and Dilini as they'd do their pooja. Sometimes, I'd pretend to sing with them. I didn't know the words so I would just hum along.

Mama jaan explained this wasn't our God or our words, and we mustn't pray to someone else's God.

"Our relationship to God is a special one, between us and our God, maano," she said. "Our God is Allah."

"I know. I don't really pray to Ganesha or ask Ganesha for things when I'm sitting next to Ranjini Auntie, Mama jaan," I had offered. "I just like to be there with Dilini, and sometimes when Dilini and Ranjini Auntie are not looking, I pray to Allah and ask him to please give Auntie and Dilini whatever they are asking for."

"Tsk. You are a silly girl," Mama jaan said with that beautiful smile of hers.

"Mama jaan? When are we going to visit Naano jaan? There is so much I want to tell her."

"When it's too hot to go to school, we'll go visit Naano," she said, kissing my forehead.

Every morning on my way to school, as I stick my face out to feel the wind, I wonder if it's hot enough for us to go to Lahore yet.

What Water Knows

It's wudu that taught,
guided by his kind words,
held in intention and care, and knowing.
Water touching parts of her that needed to know
of things greater than her.

Washing her hands,
of the want to have her mother all to herself,
her little mouth of complaints
when their cries muffle her mother's voice,
her face of the frowns
that came with missing her mother's stories.

Washing her little arms,
so they can hold what was gifted to her,
a knowing, a kind understanding.
A knowing that her little brothers will be there
beside her, shoulder to shoulder,
facing the same world,
praying for the same things.

Lahore

Every summer, as the school year inches towards an end, we start preparing to go to Lahore. The odd time, we'd go during the school year too, but that was only if there was a death in the family. Those times were always a little confusing as they would make me sad and happy at the same time.

Four giant suitcases would sit in the corner of our bedroom, new things added to them every few days. We'd bring gifts for everyone. Some imitation jewelry and makeup for my aunties to add to their dowry baskets, perfumes and watches from the vendors in the souqs for our uncles, some fabric for a shalwar kameez and new sandals for Daada jaani, my paternal grandfather, and some beautiful fabrics with sequins for Naano jaan. I picked out her and Daada jaani's gifts myself and would wait in anticipation on how they would react to them. They always loved them, and I loved that. For all the kids, of which there are many, we brought chocolates.

One summer, as I turn eight years old, it is finally time to go to Lahore. On the day we are to leave, I get picked up at the school early, I change in the back of the car, and we head straight to the airport. It is the best day ever. I don't even know what is coming out of my mouth. My words pour out of me as if someone is trying to pour water into a cup that is already full. As we check in at the Sharjah International Airport, Baba jaani reminds me that he will only be joining us in Lahore for two weeks and that I am to take care of Mama jaan and my brothers. I nod but am barely listening. The plane ride is fun. The flight attendant aunties are so nice. They give all the children crayons and papers to colour on, though I feel I am a little old for these. I prefer to read the books Mama jaan has packed for me, but I say thank you and smile broadly. Maybe these aunties don't know that I can read.

Mama jaan is carrying one of my brothers and Baba jaani is carrying the other one. Mama jaan looks so happy today. She is wearing a deep-green shalwar kameez with a beautiful floral print that carries tiny flowers with pink centres and white petals. The edges of her neckline are detailed with a dainty silver lace that pulls the whites of the floral print, sparkling in the sunlight making its way through the airplane window, adding a festive touch to her outfit. Mama jaan is smiling easily today, every smile easily spilling over into laughter. She seems light, her eyes dancing.

She looks like a queen, and I love her so much.

We are served food in little containers, and I get my own tray. There is some lamb biryani, a little dish of salad, some kheer for dessert, and some fresh naan.

I eat everything. Every grain of rice. Every piece of bread.

It's good, but not as good as Mama jaan's, and I quietly tell her that. Mama jaan smiles at me, winks, and puts a finger on her lips so I don't say that too loud. We giggle.

As we step outside the Allama Iqbal International Airport, Lahore welcomes us in all its glory. So many family members have come to pick us up at the airport. They shower us with garlands made of roses. Even I get a couple, though they are big and reach down to my knees. In the hot air, they offer such coolness. I breathe deeply, the smell of roses taking over me.

I spot at least nine of my cousins, two of them older than me. I spot three of my chachas, or uncles, one of whom is Baba jaani's brother and another one his cousin, and two of my phuphos, Baba jaani's sisters. I am introduced to new chachas and aunties I don't know. Two of my baby cousins are clinging onto me and saying things I can't even understand, and I find myself nodding and smiling just because they are smiling.

Everyone is laughing, and hugging, and smiling, and crying, and there is just so much light around me.

Our family doesn't own cars in Lahore; we just have Miyan Ji's donkey cart, Daada jaani's bicycle, and Taya jaani's rickshaw. I figure my uncles must have booked two vans to get everyone here to pick us up.

My parents and brothers are piled into one van, and I jump into the other one with my cousins.

We drive through the streets, as my cousins point out things to me. I see where they now go to school, where they went to buy gifts for my phupho's dowry, where they went to buy bangles for the wedding, where they went to buy the dress that I am to wear for Phupho's wedding. They also show me where there was a bomb blast last month and so many people died, but now the grounds are empty, so maybe there will be a mela there soon, a carnival, and how we should all ask Taya jaani to take us there on his new rickshaw. They argue about how many people we can fit in the rickshaw and who all should go. After much back and forth, they settle on ten people, including all nine of them, of course, and ask me what I think. I laugh, bob my head, and say, "Theek eh. *Sounds great.*"

I am then told it would be up to me to convince Taya jaani of this plan, but that they can help with when to ask, and how. I learn that Taya jaani is most receptive to requests such as these after he has woken up from his afternoon nap and is enjoying his doodh patti, a milky cardamom chai, and that I am the best suited to ask as I have just arrived.

I nod in agreement, making mental notes. I am worried I will run out of space to keep it in my head soon. I take it all in. Every word, I feel the joy, I feel the happiness.

In the middle of all the noise and chatter, the littlest of my cousins, Anaya, is the only quiet one. I guess that she is now three years old. She is sitting across from me, next to Guddi Baji, my cousin-sister, who is eight years older than me.

Anaya stares at me with her big brown eyes, smiling shyly whenever I catch her looking at me. I hold her gaze, smile back, and she retreats just a little, burying her face in Guddi Baji's arm. She opens one eye and bursts into giggles when she sees me staring right at her. I lean forward, put out both my hands, palms up, and say, "Anaya jaan, kaisay o? *How are you?*"

Her smile broadens, taking over her entire face. The top of her head quickly bobs to one side and back, she leans forward, putting her little palms down on mine, and says in the squeakiest, tiniest voice I have ever heard coming from a person, "Theek hon, Baji. *I'm good.*" Her voice sways and swings as if from one tree to the other. My heart fills with roses and colours, and warmth and coolness, and everything beautiful around me.

Mama jaan says we shouldn't pick favourite cousins, but my baby cousin, Anaya, *is* my favourite. I just won't tell Mama jaan.

As we meander through the bustling streets of Lahore, making our way to the family house, the sounds and smells and feels and the magic of the city settle into every part of me.

I know I will likely see my parents and pesky brothers only a handful of times for the rest of the summer. While they visit with their friends and cousins and pay respects to families who have lost loved ones, and bring gifts for dowries for the many families whose daughters are getting married, I'll be spending time with my cousins and aunties and grandparents, doing whatever it is they are doing all summer.

And it is the best thing ever.

I sleep on the highest rooftop under the stars, my manji next to Guddi Baji's. Guddi Baji is my taya jaani's daughter. Taya jaani is Baba jaani's older brother. If he were younger than Baba jaani, I would have called him chacha. Guddi Baji is his oldest daughter, and I go everywhere she goes.

I like sleeping on my manji. It has a simple wooden frame with woven jute, with short legs so we're two feet off the ground. My manji usually has a thick quilted cover that makes the old jute less prickly to sleep on, and a small pillow. And even though it cools off at night on the rooftop, it is still pretty warm, so I have a thin cotton sheet I can pull over me. Every night, I help Guddi Baji lay out all the manjiyan for us and our little cousins. Usually, we all just hang out on a couple of manjiyan till it's time to retreat to our own.

I tell my cousins all about Mama jaan's stories of the raja and the rani and how all the stars we see are in fact words of kindness and compassion and love and care from the stories told by people in their court. I tell them all about Dilini and Ranjini Auntie and my teachers in school. I tell them about the gayatri mantra and how Ranjini Auntie has a different God, and they all gasp. Out of nowhere, little Hammad asks if that means Ranjini Auntie will be going to hell and burn like his teacher says happens to anyone who doesn't pray to Allah, and we all stare at him in horror. Guddi Baji is the oldest amongst us, so we turn to her with our questioning eyes.

It seems like we're all a little unsure.

Guddi Baji clicks her tongue and says to Hammad, "Tsk, tsk. No, you silly boy. God is kind, no one can go to hell for praying to their God. And Ranjini Auntie sounds like a good person. Allah doesn't put good people in hell." We all breathe a little more easily. Hammad seems relieved too.

Over the hours that flow by, they sing to me songs they are learning in school, and I realise these are different from the ones I learn in school. Mine are in English. But the ones they are singing are the same songs Mama jaan and Baba jaani teach me at home, so I know them and can sing with them. I then sing for them songs that I'm learning in school, and they don't know them but bob and sway and clap and hum as if the words don't matter. And I guess they don't. We can celebrate without knowing.

We all sing to each other. Guddi Baji grabs a dholki, beating it in a beautiful rhythm, and soon we're having a little party on the rooftop. Guddi Baji plays the dholki as we sing one song after the other. Soon these are not even songs anyone sings at school but songs we just all know. Songs from weddings, songs from the movies, songs our mothers and aunties and grandmothers have sung to us, songs we don't even know where from, but we sing. We sing for hours.

Every morning, we all help Guddi Baji put the manjiyan away and then head downstairs to the courtyard. While everyone enjoys breakfast, I wait impatiently next to Naano jaan, who walks a few houses down the gully every morning to come get me for the day. Daado jaan, my paternal grandmother, insists I quickly shower and dress so I can go, while Naano jaan enjoys the doodh patti and rusk Daado jaan will serve her.

Some mornings, Naano jaan insists she can't stay long and I better hurry. Daado jaan insists that doodh patti will only take a minute to make. Naano insists back and offers that Daado jaan knows she can't accept even a glass of water in the home she has married her daughter into, as that would be breaking tradition.

Daado jaan clicks her tongue and says, "That is how people used to think in the old times. Now times are changing, Arisha."

And Naano smiles and softly says, "Yes, you are right. I hope not everything changes, though," and Daado jaan nods as she brings Naano jaan her doodh patti.

Some mornings Naano jaan brings meetha paratha, a sweet fried flattened roti, that she has made with sugarcane sap and cardamom. And Daado jaan asks her how they can accept this when Naano has already gifted them her beautiful daughter, Zooni, my mama jaan. And Naano smiles and says, "My Zooni is a gift, yes, but it is a gift that comes with some side gifts, such as this meetha paratha, and this little brat," and she pulls me into a big hug.

"That is true," Daado jaan says as she accepts the meetha paratha.

Daado jaan is the matriarch of the household. It is her responsibility, not Daada jaani's, to make sure all protocols are followed properly. This responsibility was passed on to her by my bebe ji, my great-grandmother, when she brought Daado jaan home as a young bride. While she still consults my bebe ji on all matters, it is Daado jaan, not Daada jaani nor any other man of the household, who represents our family at funerals and weddings. She decides what gifts we bring to weddings and births in the community. It is she who decides what offerings to bring to funerals. When a possible suitor for any of my phuphos visits, it is Daado jaan who decides if this could be a good match. It is she who decides how much dowry we can afford so Daada jaani can go talk to the suitors once a match has been decided.

It is Daado jaan who hosts the hundreds of guests who pass through our courtyard every month.

It is Daado jaan who decides how the family's wealth, however vast or meagre, gets spent.

It is Daado jaan who people come to when they want to borrow some money for a daughter's wedding. Or for some new bricks for their kilns on their rooftops.

It is Daado jaan who is responsible for our place in this society.

It is Daado jaan who has given up her life, perhaps her desires, perhaps her dreams, perhaps her freedoms to be the woman we all come to, to be the woman who always shows up, never gives up, no matter how tired, how achy, how worn out, and owns responsibility for our place in our society. It is Daado jaan who does it with grace, with beauty, and with power.

Each morning, they dance this dance of customs and codes, my daado jaan and my naano jaan. Each morning, Naano jaan eventually accepts doodh patti, and Daado jaan accepts whatever food Naano jaan has brought her as a gift.

But without the dance, the words, the reminders, the intention, the gratitude, the expressions, there would be no custom, no tradition.

Soon, summer is coming to an end, and it is time to return to Sharjah. All summer long, I have had henna on my palms, coconut oil in my hair, and gajaray and bangles on my wrists. I have danced and sung and laughed enough to last me many lives.

We all cry at the airport when it's time to leave Lahore. Mama jaan cries. I cry. My cousins cry. We promise to return soon. I tell my cousins I must wait for it to get really hot in Sharjah again before I can return to Lahore. And we wish it always stayed hot.

As we land in Sharjah, I am excited to see Dilini and tell her all about my trip. While I was in Lahore, Dilini was visiting her family in Sri Lanka. I am excited to hear all about her visit to see her ammamma, her grandmother, and I am excited to tell her about everything Naano jaan has shown me. She'll tell me about her cousins, and I'll tell her about mine. We'll trade stories about places we visited, and things we saw, and all the amazing food we ate. We'll start school again in a couple of days and visit the rest of our friends there. Suddenly, I'm not so sad anymore.

Lahore

Lahore hums in laughter,
in voices that spill from rooftops,
in hands that press love into the folds of dough,
in aunties who braid care into the hair of little ones,
pulling, twisting, weaving,
their fingers knowing the rhythm of belonging.

Here, the air smells of cardamom and rain,
of roasting sitta and songs sung for centuries,
of amrood split open on street corners,
sweet and stubborn like the city itself.
Dry-fruit stalls rising in golden heaps,
almonds dancing like raw secrets,
walnuts cracked open like promises,
pistachios waiting to be pried open,
their laughter tucked between shells.

At dusk, she glows,
her lights flickering against red bricks,
rickshaws rattling like drums,
bazaars celebrating the rush of bodies and bargains,
the Azaan folding into the city's endless song.

And when night drapes over us,
the sky thick with saffron and smoke,
little ones sitting with their grandmothers,
the chirp, the laughter, the wisdom,
wrapped into one
like silk spun in love,
like a city that never forgets its own.

Rail Gaddi

The Train

By the time all the guests left, it was well past 10:00 p.m. And we were out of milk. Agha Uncle wouldn't deliver at this hour, so Mama jaan asked me to grab some from the grocery store. I had done this a million times, so I got in the elevator, went downstairs to Agha Uncle's grocery store the next building over, and picked up two packs of Lacnor milk. Just two weeks earlier in Lahore, we were indulging in the freshest of milk from the cows at home, but now we were back in Sharjah, so Lacnor it was.

Agha Uncle was so kind. Baba jaani called him Daal Khor Bhai, my lentil-eater brother. And Agha Uncle would laugh, shake his head, and say if Baba jaani came to Afghanistan someday, Agha Uncle would make him kabuli rice with lamb. "Then we'll see who Daal Khor is," he'd say. And they'd both laugh.

Baba would say it would be his honour to visit, and Agha Uncle would say it would be his honour to host us.

"Honour." I liked that word.

I liked Agha Uncle. He said his daughter Afra was my age and as beautiful as a sapphire. My wurra neelam, my little sapphire. He showed me a photo of Afra once.

Afra's eyes were the bluest eyes I had ever seen. The colour of the water at the corniche beach midday. The deep blue green of the ocean. I wondered if Afra also liked the water, like I did. Surely, she must. She must see her eyes are like the ocean! I wished I could meet her someday. We could be friends, just like Dilini and I were. And then Afra could bring us stories from Kabul as I would share stories from Lahore, and Dilini from Colombo.

Agha Uncle must miss Afra dearly, I would often think. He only saw her once a year when he could go visit.

Grabbing the milk, and thanking Agha Uncle, I tell him to pass on my salaam to little Afra, and he nods with a big smile.

Walking past Security Uncle, who nods his head as I hop by, I step in the single-door elevator with its small glass inset on the one side and press 8.

I'd often put my head against that glass inset and watch the floors go by. Only if I was alone in the elevator, of course. It was like being on a train. Only instead of going sideways, you'd go up and down like you were going deep into the earth or up into space.

Just as the blue door was closing, a hand reached in and a tall, very dark brown man stepped inside and pressed 7. He smiled at me. Something about that smile gave me the shivers. It was not winter yet, no reason for the shivers.

I do not like him, I decide.

We don't decide till we know, puttar, Baba's voice says in my head. I try to breathe and wonder if I am allowed to disagree with Baba jaani. I should ask Baba jaani when I get upstairs.

I didn't like how he looked at me. I don't know why he was walking around in his lungi. People wore that at bedtime. But then again, I was walking around in a fancy dress that Naano jaan had made for me just two weeks before when I was visiting her in Lahore. So, I guess it was okay.

A second later, he pulls open his lungi. That smile, that sickening smile. The moustache. The sickening bloodshot eyes. Afra's eyes were beautiful. Her eyes would give anyone strength, I thought. This man's eyes were bad.

"You are beautiful," he says, touching himself.

"I will tell Baba you are a bad man. I don't like this." I am shaking.

He slaps me across the face. My ears start ringing.

The elevator stops on the seventh floor. He drags me by my shirt into the electrical room. I try to scream but I can't.

He tries to put something in my mouth. I throw up all over myself. All over my new dress. He rips my beautiful dress. It makes me so angry. Did he not know how hard Naano jaan worked on sewing it? I clutch the edges of my dress. It gives me strength. My beautiful dress. The deep maroon and gold of it was so pretty. As I hold it, I called out to Mama jaan. Could she sense I was hurting? She was only one floor up.

Baba? I call in my head. Could he hear me? Surely, they could.

Naano jaan had spent days sewing my dress. It made her allergies so much worse, but she had said she wanted her Laachi to look like the most beautiful queen in the kingdom. I imagine Naano jaan's smile. It gives me strength. My naano jaan was the most beautiful queen in the kingdom.

As I cling to my torn dress, he paces nervously in the electrical room. Was he looking for something? Was he going to kill me?

My head is throbbing. I try calling Mama jaan in my heart.

Mama jaan, can you hear me in your heart? No response. I did not really know how these things worked. Was I supposed to hear her back? I had never tried calling her from my heart before. She would always say if I ever needed her, I should close my eyes, and she will hear me.

He grabs my throat. I raised my finger.

"One minute, please, sir." My voice barely comes. "Don't hurt me, please. I won't tell anyone. I promise. Baba says if you break rules, they send you home. If you hurt me, they'll send you home. Baba says our families depend on us. Don't hurt me, please. . . ." I am shaking. No more words come. I try. Nothing happens.

Those burning bloodshot eyes. That smile. He slaps me again. Again. And again. He grabs my hair and pushes my head against the wall. It hurts so much.

Mama jaan, can you hear me? Baba? Help me, please.

And then it all goes black.

I do not know how long it is before I come to. Everything hurts so much. Blood is pooled between my legs. I throw up again.

Mama jaan? Baba? Can you hear me? I'm under here. Could they hear me?

They were just one floor up. I could do this. My maroon dress. Did I still have my hair, or did he rip it all out? The gold ribbon. Naano jaan and I had gone to the market together to pick it out. I would have to tell Naano jaan what happened. Maybe she and I could pick another ribbon to fix this dress.

He ruined my dress.

Tears came. Why was I crying? When I'd trip and fall, Naano jaan would tell me I should get up.

"We always fall, don't we?" she would say. "But do we stay there? Nah, jaan. We get up. We get up to tell someone why we fell."

If she were here, *Get up, Laachiye,* she would say.

Was Naano jaan there? Was she talking to me? Had I somehow connected to Naano jaan instead?

Naano jaan? Can you hear me?

I try getting up. It was so difficult. I get up. It was only one floor up. I could get back in the elevator. I did. The Lacnor was still on the floor outside the elevator. My brothers would need milk at night.

My eyes land on my parents just as the ugly, bloodstained blue door of the elevator opens. Mama jaan and Baba jaani are outside the elevator door. Mama jaan's face is swollen. Has she been crying? And my dress, which I am clutching so tightly under one arm, now off my body. I drop the milk. I can't carry anything anymore.

I can't carry myself anymore.

And then it all goes black again.

I was eight years old.
 I lost my words.
 I stayed in a hospital in Sharjah for two weeks.
 I started wetting the bed.
 I met nightmares for the first time.
 I learned the word "rape."
 I tried to speak but no words came. No voice came.
 I wet my clothes in school.

I wet my clothes every time I saw a very dark brown man with a thick moustache.

I woke up many times in the middle of the night, gasping for air. Rocking.

My parents started locking our bedroom door after finding me curled up on the floor of the balcony off our living room one night.

Baba jaani brought me to many hakeem uncles—healers—then. To doctors. To specialists. To anyone who would say they could heal me.

I did not understand what needed to be healed. I was fine. I just couldn't speak.

Every couple of weeks, Mama jaan would put me on the phone with Naano jaan back in Lahore. Voice dipped in jasmine and rolled in cardamom and rose water, Naano jaan would say, "Laachiye, kee hoya, puttar? Bol di kyon nai?" as she would choke back tears. *"Laachiye, what happened, my little one? Why don't you speak?"*

And as if the oceans had found a drain right at the bottom, with the sound of Naano jaan's choking voice, my tears would flow and flow and flow.

But no words would come.

Water, You Must Know

She doesn't smile the same.
He looks away too long.
Their voices sound like whispers,
afraid of waking something up.

The little ones pull at her sleeve,
but she doesn't scoop them up like before.
She used to laugh when they wrestled,
kissing their scraped-up knees,
smoothing their hair,
calling them bundles of life.

Now she just nods.
Sitting by her wudu bucket,
letting the water run through her fingers,
watching it slip away.

Water, do you know?
Know if wudu can teach to share,
to love, to know.
Can it make one smile again?

Ik Si Raja

There Once Was a King

Months later one night, Mama jaan asks me if I want to listen to a story. I nod and sit in her lap as she rocks me.

Once, when the prince was little, he was out playing in the fields. He would run from one end of the mustard field to the other, laughing as the bright-yellow flowers absorbed him in a golden sea. He loved how the soft brush of the delicate mustard flowers felt against his arms and legs. He could smell the blossoms. Occasionally, his foot would land in an uneven spot, and he would trip and fall and laugh even more. It was so much fun to play in the fields. These fields were his friends.

One time, the little prince was having so much fun that he lost track of time. Suddenly, he was surrounded by these four big, burly men. The little prince didn't like them.

And these men hurt the little prince.

When the prince woke up, he was in the middle of the field and in a lot of pain. Everything hurt. He called and called and called for help, but no one heard him. Finally, a little bird up in the tree chirped. The prince said to the bird, "I don't speak your language, little bird, but can you help me? I can't walk."

"I am so little, I can't carry you, my prince, but I will bring some help," the bird chirped. And off it went.

The little bird came back with some friends, more birds. Together, they tried to lift the prince, but even though he was just a child, he was too heavy for them.

The birds chirped and chirped about what to do as the little prince listened. Then, without telling him what they were going to do, they all flew in different directions and before long returned with more birds, one drop of water, one breath of air, and several little people who the birds explained were the two-spirited children with special powers. The prince still couldn't understand how all these beings could help carry him.

As if they heard his question, the little two-spirited beings came up to the prince and sat down gently in front of him, looking up at him.

"Tell us what happened, little prince. Are you hurt?"

"Yes," the prince said. His voice rose and fell, his sobs turning the one breath into strong howling winds.

His tears flowed and flowed, and turned the one drop of water into deep, flowing rivers.

His words made the two-spirited children grow bigger and bigger around him.

And as the prince's story made them all stronger together, they were all big enough and strong enough to carry the little prince home to his parents. Together.

The prince asked them to stay with him so no one could ever hurt him again, but they said no, and that they had to return to their duties. There were other little children who may need their help. The prince understood this and asked, "But I don't want to lose you, my friends. You have saved my life."

"You won't, our prince. Whenever you need us, just write to us. We will leave you this," the birds said as they carried a little yellow pencil to the prince.

"But I only know a few words," the prince said, his face filled with worry.

"Write those few words then. And think about the rest. We will be there with you, young prince. In love, in care. In every tear you shed, in every word you speak, in every word you write, in every curiosity you carry, we will be with you."

I look up at Mama jaan, and she looks back at me, holding out a fist. I tilt my head with a question in my eyes, and she nods. I carefully open her fist, and there is a little yellow pencil, and I gasp, touching it. I look at Mama jaan, and she says softly, "You can have it."

I look at the pencil for a long time, and then say my first words in several months.

"What if I run out of the pencil, Mama jaan?"

Mama jaan's eyes fill with tears as she tries to speak through her gulps of breath. "That's okay, maano jaan. The magic is not in the pencil, meri jaan. It is in *you*. Any pencil you pick up will have your magic. Just try it, okay?"

I nod.

That night, I write my first words.

Me:
Hi. Can you help me?

The next morning, I see more words on the paper.

Magic:
Hi, Emahn. I don't know if I can help you. Let's try that together.

Me:
Okay. How?

Magic:
Tell me a story.

Me:
There was a bad man.
He hurt me,
made my mama jaan cry,
my naano jaan cry,
Baba jaani too.
My brothers don't know.
But I do.

Magic:
That is a beautiful poem. I'm so sorry that happened to you, Emahn.
You are so brave.
You should write more. I would love to hear your words.

Me:
Okay.

Magic:
May you find the power within,

the power of secrets
etched in poetry, dreams, and words.

May they find you too,
so you may have someone to trust,
to love, to hold,
to be loved,
to be held.

Karray

Clay Pots

Writing becomes a nightly routine. I write poems, stories, and songs.
I try singing them too, sometimes.
I share a bedroom with my brothers. Mama jaan and Baba jaani are in one room, and we have one spare bedroom, where my brothers play and I do my homework. Dilini has moved into a flat across from us, still on the same floor. We don't visit as often, but I do see her sometimes. We still trade stories, and eventually I learn to laugh again. My nights are still filled with night terrors, and I still wet the bed. But I have my words. My days are filled with school, which I enjoy. My teachers are all very kind, and I am very diligent with my homework.
Sometimes, I do my homework with my magic pencil.
That year, 1992, the impacts of the Gulf War linger on, with fear of more conflict erupting, and there are very few of us left in class. The streets are quieter. The fruit and vegetable markets are sparse. We have been stocking sacks of rice and lentils and bottles of drinking water at home. We don't eat meat much anymore. Baba jaani works longer hours.
One night, Baba jaani returns with gas masks, just in case we need them. He shows Mama jaan and me how to use them in case he's not around.

Sharjah feels more and more like a waiting room. People stay for a bit, but not for too long. Baba jaani says if the war gets worse and the schools close, he may send us to Lahore before it gets too hot. I hear about people losing their homes in Kuwait from the uncles talking in low tones outside the masjid, shaking their heads, rubbing their beards, glancing at us kids like we aren't supposed to hear. But we always hear. The war sits between us at dinner, in the long-distance calls made late at night, in the sighs Mama jaan swallows when she thinks no one is looking.

During the day, life moves on. I go to school every day and focus on my homework. Mama jaan packs Milco juice boxes with our lunch instead of freshly squeezed orange juice. I don't like the taste of the juice box—it is more sugar than fruit—but I don't complain. Sometimes, at night, we stop by the corniche, the lights from the dhows flickering on the dark water. I wonder if the water remembers all the people who leave because of war, if it carries their stories like secrets in its waves. I want to ask Baba jaani, but he looks too tired.

We can't rent new VHS cassettes from the rental store anymore, so every few days, I watch *Aladdin* again. Every time I watch it, something new lodges in my brain, and it plays it over and over again, like a new lesson. Sometimes, I imagine I am Aladdin and want to fly far away on my magic carpet and find new friends. Sometimes, I imagine Baba jaani is the genie—always protecting me. And then my heart hurts with the thought that anyone would ever try to trap my baba jaani in a lamp.

Every night, despite the curfew, we join Baba jaani wherever he goes. He works at the palaces sometimes, so we play in the gardens outside. I always bring my homework with me. Sometimes, when my homework feels difficult, I do it with my magic pencil.

I write every day. About the flowers I see, the colours I like. I write about what I'm learning at school. About my teachers. Sometimes, I write letters to pen pals I have made through *Young Times* magazine. One of my pen pals, Emily, lives in New Jersey in the United States. She tells me they have lockers in their school that they put posters on, and I wonder if I can put posters up in the room my brothers and I share in the flat. I tell her how Mama jaan and I make keemay alay parathay, stuffed ground-meat breads, every Friday after Jumah prayers, and she tells me she thinks her parents don't love her. I tell her that is not possible.

Sometimes, I write letters to Naano. Though those are in Punjabi, and they take me longer. Sometimes, I write about my brothers. Sometimes, I write about my friends.

I laugh sometimes too.

Sometimes, I share the poems I write with my magic pencil and leave them out beside my mattress at night. Occasionally, I get a note back.

That spring, while the Gulf War slows down, fears linger about Iraq's ruler using his weapons to hurt United Arab Emirates because it supported Kuwait. Baba jaani and Mama jaan decide that she, my brothers, and I will live in Lahore for at least a few months, till the situation in the Gulf improves and we can return to Sharjah. Many of my other friends in school return to their countries while their fathers stay. My teachers make sure I have enough homework to last me a few months, and just in case we end up staying longer than expected, we pack books for the next grade with us so I can keep studying. Baba does not join us on this trip. He stays back to work.

Being in Lahore is like being back in the middle of everything beautiful. I spend my evenings with Guddi Baji on the rooftops, moulding clay into pots and plates, firing them.

I laugh again. I giggle again.

"Hold it like you care about it," says Guddi Baji, as she hugs her clay pot close to her. "Kiss it, even, like this," she says, gently bringing her red-clay-caked hands with the pot close to her lips.

"Hain? Why would I kiss my plate, Guddi Baji?" I ask, barely able to contain my laughter.

"Oh, pagliye! So that every time the pot becomes home to something delicious and rich with flavours and colours, it knows it is loved. Every handful of rice will carry that love, every scoop of korma more delicious than the one before," she says, with a beautiful smile. I wish she would smile more often.

"Wouldn't the person using it have to show their love to the pot, Guddi Baji? Why us? We might not even use it."

"Tsk," she says, clicking her tongue. "They'll show theirs, Laachiye. You show yours. Love is love. And yours is special."

"Is it?" I ask, grinning.

Holding my carved plate up in my palm, I bring it to my lips, and tell my plate I love it, and wish that it offers the best rotiyah and parathay anyone has ever had. Bobbing my head, pleased with myself, I then pass it to Guddi Baji to place it in the kiln, right next to her pot.

Next to her real-size pot, my little plate for my pretend house looks silly.

"I don't know how anyone would make a roti on that, Laachiye. Certainly not a roti for you. You'll need twenty of them!" she teases, poking my tummy.

"Or thirty, if I've been hauling things for you!" I squeal, both of us bursting into laughter. Our bellies finally settle from the laughing, and I lean over. Wrapping my arms around her, I say, "I love you. More than the plate, Guddi Baji."

She looks down at me and shakes her head, with that warm smile I love so much.

"Your love is so pure, Laachiye," she whispers, eyes filling with tears. "Dobara nazar na laggay. *May the evil eye never get you again.*"

I want to ask her about the evil eye but let it sit. I can ask Naano jaan.

We watch the fire warm and harden her pot and my little plate, and I wonder if the fire hurts my little plate. It must. But my plate needs that fire to come alive, to be, to become. Just like the pot. To be able to cook saag over a low flame for hours, the pot needed to know the heat. All those spices would need to dance in the heat of the flame, teasing each mustard leaf till they were hugged, absorbed, accepted.

Yes, the pot had to burn, had to *know*, had to learn the touch of fire, had to have *felt* fire, breathed it, absorbed it, become it.

Fire was life.

Fire is life.

Fire and Water

Fire devours,
teeth sinking into walls,
swallowing wood, cloth, bone.
Feasting on cities,
spitting out ash where homes once stood,
blackening the sky, leaving war in its wake.

Fire rages,
bursting in the night,
a soldier wide awake, a lover never letting go.
It does not ask, just takes.
And yet fire nurtures,
breathing life into dying embers,
coaxing spices to dance, turning raw into ready,
cold into comfort,
kindling into light.

Then comes water,
slipping through the cracks, moving like a whisper,
crashing like a storm,
cooling the burn, drowning the rage,
softening war's rough hands.

Water, do you know?
If fire becomes war,
can you become peace?
If fire takes,
can you return what is lost?
Or do you only carry the ruins,
folding them into your waves,
telling the skies what you could not save?

Khoya

That year, while I'm in Lahore, I talk to Baba jaani back in Sharjah every few days. He calls the home phone, and usually I'm somewhere on one of the rooftops, so I hear, "Maaaaaaanoooooo, Baba!" and I drop everything and run multiple flights of stairs, usually barefoot, to get to the phone, breathless, ready to tell Baba jaani everything I have learned, and all the darbars we have been to, and how I learned how to make parathay now, and how I am learning new songs. I even sing one for him.

Mostly Baba jaani just laughs, though I'm not really telling him jokes. I ask him how things are in Sharjah, and he tells me he has been travelling to Kuwait, to Iraq, to Sudan, to Bahrain, to Saudi Arabia. I have seen these places on a map, but other than Saudi Arabia, where we have been a couple of times for Umrah and once for Hajj, I don't really know what they look like. I ask him if he misses Mama jaan, and he's quiet for a second. I wonder if the line has dropped.

"You know when you get really hungry, puttar?"

"Mmhmm."

"And you want to just fight with your brothers because you're hungry?"

"Mmhmmmmm?" I say, feeling a hint of defensiveness creeping up in me.

"That's how I feel without your mama jaan," he says. "I either don't want to speak to anyone or just fight with them."

"Tsk, aw, Baba jaani. She's the same. Always picking on me."

"That's different."

"No, she tells me I need to sit like a girl. What does that even mean?"

He sighs. "Never mind."

"No, no. Mind mind," I say. "I mean, she misses you too, and we hope we can come back soon. We miss you too, Baba jaani. I'm sure it's safe enough. Plus, if anything happens, at least we'll be together. We should come back!"

"Hmmm," he says. I can tell his heart wants to say yes, but he hesitates.

We talk about a few more things, and then he hangs up, and I feel a little sad. Baba is lonely without us, and I wish I could be with him. I feel like being alone for a bit, so I grab a book and go sit by the motia bush. And soon I am carried away by a story of a land far away with fairies and elves and trees that move during the night while the world sleeps.

"Ay kee?! Chal, main Layla di kaani sunanna wan." Daada jaani interrupts my dreamy reading time. *"What's this? Let me tell you a story about Layla."*

I look up at him, and his eyes are dancing as he asks me. Wrinkles hug those dark eyes of his. There's mystery in those deep wrinkles. They deepen when he smiles, each wrinkle telling its own little story. Sometimes, I wonder if the stories change over time. Do the wrinkles deepen as he adds more colour, more texture, more nuance to each story? What if he ran out of space around those eyes? He must carry those stories elsewhere. Maybe in a secret treasure basket somewhere, or in his little black diary, where he saves phone numbers and names of people he meets in his travels.

Or, maybe, we were supposed to carry them? In our wrinkles? But we didn't have any wrinkles. I was a child, and children didn't have wrinkles, *did they?*

Layla was Daada jaani's mare. And any time stories involved Layla, it meant Daada jaani was mediating a community conflict of some sort. So, while every story time was special, story time about Layla was extra special.

I run out onto the veranda and invite all the kids to gather on the rooftop for story time. Story time was starting earlier than usual today, which could mean Daada jaani was planning on making burfi as he told the stories. As if he heard me, he asks Daado jaan to send someone to the rooftop with a pot of milk from that morning so he can make burfi.

The midafternoon sun offers much-needed warmth in the winter months. I watch Daado jaan closely as she pulls out a large valtoyee. It's a beautiful thing, this valtoyee, I think. Its large and round golden-brass body carries milk just like a mother's swollen womb carries a little one. Its little neck is small, and protects the milk from spilling out, and allows the pour to be carefully measured. The bottom is round and flared, allowing a flat donut ring to sit under, holding the pot. This also allows the women to carry the valtoyee on their heads, should they need to transport the milk. Daado jaan gets one of us to grab a large metal pot, another one to grab a large wooden spoon, someone gets to hold a couple of large bamboo fans, a muslin cloth, a sack of coal, a large box of matches, some fresh nuts, plates, a handful of knives, a mortar and pestle, and some other supplies she thinks Daada jaani might need.

Sighing contently as she does an inventory of all the supplies distributed amongst us little ones, she grabs a ring off a hook in the veranda, places the ring on her head, bends over to pick up the milk-full valtoyee and gracefully places it on her head in one swift motion, and starts her journey up to the rooftop, a bunch of us little ones in tow like a tiny army of random supplies.

Once on the rooftop, she sets the valtoyee down, its stunning gold shimmering in the late-afternoon sun, and pulls out a puwwa, a metal measuring cup, to measure out eight ser of milk.

Laying all our supplies around the brick kiln in the middle of the rooftop, we watch Daado jaan as she assigns the chopping and slicing of the nuts to the older kids, and to the ones slightly younger, she asks to help the older ones with whatever they need to get the job done.

To me, she hands over the mortar and pestle and a bag of pistachios and reminds me that the process should not be noisy if I do it right. I frown, knowing this will be hard. How does one beat down pistachios into a powder without making any noise?

She assigns Anaya, my little cousin, to help me. Anaya looks up at me with those gorgeous brown eyes with the longest eyelashes I have ever seen on a child, keen, eager, a grin the size of the Karakoram range on her face. I tell her she has two tasks. First, grab as many pistachios as she can in her tiny little palms and toss them in the mortar. Second, when I say so, drop the crushed ones into the plate Daado jaan has given us.

As minutes go by, and the preparations proceed, some of the aunties join us with their little ones who are barely learning how to crawl. I always wonder if the littlest ones understood Daada jaani's stories. Sometimes, they fell asleep as their mothers swayed them.

I wonder if the stories are for the mothers. Perhaps for both. Maybe this is how mothers were showing the littlest ones how to listen to Daada jaani's stories.

Preparation of the nuts assigned, Daado jaan carefully lays out fresh coals in the kiln. The kiln is one of my favourite parts of the house. The bricks and clay come together in a cradle, like a perfectly imperfect puzzle, waiting to awe the next person with what this cradle can give life to. Each brick sings a testament to the hands that have laid it, a testament to the fingers that have repaired any cracks with clay as it wears out over the years.

Suddenly, it dawns on me that perhaps it is the kiln that also holds all the stories Daada jaani tells. The magic of that thought warms every being of me. The bricks have been listening this whole time! To the stories, to the giggles, to the cries, to the gasps, to the hearts that beat with every word Daada jaani says. When it's time for a brick to retire and a new one to take its place, the old ones must tell every new brick that joins the kiln the stories that have been told over the years, the decades, the centuries. As the years go by, in this way, each brick in this cradle of magic becomes a teller and a keeper of stories.

As the late afternoon inches towards the evening, the coals are softly crackling, and the metal pot of fresh, heavy milk sits atop. The stirring begins, a sign for the little kids with unassigned tasks to gather around so the story can begin.

"Layla," he begins, with his warm voice, rich like the soils of Punjab, "was stunning, my little ones. Her big brown eyes, soulful and curious, framed by long, luxuriant eyelashes, were envied by those near and far. She smiled every time she saw me." His eyes dance with those wrinkles I so deeply adore.

"Layla was so wise, so intelligent, and so playful. So very playful." He laughs. My heart feels so warm when he laughs. "She knew how to get away with a lot." He pauses, his eyes widening, his brows rising as if a particular memory rushes to him but stops just before it touches his lips. He sighs, looking down at the milk, still dancing away, swirling as if humming a soft tune, garnishing his story.

"Layla navigated so much conflict in her life, my little ones," he continues. "With each conflict came more wisdom, which Layla just seemed to gather, as if picking cotton in the fields and dotting it carefully, beautifully, along her path, so next time, she knew where to go. Each conflict seemed to make her stronger, wiser, more powerful, more responsible, as if conflict for her was like milk for us, feeding us, fueling us, making our bones stronger, my little ones." He flexes his bicep, and we all giggle, some of us quickly starting to flex our biceps to show the others.

He's a slight man, Daada jaani, even slighter now that he is getting older, his beard and eyebrows all silver. Yet every morning, he hops on his bicycle and starts his day by hauling eighty ser of milk, going door to door, greeting people, asking how their old ones are faring, if the littlest ones have teeth yet, how the house repairs are coming along, how their livestock is doing, how their daughters are doing, if their sons who are overseas are able to send enough money back, and if all in the house of many are keeping healthy. And in this way, he knows when anyone in the community is unwell, needing a visit, needing to know that they are not alone.

"Ahem, ahem." He clears his throat, and we all hush.

"In fact," he continues, "Layla was so wise that sometimes she was even asked to help others see better, find a path forward. She listened with patience, with compassion, sometimes for days, my little ones. Can you imagine listening to this old man for days?" He smiles and we giggle.

He falls silent for a bit, the milk simmering and swirling as he stirs with his wooden spoon in gentle, patient motions. Playful wisps of steam rise, curling into the air every time Daada jaani switches the direction of the stirring spoon.

The coals crackle playfully as he speaks again.

"One time, Layla was confronted with a particularly difficult issue.

A young, widowed father wanted to marry his young daughter Aliya off to a much older man, because he couldn't afford to provide for Aliya and the older man had agreed not to take a dowry. Aliya had come to Layla and cried for days, her tears breaking Layla's biggest of hearts. Aliya's little heart was terribly scared and confused. She wept and wept and wept some more, promising to Layla that she would never disobey her father, but that this man was so old, and little Aliya was so scared. She promised she would never eat again so her father didn't have to worry about providing for her. She would never ask for new clothes or new bangles, or anything. She just wanted to stay in her home and take care of her little brothers, because if she didn't, who would?

"But what could Layla do? Could she hide little Aliya and protect her? But then her father would come looking. Could Layla talk to the old man and ask him to shoo away and leave little Aliya alone? Could Layla talk to the poor father and find a way to support him in raising little Aliya?"

Daada jaani falls silent again and looks at us. Softly, he says, "Nikki duniya, kee karay Layla? *My little worlds, what should Layla do?*"

A long silence follows, as we watch Daada jaani's face, now, with the sun set, glowing just in the light from the kiln. He's watching the milk closely now, time stretching, each moment infused with care and patience.

His wooden spoon coaxes the milk slowly, tenderly, urging it to thicken and condense. Each stir is the gentlest of caresses, a loving nudge, guiding the milk on its journey, honouring it. Every now and then, he pushes a little faster, as if reminding the milk that it can't get distracted by the beauty of the story. It must keep moving, for moving will allow it to grow into its new form. The milk, now heavier, seems to take more effort. It's thicker now, darker too.

"Hmmm?" he says, looking up, and we know the bravest amongst us must speak.

Pa'ji, my older cousin, speaks first and the rest of us follow.

One by one, we say what seems fair to our little minds. Daada jaani patiently listens. His eyes shuffle between us and the rapidly condensing milk, a thick paste now. Our solutions range from sending firecrackers and roaches and frogs and lizards to the old man's place to scare him and leave little Aliya alone, to bringing everyone together to help the young father, to maybe inviting Aliya to live with us, in our home, where she would be safe and could sleep in our manjiyan under the stars, like us. Every solution invites reactions and much conversation, sometimes laughter, sometimes fury, and everything in between.

Daada jaani doesn't say much, just watches us, and we all watch him as every solution is voiced, looking for the slightest twitch of a muscle, the slightest curl of his lips, the gentlest little nod, the most subtle raise of the eyebrows, to know if this could be a solution worth exploring.

We have all been in this story time enough to know every solution stands as a possibility.

And then, as if the kiln has heard us enough, the doughy parts start separating from the walls of the pot, and Daada jaani asks us to come closer carefully.

We watch as the sacred pot, once brimming with milk, now holds a dense, luscious, creamy mass. It is as if all that strength in the milk boiled right down into this one small lump of strength, and why wouldn't it? Daada jaani had poured so much love and story and care into it.

This lump is khoya, the base of hundreds of our desserts.

Next, Daada jaani adds a wad of ghee and a cup of gurr that melts instantly as it touches the khoya, and as if we all knew, we all send our assigned little ones to drop the nuts in the pot, a heap of crushed almonds, powdered pistachios, ground cardamom. Daada jaani thanks each little one, and they grin proudly. He then looks at each of us who sent the little ones forward, nodding in approval.

He mixes everything together, in what seems like the perfect harmony of spices dancing in celebration, the deeply intoxicating aroma taking over us all. We breathe it all in, our souls smiling, our mouths watering, our tummies grumbling in anticipation.

This is burfi. The dessert of the Gujjars. The dessert of my people.

As the pot comes off the coals, they glow softly, as if gleaming in joy with what they have accomplished. At that moment, I know the answer to where the stories Daada jaani tells us go. They lie in those wrinkles, in the bricks and the clay in the kiln, in the decisions he makes, in the deliberations he facilitates, in everything we learn each time we think about what Layla would do.

The stories are carried in us, in our hearts and minds, in our actions, in our conversations, in our dreams, and in the burfi we share with those we love.

They are carried in the wisps of air rising from the pot, in the air that becomes the wind, travelling miles and miles away, settling on another rooftop, connecting us all.

As we wait for the burfi to cool just enough so our mouths can handle it, Daada jaani reminds us that there is never a perfect answer to a question. While it may seem obvious to each of us how the matter of Aliya and her young father and the old suitor should have been resolved, the answer is never simple.

The answer is somewhere in between what the person, the community, and the society is ready to hear, is ready for, believes to be right and moral and acceptable, and deep within our hearts, what we who are asked, who are invited to be in the middle of it, believe might seem like the best thing to do.

We nod, as if we understand. I won't for a long time yet.

Burfi

Under watchful hands
with patience and steadiness,
a spoon tracing circles
in the quiet rhythm of waiting.
No rushing, no forcing,
just time, just care,
the scents of something becoming
what it was always meant to be.
Born from hours,
from ritual, from love,
from knowing that it is made with care
no other way to be,
but sweet, tender,
and sacred.

Takhti

The Wooden Board

Monsoon in Lahore was my favourite season of the year. It came with a sense of anticipation and relief, transforming the landscape with its arrival. With intense weeks of heat inching towards it, the arrival of the monsoon meant distant rumbles, the skies shifting from bright blues to brooding greys with thick clouds meeting in the skies as if readying themselves for battle. The winds would then pick up, as if warning the clouds that battles fought in the skies came with rules that must be followed. With the winds also came the deeply comforting smells of wet soils, a hint of what transformation would feel like, smell like, taste like.

And then the magical rains would come.

In sudden bursts, the drops would drum on rooftops, splatter against windows, and cascade from the edges of trees in the courtyards. Streets would fill quickly with water, turning into small, swirling streams, inviting laughter from children splashing around.

The world around me would seem to breathe again, as the parched earth would drink deeply, plants unfurling their leaves, their greens deepening and brightening in gratitude.

Like the leaves, I would submit to mother earth's love too then.

Sprawling on the cool brick floor of Naano jaan's rooftop, my face up to the skies, I'd watch as the rain fell in gentle sheets around me, the bricks, warmed by the earlier sun, now soothing under me.

I'd watch the raindrops, each one pelting down, creating a dance of tiny splashes, echoing a gentle, playful strum in my soul. If I listened closely, the melody of the raindrops was like a melody from the seventh sky, a melody wrapped in wonder, in awe, in beauty beyond this world.

I'd wonder if Rani, the queen from Mama jaan's stories, could also hear this melody as she floated across the skies.

The melody of the monsoon rain was all my happy colours dancing with me, around me, in me. Each drop that touched my skin was a soft kiss from the skies. Each rain brought a thousand kisses, enough love to last me many lives.

One morning in mid-July, playing around on Naano jaan's rooftop, I hear her call me to her room. This was usually her afternoon nap time, so I think maybe I am making too much noise and woke her up. I go in, expecting Naano jaan to tell me how we must move around with gentler feet when others are resting, something she has tried to teach me a few times this summer.

"Walk like goats. Do we ever hear them stomping? They can be up the side of mountains. Nimble. No one even hears them coming," she'd say, barely containing her laughter. "You, pagliye, stomp like a baby elephant!"

Giggling, I'd remind her how cute baby elephants were and how cool it would be for me to be a real elephant. "They're so beautiful and graceful, Naano jaan. They walk like this." I'd stomp and sway at the same time, and Mama jaan would say from the corner of the room, "Waikh lo ainu appa'yee hun. Tussi samjhao su, meri te koi na sundi eh kuri. *See for yourself now. You explain to her. This girl doesn't listen to me.*"

"I want everyone to hear me coming, Naano jaan. Like this!" And I'd stomp and sway and stomp some more till we were all laughing and I couldn't laugh anymore.

As I walk into her room that day, I find Naano sitting on her manji, the hot air in the room clinging to us.

Entering Naano jaan's room now, I quietly say, "Hanji, Naano jaan, bulaya tussi? *Yes, Naano jaan, you called me?*"

"Idhar aa, puttar. *Come here, little one.*" She gestures for me to join her on her manji.

Naano jaan has been sick for a couple of weeks now, and I'm worried about her. She looks tired. Her wrinkles, which usually carry so much love and laughter, today seem to carry more worry, more weight.

"Are you okay, Naano jaan?" I ask her.

She smiles wearily, kissing my forehead. "As long as I have the love of my kamli Laachi, I will always be okay."

"Well, in that case, you're set for the next hundred lives, Naano jaan!" I say. She smiles a smile so warm she looks years younger.

I wrap my arms around her, squeezing her, and she coughs, and I let her go, worried I have hurt her. She laughs softly and gets up slowly. Walking across the room, she pulls out a wooden board, smooth and polished, its surface showing faint marks of some sort.

"You know how you have a magic pencil?" She looks at me, holding my gaze.

I hold my breath.

"This is my magic takhti."

A takhti is a traditional wooden writing board used for practising writing and calligraphy. Made from a smooth, flat piece of wood and often coated with a layer of grey claylike chalk called gaachi, the takhti is an important part of who we are. One would write on it with a chiselled qalam, a wooden pencil, dipping the sharpened, chiselled edge into a small container of black ink typically made with soot and water. Tapping off the excess ink, the qalam is placed firmly on the board, in an act that is gentle, focused, and steady.

As our little ones write out their alif, be, pe, te, the older ones write couplets, short poems, short stories. Once done and our work shared with our aunties, we'd rinse off the board under warm water and coat it with gaachi, ready to be used the next day. I had a takhti with me in Sharjah too, but it wasn't the same. Sitting in a quiet flat on the eighth floor of a building was no match for sitting on the mud floor in a courtyard by the motia with my cousins, their chatter, their laughter, their endless banter.

Naano jaan's eyes crinkle at the corners with something I have not seen before. It is somewhere between joy and grief, between accepting and refusing, between wanting and giving, between curiosity and knowing.

"When I was your age, Emahn jaan, something bad happened to me too," she says, looking at the board in her hands, her fingers lingering over the wood, as if tracing old lines, as if she could still see what was on it, as if she was visiting an old friend she had shared secrets with.

Everything grows dark around me, the colours of the afternoon suddenly disappearing. My mouth goes dry, my heart starts racing. An unexplainable darkness comes at me from the inside out.

Something bad happened to me, she said.

Someone had hurt my naano jaan.

Someone.

Hurt.

My.

Naano jaan.

Those words churn in my head as if not fitting in the space they need to be able to turn and twist, so they just scrape at the edges of my brain.

I blink hard, pushing back, pushing down, pushing away the darkness coming at me. I must listen. I breathe, trying to force my lungs to do their job.

Ffff. Pfff.

"What happened, Naano jaan?" I ask her cautiously, my breaths shallow.

"What happened is not important, Laachiye. Pain is pain. A little more, a little less, doesn't matter, puttar. Our hurts are all different. What hurts me more may hurt you less. Hurt is hurt. Shame is shame. What shames you more may shame me less. Shame is shame. Bad men hurting little girls is bad men hurting little girls. The how and what is not important. It's what we do with it that is more important."

She looks up at me, her face contorted, her eyes wider, as if blinking them will open floodgates she's holding shut with all her might.

"My takhti became my best friend. I told it all my secrets. I wrote on it every day. And then waited for the ink to dry. And once it was dry, I kissed my words. And then I washed it, knowing my words were now a part of the wood, a part of the universe. A part of me I had shared so I wasn't carrying my pain alone. Here, I want you to have it."

She is out of breath. She has used all her words. I cannot imagine how long she has been playing these words in her mind. How heavy they must have been for her.

She looks relieved. Tired. Sad. But lighter.

She holds it out, and I take it from her, kissing it.

"Merbaani, Naano jaan," I say.

I know I am holding a bridge between Naano jaan's grief and mine. This takhti wasn't just a board. It was a piece of her, a symbol of her strength, a keeper of her words, a keeper of her magic.

"Mama jaan says the magic is not in the pencil, Naano jaan," I say softly.

"She's right, puttar. Magic is in the ability to see beauty in everything around us. In the ugliest of things. In the most difficult of things. In the hardest of things. Everyone can see beauty in the obvious. Seeing it, hearing it, telling it you see it, welcoming it, knowing it, where no one else can, *that* is the magic, Laachiye. *That* is magic."

At that moment, I understand the expression on Naano jaan's face. In the endless hours in the kitchen, surrounded by all her spices and stories, surrounded with love and laughter and endless chatter, she had passed on all her teachings in life to me. And now, by gifting me the takhti, she had just honoured me with the story of her pain, the courage of her survival.

She had written on this takhti in moments of darkness, in moments of joy, in moments she didn't understand.

With her own hands, Naano jaan had dipped the qalam in ink, and watched the ink dry, over and over again.

She had touched the ink as she had watched it wash away and felt its silkiness on her fingers.

She had written from the depths of her heart—with love, with anger, with grief, with joy, with passion.

With magic.

Naano jaan passed away that summer. I was with her as her eyes closed. As she took her last breath.

I held her hand as the skies welcomed her home.

At her funeral, as my insides scraped against me in an agony I had never felt before, as my insides burned as if eating every muscle bit by bit at the loss of her, as the cries and wailing of everyone around me reached my ears, I sat and listened and looked for the beauty in this darkness.

As she lay there, facing the skies, I noted the richness of the jasmines and the roses that lay on her, holding her carefully in their love. I thanked them for being there with her. For caring for her. For reminding her of the beauty around her.

I noted the calmness on her face, the gentleness, the tenderness with which she had welcomed death.

I noted the wrinkles on her face. Each carrying a lifetime of wisdom, of lessons, of messages Naano jaan wanted me to believe with every cell in my body.

And I received them all. In a basket I would never let go.

I noted the gentle breeze that touched her, touched me, reminding me we were never separated.

I noted the rustle of the neem tree, as if the wind was urging it to make sure I was okay.

I was okay. I was going to be okay.

Ffff. Pfff.

When the most important person in our life dies, what is it that we lose? The sound of their laughter? The warmth of their touch? The comforting scent of them? The sound of them telling us everything will be okay?

As I watched her, wrapped in two sheets of unsewn white cloth, I wondered what it was *exactly* that I was losing.

I wasn't losing Naano jaan. No.

I would no longer need to wait for weeks for Mama jaan to call her so I could hear her voice on the phone. I would no longer need to wait for hot summers to run into her arms, spend hours in her kitchen, dance with her spices, dance with her voice, hear her laughter.

No. I now had her with me, *any time* I wanted. She was now a part of me I could visit any time.

She was now *me*. And me, her.

Pain and darkness could live in harmony with many things, I decide.

That night, with Naano jaan returned to mother earth and her entire being intertwined with mine, with hands that wouldn't stop shaking, with tears that wouldn't stop flowing, I wrote on the takhti.

To Naano Jaan's Takhti

You knew her too,
just like me.
Better than me,
perhaps?

You held her,
comforted her, loved her, showed her
the beauty that wasn't, the love that wasn't,
the comfort that wasn't, the care that wasn't,
perhaps?

You made her believe
in joy over grief, rain over drought,
love over hate,
perhaps?

You made her believe in beauty over darkness,
glimmers over sorrow, strength over weakness,
embers over ashes, life over death,
perhaps?

For that, I love you.
I honour you, I gift you to keep
my secrets with hers,
my ink with hers, my words with hers.
Our inks together, our words together,
woven through them all,
the lives she and I have lived,
the lives we live today,
the lives ahead.

Nezaam

Rules

The Gulf War winds down, and we return to Sharjah a few weeks after Naano jaan passes. Sharjah seems more tired than when I was last there a few months prior. Everything seems to move more slowly, a little cautiously. There are many families from Kuwait and Iraq in the country now. There seems to be some relief that the war has ended, but everything seems more measured, as if speaking of the end of the war would bring an omen no one wants to know about. In our small flat, we put the gas masks away. The souqs feel fuller and louder. Women bargain at shops like they never forgot how. There are fabrics in the souq we hadn't seen before—bright saris from India, stiff lawn from Pakistan, shawls from Yemen embroidered with orange-gold threads. The shopkeepers seem to call out louder, knowing people's pockets are starting to fill up again. Sharjah seems to be moving forward. The souq says so.

As things settle back into a routine, I throw myself into school.

Every recess, instead of spending time with friends, I go to the library.

I learn a lot about rules over the years that follow.

Rules. We didn't really have a word for them in Punjabi. And if we did, I hadn't learned it yet. The closest one I knew was nezaam. A system of sorts, protocols, codes of conduct, relationships, social order. At school, these were principles we as students would follow. At home, these were principles we as a family, as children, would follow—how we were expected to behave as good humans, to promote harmony, stability—something that would be acceptable in society.

It was always intriguing to me how so many words were needed to describe a word from the language of my ancestors.

At school, the back corner on the floor of the library was my favourite place to be. It was a small, quiet spot, tucked away from the rest of the classroom, and though it wasn't where students were supposed to sit, Ms. Zahra knew I liked it there. She let me be, even though it went against the nezaam about where, how, and when we should sit. She'd glance over sometimes with a soft smile, an understanding in her eyes. Every now and then, she'd bring me a new book the school had recently acquired, the pages still crisp and fresh, smelling of paper that was young, paper that hadn't been touched by the many readers who would over time trace the lines with their fingers. She would sit on the floor next to me for the forty-five-minute recess as I touched the pages. We never really spoke. We didn't have to. Sometimes, in the silence, words float around us, making meaning without needing to be said.

My name would often be the first written on the library log to check out a new book. I would see words, many of them words I knew. Others were new. With every new book, I learned new ways for how words could come together to explain the vastness of who we were as humans.

Then there was the nezaam about how long we were allowed to keep a book—strictly two weeks, no more, no less. But I never needed that long. A few days would pass, and I'd already have devoured it, ready for another. So Ms. Zahra and I bent that nezaam too.

I wondered what nezaam my books had, their pages filled with stories and worlds I could float into whenever I needed an escape. The characters, their journeys, weaving their way into my poems, my dreams, and sometimes my nightmares. They had beauty in them, these characters, their journeys unique and curious. I wondered what nezaam governed these characters.

I loved school. I loved the order, the structure, it offered, the sense of calm that came from knowing what to expect. There were no surprises here, no unspoken rules. If I did my homework, put in the time, paid attention, and carefully and respectfully asked the questions floating in my head, the care would be returned. The teachers noticed; the system worked. It was a relationship of mutual respect, one I could count on. The nezaam was clear.

My teachers loved me too. There was a beautiful simplicity in this relationship—between me, my books, and my teachers. We were always taught that our teachers were our second parents, and for me, that was true. These were the people who knew more words than me, who had seen more of the world than I had, who had perhaps asked more questions of the universe than I could even imagine. They brought with them the knowledge of their worlds, the knowledge of their grandmothers and grandfathers, the knowledge of their lands. That thought alone kept me in constant reverence of them.

School was not just a place of learning for me; it was a sanctuary.

We were only allowed to speak English, unless we were in a language class, and that was okay. My thoughts, my questions, my curiosity—all of it flowed out in the language I was required to use, and it felt fine, a way to belong. All our English was different anyway. Every word was pronounced in a dozen different ways—the South Indian way, the North Indian way, the Lahori way, the Pashto way, the English way, the Egyptian way, the Qatari way, the Bahraini way, the Palestinian way, the Sri Lankan way, the Moroccan way, the Israeli way, the Nepali way, the Bengali way. And none of us questioned it or mocked each other for how they said a word, or winced every time something was said differently from how it rolled off our tongues.

Each word had a life of its own on the tongue of the keeper of the word.

While some students rebelled against the rules, I followed them. Perhaps there was thrill in rebellion, in pushing back, but I didn't need that. Not yet. I needed to understand the world first. One day, I would probably have to break the rules, the ones the world around me would lay on me, the ones about what it meant to be a woman, a daughter, a sister, a mother, perhaps even a grandmother. Those were the rules that sought to shape me, to define what I could or could not be. I would break them in my own time. In my own way.

But the rules at school? They were different. I found comfort in them. They were like the steady lines on a page, offering a structure for me to fill with my own words. There was something curiously elegant about following them, about understanding their purpose. They helped me see the world with clarity, to navigate it without the chaos of confusion. There was a certain beauty in that simplicity, a calm that came from knowing where I stood.

Plus, if the *why* of the rule didn't settle in me, if it felt unjust, I could always learn to change it. Daada jaani had taught me that in his stories. To understand a rule fully was the first step in moulding it, in reshaping it to fit a more just and compassionate world. It was like the karray, the clay pots, on the rooftop with Guddi Baji. We had to learn to speak to the clay, feel it in our hands, around our fingers, letting it show us what it was meant to do, and how. And then, once we understood each other, we could build something. Our fingers shaping it, the clay letting us.

For now, though, in the safety of the classroom, with its steady hum of routine, I let the rules guide me. All of them. The shuffling to get on our feet every time class changed to greet the new teachers arriving for the next class.

The bells every forty-five minutes to mark the end of one class and the beginning of the next.

The perfectly straight lines in the morning assembly, with each student standing equally apart.

The perfectly uniformed marches around the school grounds. Hands rising and dropping to the same height, our strides the same distance.

The perfectly identical uniforms.

The perfectly identical way our hijabs were worn.

The perfectly identical lack of makeup on our faces, or polish on our nails.

The perfectly identical shoes every day of the week.

The perfectly identical arrangement of desks and chairs in every classroom.

The perfectly identical brown covers on each notebook.

The perfectly hidden secrets I carried. At school, no one needed to know about the bad man. At school, there were no nightmares. No dark tunnels. No bitter tastes in my mouth.

School was a treasure map, showing me the path to many more worlds, until one day, I'd be ready to draw my own.

Zindagi da Nezaam

There's a rhythm to it,
a silent guide,
a steady beat.
Marking the lines we walk each day
in quiet tones,
muted colours
shaping our way.

Some rebel,
some fight their form,
raging against the storm.
For me, there's a grace,
a path, a rhythm,
a steady pace.

For every nezaam,
there's a reason tucked,
threads weaving through,
some smooth as silk,
others frazzled and frayed,
tired and old,
ready for something new.

Some rules are walls,
some are doors,
some fail,
but they all shape
and mould and guide and show.

In their dance,
we find a way,
sometimes to follow,
sometimes to sway.

Akhiyaan

The Eyes

On my fifteenth birthday, as my teachers celebrate my breaking of all academic records in the Gulf, talks about my marriage start at home. I don't really pay attention. I'm too busy with my books, my tests, and my lessons.

Well, and a secret boyfriend.

A boyfriend with eyes that make my heart flutter like the wings of a hummingbird. A boyfriend with a smile that makes me stop breathing. He must remain a secret in my world, of course. Girls are not allowed to love without permission. And I don't know how to seek that permission, or *who* to seek it from. I imagine asking Naano jaan the question, but I don't really get an answer other than to just be.

So, I be.

Every Wednesday after school, I ask for permission to go to a public library and instead spend time with Yawar.

Aaah, Yawar.

Yawar is like a gentle, cool breeze from the mountains of Kashmir. He is tall, so painfully handsome, with a mop of messy, wavy raven-black hair, and eyes that are a clash of browns, greys, greens, and hazel against his light skin. He looks at me with a curiosity *so* deep, so respectful, so gentle, yet so strong, that I want to tell him all my secrets. I tell him some. Some are mine to keep.

I tell him about my rooftops in Lahore, about the fields of Punjab, about the narrow, meandering streets, about the colours of the sky on Basant. And he tells me about the valleys of Kashmir, carved in beauty that must have taken centuries, for every detail to be so perfect. He tells me about his towering mountains, their snow-capped peaks touching the clouds, standing proud and loud around the valleys, their white tops playfully contrasting with the rich greens below. I imagine them to be my happy greens.

He tells me about the valleys that stretch wide and deep, cradled lovingly, carefully, by these mountains, holding quiet serenity wrapped in grandeur.

He tells me how in the spring, the valleys bloom with colour, rich fields of wildflowers swaying in the gentle breeze, seas of reds, yellows, and purples stretching as far as the eye can see. He tells me how every fall, the chinar trees turn a fiery red, their leaves carpeting the ground in a blaze of orange and gold.

He tells me about the rivers that run clear as glass, winding their way through the valleys, their waters shimmering playfully in the sunlight as they carve gentle paths between meadows and villages. His rivers speak in soft murmurs as they flow by the weeping willows, he says, their sound blending with the songs of birds that call the valleys their home.

I imagine sitting by the willows with him someday, tracing our fingertips together over lines of Rumi's poetry.

I love listening to him describe his home, which he left just two years prior, his family being the unfortunate ones, he says, chosen to leave the homeland to slog for the rest of their lives.

I can tell he misses home.

I have often asked Mama jaan to tell me about her Kashmir, but she always hesitates. She says she doesn't remember much, just that Naano jaan was a little girl when they had to leave after her father was killed and their house burned down during the Partition riots. I tell myself that perhaps Mama jaan is not ready to tell me. Or maybe she doesn't know. Or maybe what she knows is hidden too deep down, too far away from where she can pull it from, mould it into words to share with me.

She'll tell me in time, I tell myself.

For now, I learn about the beauty of my mama jaan's homeland from Yawar. I imagine being there with him someday, seeing it through his eyes.

Ahhh, those eyes.

One Wednesday, as I'm telling him about the latest happenings at school, I tell him I wrote a poem for him.

"Well, I feel honoured to have finally made it into your poems, Emahn jaan," he says, with a smile that turns me into mush. My face gets hot. I love the sound of my name on his lips. He pronounces it a little differently than my parents; it's lighter, less rounded, sharper, but gentler.

"Well, yeah, I suppose some things take time." I giggle. "Can I read it to you?" I say, feeling a hint of courage. I should have just given it to him, but here we are.

"Only if I can stare at you as you do," he says, his voice barely a whisper.

"Fine. Only if I can stare right back at you," I say, feeling braver.

"Oh my. Deal." He laughs. God, I love his laugh.

I take a deep breath in. With my left hand, I tuck my hair behind my left ear, and with a voice that is a little shaky from all the giddiness coursing through me, knowing his eyes are on me, I begin.

"I call this poem 'Akhiyaan.' It's about your eyes."

> In the hazel of your eyes,
> I see the dawn,
> light shifting gently,
> subtly,
> a quiet flame,
> where dreams take shape.
>
> In the green of your eyes,
> I see the wild,
> the untamed,
> the pine trees in the forests,
> whispering their secrets
> to those who listen.

In the greys of your eyes,
I see the rain,
the calm,
the gentle pause
between the storms,
where peace settles,
sometimes lingers.

In the brown of your eyes,
I see the homeland,
the earth,
steady and warm.
I see my fields,
my muddy rivers,
my rooftops.

Each colour of your eyes
tells me a story,
softly unfolding,
and in your eyes,
Yawar jaan,
I find my world.

I look up. "What do you think?"

His eyes are filled with tears as his smile widens. Oh, that smile. I'd do *anything* for that smile. A smile ever ready, just waiting for the next opportunity to land on his lips as it spills out of his heart. Some people wait for something to smile about. This beautiful man's heart lives in the field of smiles.

I will him to keep looking into my eyes as I shift my gaze from his left eye to his right and back. The air is so comforting, holding us both in its embrace. It's as if the whole universe is holding its breath, converging, the sky blushing as its colours come together in a delicate backdrop.

"Tsk, tsk. Oh ho. Why the tears, meri jaan? It's a happy question," I whisper, leaning forward, bringing his hands to my lips, kissing them ever so tenderly, as we sit cross-legged, facing each other, our knees touching, staring into each other's eyes, holding hands.

He sighs. "Because you just pour out love as if you have a bottomless cup, Emahn," he says, holding my gaze. "I don't know where it fills from." He has a muddled expression that looks like half a frown trying hard to cut through the smile.

"Oh, that's easy," I say. "Some of us were born with baskets, not cups. Baskets that fill every time something little, something beautiful says hello to us, like this little one!" I lean in and kiss the tiny mole on his cheek I have adoringly kissed a million times.

"See? Basket all full!" I laugh.

In that moment, his eyes pull me in so deeply, so powerfully, so intimately, yet so timidly, that even if I tried, I knew I wouldn't be able to look away, warmth surging through my body. Beautiful fuchsias, marigolds, greens, with gentle streaks of shimmering gold, flow through me, dancing and twirling.

Joy. Those must be the colours of joy.

I feel so much joy and so much love in that moment that I'm worried my heart may just forget how to beat. Is it possible that joy and love can hurt? I feel so much love for him that every cell in my body wants to pour all the love it's carrying into him.

A few weeks later, I muster all the courage in my bones, from the air around me, from the poems I have written over the years, and decide to talk to Mama jaan. I pick a time I know it'll be just her and me in our flat.

She's busy peeling some potatoes, so I sit across from her and start peeling them with her. She looks up, looks at me, looks through me, and says, "Mmhmm? I'm listening."

"Mama jaan, I want to tell you something." My heart is racing so fast I'm worried it will jump out of my chest and run away from me. My face feels hot. The air feels thick. I feel like I'm at the edge of a cliff and if I jump, I won't know where my feet are, where my hands are, or where I am.

She keeps looking down at the potato in her hand.

I start, "Mama jaan, I have a friend. A boy."

She keeps peeling.

I take a breath in and continue.

"He is Kashmiri. From your home, Mama jaan! He is very kind, so respectful. He is so beautiful. I feel safe with him. He adores me. His mother is very kind to me. His sisters are younger and adore me. I met his daadi jaan, and she is the gentlest soul and would love to meet you and Baba jaani someday. He says someday, we can move back to our homeland together...."

Mama jaan looks up, tears in her eyes, and I stop talking.

My heart sinks.

She keeps looking at me for what seems like an eternity. I see her expression dance between love deeper than the depth of the universe, to protecting me with everything she has, to anger, to helplessness, to wonder, to sadness again, and my heart doesn't know what to make of it all.

She clears her throat, blinking hard, as if blinking will take her away, anywhere except where she is.

"You're not allowed to dream, Emahn. You have been promised to someone else," she says, looking down again, her hands shaking. She brings her knife to the potato to keep peeling, but it just shakes. Her voice has a sadness to it so vast, I can't find the edges of it to fold it for her, to fold it for myself.

"But Mama jaan, Yawar is Kashmiri. From your home. And I feel safe with him." I am already sobbing, knowing this is a lost cause.

"Yawar. That is a beautiful Kashmiri name. Emahn Yawar. That would have looked beautiful together." She is smiling and crying. And I don't understand.

"It is a beautiful name. He is so tall, Mama jaan. He has those eyes with a splash of green that you always talk about that come from the Kashmir valley." I laugh, but I'm crying too. I have already jumped off the cliff, and I know I am headed for darkness.

This bird is not about to take flight, I know. I know it deep in my bones. I can feel the harsh, unforgiving, cutting edges of my universe digging and gnawing themselves from the deepest insides of my being. I can feel it in the air around me.

This bird is in the wrong nest, on the wrong cliff, and there's nowhere to go.

Mama jaan puts the potatoes aside and asks me to put my head in her lap. I do. Running her fingers through my hair, she says through her sobs, "Love him quietly, meri jaan. In your heart. Like another secret you can never tell anyone."

"I'm so tired of secrets, Mama jaan," I say.

Smiling, she says, "You'll get used to them. You are destined to push boundaries that make bigger circles for more. Every time you push, you'll hold more secrets. Some yours, some others'."

I don't understand. I tell myself that someday I might.

"You will be asked if you agree to marry the man who has been selected for you. Choose your words very carefully, Emahn. We don't choose for ourselves. We choose for the family," she says, kissing my forehead and rocking me back and forth as if that will help me drown all my dreams.

And it does.

Yawar is not the man I am to marry. I am to marry the man chosen for me. I am asked if I agree. But no is not an option in the answers I am to choose from.

In a few months, before I turn sixteen, I am to have my nikah, a marriage contract signed, between me and a man I don't know. In the eyes of Allah and our community, this will make this stranger and me husband and wife. My ruksati, my departure from my parents' home to his and the consummation of our marriage, is not to happen till I turn eighteen. But within a week of my ruksati, I am to leave with him for Canada to start my new life as his bride, I am told.

His family will let me continue my education, I am told.

His family has a good reputation, I am told.

His family is successful, I am told.

His family has political influence, I am told.

His family will provide a strong economic alliance, I am told.

He is the oldest sibling, just like me, I am told.

By accepting this marriage, our respective families will be able to advance our places in the community, I am told. It will bring much-needed technological advances to our family's small milk-and-dairy operations in the homeland, I am told.

They are progressive, I am told.

I am lucky I don't have to live with his entire family in their joint household in Pakistan, I am told. I will just have a short week with him in Sharjah before we board our planes for Canada. Just as our parents left their homes for the family, so will we, I am told. I am one of the oldest of many young cousins, so this is my duty, I am told.

If we work hard, our baby cousins might be able to follow, setting everyone up for livelihoods beyond our humble ones. They wouldn't get swept away with the turmoil in the region; they may have bigger incomes, steadier livelihoods, I am told.

I am lucky it will just be me and him in our flat in Canada, I am told.

He will love me, I am told.

I will learn to love him, I am told.

I visit Yawar for the last time one week before my nikah with the stranger. Yawar places a little motia in my hair. "When the world tries to dim your light, just remember where your light is. It's here. In you," he says, running the tip of his index finger across my forehead. "I'll always love you, Emahn jaan. In our next life, I'll wait for you by the weeping willows. Meet me there?"

I nod, tears running down my face, my world shattered into a million little pieces I won't know how to find. We hold each other as we weep together, our tears becoming one.

Aarzoo—a gentle, innocently pure longing, filled with hope—is how I had carried my love for Yawar.

Ghattan—a deep suffocation that makes your lungs forget their purpose—is how I will carry my love for him.

I will meet him in the next life, in the skies, amongst the stars, I decide.

For months, I grieve in silence. I cry till my eyelids can't carry the weight of my grief. I cry till my soul doesn't know how to cry anymore. I cry till I can cry no more.

Seij Sajao

Adorn the Bridal Bed

My husband, the stranger, lives in Sharjah with his father, mother, three sisters, and a younger brother. He is the oldest of his siblings. Both our families have significantly larger extended families in Lahore, so our nikah happens in Lahore. I only meet him once in Sharjah before our nikah. I don't say much when I meet him, just smile and nod as Mama jaan has firmly instructed me to do. She reasoned that I would have two years to get to know him between nikah and ruksati.

Later, I hear Mama jaan telling his mother I'm just a little shy and it will take time to feel comfortable.

I meet him several times over the two years leading up to my ruksati. They visit our flat on Eid, on birthdays, and sometimes just because. His sisters take me to the souq several times to buy me new clothes that I can bring with me to Canada. I'm not sure how I'd wear these clothes in Canada. While the clothes are stunning, I had only seen women in Hollywood movies wearing pants and shirts, and sometimes long dresses, but certainly not extravagant shalwar kameez and patiala suits with intricate embroidery. But I thank them profusely regardless. They tell me their brother is lucky to have a beautiful wife like me.

I like his sisters. They seem kind, they laugh easily, and we often end our trips to the market with ice cream at Baskin-Robbins at Sharjah Mall.

A month before I turn eighteen, as our families pull together a final celebration for the ruksati and our departure to Canada, his mother takes me to get my nose pierced for the occasion. The piercing is important so I can wear the nath, a bridal nose hoop, that had been gifted to my mother-in-law by her mother-in-law, who in turn had received it from hers. Because I am now the oldest son's wife, the nath is going to be my responsibility. I feel the weight of the responsibility and wonder if and how I'd ever fulfill it with a broken heart that still hasn't stopped thinking about Yawar.

Our families together decide that the ruksati does not need to be a big affair and a small celebration with friends and family in Sharjah should suffice. I don't object to anything. Because his family lives in a small flat with limited privacy for the bride and groom for their wedding night, his family books us a hotel room overlooking the Arabian Gulf for the week. They suggest this can be our honeymoon before we jump into the fast-paced life in Canada.

As I sit in the hotel room, decorated with jasmines and roses that would typically line a bridal chamber, I look at the beautiful deep brown of the henna on my hands. My husband's initials are drawn in for him to find. My friends had giggled as the henna artist drew them in, teasing me about all the tingling feelings I would feel as he would trace his fingers around my palms until he found the hidden initials. I hadn't felt their giggles in my being. I hadn't felt much.

I admire what the artist had done. Henna is what made the bride. The deep brown was meant to represent the love that would seemingly bind us together on this new path. There had been a few gasps about the yellow spots that had not quite become brown. I just assumed it was because the dried henna had probably peeled off too soon. The henna artist had gasped too—not a good sign. This rarely happened, she had said. Perhaps she could fix it, she had said, as she carefully massaged sugar-and-lemon syrup into my palms.

I wasn't too terribly worried about it. It still looked beautiful. I still looked beautiful. Perfect henna or not. Plus, my life wasn't perfect anyway. And that was okay. And the mandalas she had drawn were perfect circles. I loved circles. Circles were life. And yellow was a beautiful colour still. It was the colour of sunshine, warm sunshine on a cool winter morning. Sunshine that brought life, that bred the greens, the blues, the purples of spring across Punjab, across Kashmir.

But still, what if it were true? Was this yellow a curse? What if he was not going to love me? What if I couldn't learn to love him? I brushed the thought aside. I was pretty lovable, I told myself.

And I could learn to love him. I didn't know how. But I could figure it out.

I sit up straighter, straightening out my dress, breathing in the beautiful smell of jasmine and roses in my gajaray. Oh, how I loved jasmine. The scent of jasmine always made my heart dance. There was something so playful, so beautiful about that scent. And my beautiful red dress. Was this the red of the chinar trees of the Kashmir valley? This was a beautiful deep red, with intricate gold metal and foil embroidery.

I run my fingers lightly on the embroidery, along the edge of the skirt where the sunflowers were embroidered. Those sunflowers were so special. Each one had little sequins within it, sparkling, dancing in the light. How on earth had my aunties made something so beautiful?

And then my glass bangles, each one making a soft clink as it touched the other. I always imagined bangles to be like sisters. Mischievous, noisy, playful. The set I am wearing is particularly stunning. Mama jaan had picked it out herself. The golden bangles on the outside, twelve red ones, a thinner silver one, a gold one, another thin silver one, twelve more red ones, and another gold one.

Twelve red ones for twelve months of happiness each year, she had said. She'd smiled with tears in her eyes as she'd put the set together. I loved her smile. Her smile always gave me the strength to know nothing was ever too hard, too difficult. Suddenly, I miss Mama jaan.

He walks over to the bed. Moving the string of jasmines and roses aside, looking at me, smiling, he says, "Hi."

"Hi," I said, my heart pounding. Could he hear my heart? I hoped not.

"You look beautiful." My face felt warm. It wasn't a happy warm. There was an odd, bitter taste in my mouth. I tried to breathe.

"Why were you crying as we left?" he asked.

"Oh. I was just sad leaving my home, I was thinking of how I would miss my parents and my brothers and all their pranks. And then Mama jaan was sad, and that made me sad. And I was also a little hungry, I think. They didn't want me to eat so I could keep my nath on," I ramble.

"You talk a lot. They are not your parents anymore," he says, his smile fading.

"They will always be my parents," I say, suddenly feeling like the walls are creeping in, my mouth dry.

"No," he drawls, his voice growing louder. "My parents are your parents now."

"Yes, of course, you are right, your parents are also my parents now." I try smiling. It doesn't happen. Somehow, I can't force my muscles to do it right.

"Are you smiling?" he says. "You smile too much too. Everyone noticed."

"I . . . like to smile," I say quietly.

"Are you mocking me? Or do you really understand what I'm saying?"

I didn't. He was upset that I was sad. And upset I was smiling. Was there something else I should have been doing?

"I am your world now. You smile when I tell you to. You laugh only when I say you can. My family is your family. Your family is a thing of the past," he says under his breath.

None of it made sense. Who was this person? Why was I here?

"Answer me, Emahn. Do you understand?"

I don't. I don't like how he says my name. It feels like an angry rock, hurled at someone to hurt them. It doesn't sound like my name.

"No, I don't understand," I say quietly. "I can't just pretend my parents don't exist because I signed a doc—"

I don't even get a chance to dread my words. A sharp slap crosses my face.

And just like that, I am back in the elevator. My ears are ringing.

He is saying something. I am sure of it. He has that same look in his eyes. The beast. The bad man. The one who hurts.

I can see his lips move. He grabs my chin in his hand and puts his mouth on me so hard I feel bitter blood in my mouth.

The walls are coming in. He starts pulling my dupatta from my head. The thing was pinned in place with a million bobby pins. I try to stop him, gesturing I'll take it off. He slaps me again. He pulls it so hard I think my hair is going to rip right out of my skull.

I am suddenly really dizzy.

Everything goes black.

I do not remember what happened next.

I wake up in the middle of the night. My dupatta still on, my shirt still on. My skirt is gone. I am standing by the bed, half naked. I don't know how I got there. Had he . . . ? He must have. I felt it as I walked. My insides are aching.

He is asleep.

I pull my skirt on and walk out on the balcony of the hotel room, overlooking the Arabian Gulf. It is so peaceful. It is so quiet, so humid. The darkness has an odd sense of peace to it. The darkness gives me strength. The smell of quiet gives me strength.

Sitting on the balcony floor in my wedding dress, I start picking out the bobby pins from my hair. One at a time.

When Mama jaan had put them in, I had complained at how tedious this whole affair was. And she had smiled and said I should think of these like I think of my little books.

"All those books you obsess over, Laachiye." She made a huge pile with her hands.

We both laughed.

"All those words you chase, pick a word for each pin," she said. And together we picked a whole bunch of words I liked.

One for love. One for mystery. One for magic. One for the monsoon. One for each of the spices that were my friends.

One for kindness. One for patience. One for resilience. One for gratitude. One for respect. One for trust.

One for goodness. One for laughter. One for hope. One for the family.

One for Mama jaan.
One for Baba jaani.
Two for my brothers.
Mama jaan and I held each other and cried then.
And here I am. Picking the pins. With words I had not chosen.
I keep picking.

One for shock. One for confusion. One for disrespect. One for pain. One for grief. One for hurt. One for secrets. One for never telling anyone.

One for hell.

My pins out of my hair, I look at my hands, tracing with my eyes the initials he had not even looked for.

The Wedding Night

They said today is a blessing
wrapped in reds and gold,
with hands stained red.
A bride I was, they said.
But I feel like a child
playing dress-up
in a world too big,
a world I still have
so many questions for.

Be good, my aunties had said,
be patient, be playful.
But my heart pounds in a way
I can't quiet,
screaming in a silence
too loud to hear,
like a door closing,
locking me inside
where I don't belong.

They call him my husband now,
but a stranger he is.
I haven't met him in my lives before,
never heard his voice,
never looked into his eyes
to know.

I don't know how to feel about this world,
a world I didn't choose,
heavy, uncertain,
unknown, perhaps?

Yet somewhere inside,
I cling to a quiet hope,
a wish for a kindness
that might soften the edges,
stretch the silence.

I don't know how to feel,
so I wait for the morning,
for the light to come in
from across the seven skies,
where she lives.

Ik Si Rani

There Once Was a Queen

That week, I write my first story of the raja and his beautiful queen.

When the raja was a young prince, while out of his palace visiting the kingdom, he ran into the rani, then a poor peasant's daughter in a mustard field.

The moment he laid eyes on her, it was like the world stopped moving, hushed, to watch the magic unfold. Time stood still, as if the wind had forgotten how to breathe. Her long hair was down to her knees, like a thousand ravens taking flight. Her skin glowed with the softness of a waterfall that cuts through the seven skies. And her large, striking green eyes—oh, her eyes. Her eyes were the greens of the emeralds found only in the deepest crevices of the ocean.

He was captivated—imprisoned—like a magician who had just found the source of his magic.

She noticed him staring then, a smile slowly forming on her face like the first ray of sunlight breaking through after a long storm. It began in her green eyes, which seemed to dance with a secret she was willing to share only with those who dared to look long enough. The corners of her lips curled hesitantly, as if testing the waters, testing if he could take it. And then, as the radiance of her smile filled the skies, colouring them in beautiful greens and blues and purples and fuchsias, the world around her faded, everything growing softer, gentler.

With her smile, she gifted him a piece of her. A piece he was never going to lose.

The young prince retreated to his chambers that afternoon, refusing to speak to anyone for days. He summoned his closest advisors, the two-spirited beings, the animals, the rivers, the skies, and the winds, asking them how he could make the peasant's daughter his wife. His advisors took many days to think and finally told the young prince that the peasant's daughter was not for the young prince to have.

The prince was enraged. How could that be? He was the prince of the most powerful kingdom, after all. He could have anything he wanted.

"No," they said together. He had to earn it. He had to learn to earn it. He first had to learn what need was. He had to have the thirst of a traveller in the desert, the hunger of a beggar who hadn't tasted bread in weeks, the bone-scraping longing of a childless mother, the searching ache of a fatherless child, the dark and hopeless agony of an orphan.

The peasant's daughter was special, they explained together. Her love was sacred, and only those who were worthy could earn it.

Were all daughters sacred like that? the young prince pleadingly asked them.

Yes, they said. And he needed to learn what sacred was.

So, he tried. For months, he wrote thousands of poems for her, pronouncing his love, his promises, his commitments, his vows, his submission. He sent them to her, with pieces of his heart, fragments of his hopes, and hints of his desires.

And she rejected them.

No matter how hard the young prince tried, she read his words, shook her head, and threw them in the rivers. And his words would drown, pieces of his heart with them.

He tried and tried and tried some more. With no luck. With each rejection, his ache grew. He promised her the stars and the moon. He promised her the riches of his kingdom, as many chefs as she needed. Merchants would come to her so she would never have to set foot in the fields again, he promised.

Nothing. Nothing seemed to please the peasant's daughter. Nothing was enough.

After months of trying, he summoned his advisors again.

"Why? Why does she reject me, when all I do is tell her how beautiful she is and how I will be dutiful to her, and protect her, and shower her with all I have?" he asked them.

"You promise to give her that which comes to you easily, young prince," the two-spirited beings said. "She seeks that which does not come to you easily."

"What? What is it she seeks? I will give it to her. *Anything.*"

"Visit her yourself, young prince. Ask her."

So, he did.

She greeted him with that smile of a million stars twinkling in the night sky and said, "Finally, you come, my prince. I was hoping you'd come sooner, but I guess it takes time for those who don't know what need does to mortals."

"What can I do to convince you to become my princess? I have tried everything. I don't know what you seek. But I know I am willing to give it to you. Please tell me, my sweet."

She looked at him curiously, for what seemed like days. Her emerald-green eyes looking through his soul, into the deepest crevices of him.

"I seek not to be yours. I seek to walk with you as myself, my raven hair mine, my emerald eyes mine, my voice mine, my laughter mine, my tears mine, my anguish mine, my anger mine, my joy mine, my family mine.

"I seek to be mine. If you can honour that, I will walk with you."

And he agreed.

And so, she became the princess, his equal. He adored her and she adored him. Every time her hands carried the sacred plant of henna, it radiated in deep reds and browns and graced the winds with its rich, earthy fragrance. She walked with him; she sat in court with him. She advised with him. She counselled with him.

When he became the raja, she became Moonga Rani, the emerald queen.

It was Moonga Rani who gave verdicts in court as the raja sat next to her, listening—after they had spent several nights walking across the skies, recounting the stories told in their court.

I wished I could be Moonga Rani, and my husband, the stranger who I did not pick, my raja.

PART 2—GULAB

Roses

Phullan di Saanh

The roses in my gajarah
unfold with every breath I take,
bowing with grace,
uncertainty, not knowing.

Their colours may fade,
petals unsure, disconnected,
as they journey away,
without thorns to protect them,
to lands far away.

Gulab

Roses

In my courtyard, my dear guest, as story time unfolds, we find ourselves wrapped in the embrace of the motia. Its fragrance lingers in the air, quiet and grounding, guiding us silently through calm mornings, stormy afternoons, colourful evenings, and starry nights. Together, we journey through moments filled with a quiet kind of magic.

I imagine us moving towards the gulab de bute, the rose bushes. Deep red, soft pink, yellow, and white—their colours draw us in, their fragrance settling in our souls, wrapping us in stillness, inviting us to listen. Each velvety petal rides the winds, lingering in the air, mingling with the chatter, the banter, the laughter that fills my courtyard. It brings together all the scattered pieces of us, weaving them into something whole.

These roses are more than just decor, more than beauty blooming in a courtyard, in a land far away. In each petal and each thorn lies a part of my people, their stories. For countless moons and across countless lives, through skies, stars, and oceans, we have nurtured them, cared for them, loved them. But we've also cut them, plucked them, hurt them—only to have them dance with us as symbols, carrying meaning where words fall short. They speak of love—these roses—of beauty, of spiritual celebration, of ways of knowing that float across tribes, families, clans, castes, subcastes, classes, languages, embodying expressions too tender to say aloud.

The gulab in my courtyard tell stories. Stories of opulence in Mughal gardens, of hospitality in a host's welcoming arms. They speak of intimacy and hope in a bride's gajarah, commitment in the groom's sehra, joy under the feet of a new mother, and of sacredness on a mayyat, a body, as it returns to the earth.

These roses carry the echoes of longing for the divine in Bulleh Shah's soulful melodies, of yearning in the tales of Heer Ranjha, of sacrifice in the folklore of Sassi Punnu. They hold the magic of Rumi's verses.

They hold the uncertain light that peeks through the darkness of a woman stepping into an unfamiliar world.

In my courtyard, my dear guest, the gulab de bute—my rose bushes—tell my story. Tales of longing to belong, of longing that was hopeful but now just suffocates, of walking paths lined with sacrifices. Tales of silencing storms within, of searching in fields of thorns for a place I can quietly rest for just a few forgiving moments.

In my courtyard, my gulab speak of the yearning to love and be loved, to share my stories with those who won't hurt me, with those who will truly learn to just listen.

Pardes de Pardesi Rang

The Foreign Colours of a Foreign Land

We arrive in Canada at Toronto Pearson on a brisk fall night.

The air is sharp and new, and smells of jet fuel and burning rubber. At the immigration desk, the officer asks if I have a middle name. I tell him I don't. He gives me one. A name that isn't mine, yet somehow I carry it with me until one day, two decades later, as I am made a citizen of Canada, another officer decides I no longer need it, and takes it away from me.

I don't say anything. Just laugh at the absurdity of it all.

We are hosted by a friend in Toronto for the evening, and hop on a bus, our suitcases in tow, to a city of a million people in the heart of the prairies. Everything feels so expansive, as we travel along the highway. We expect it to change as we get closer to the city, but it doesn't. The roads are wide, the pickup trucks are massive, and the trucks carrying loads are the largest vehicles I have ever seen—much bigger than the trucks back in Lahore or even Sharjah.

This land feels different. Its colours feel different. There is much I don't understand—this land's systems, its ways, its being, its way of speaking to me. I can't find this land's voice. I listen, but I can't hear it. It doesn't reach my ears. It doesn't reach my heart.

They call flats "apartments" here.

Its voices feel foreign, like they were never meant for me.

I feel like an uninvited guest who doesn't know where the host is. I look around but can't see them. So, I keep looking. I must find the host so I can learn the nezaam, the ways of this land.

I don't understand why everyone rushes, or why neighbours don't really talk to each other. I don't understand why I can't smell mangoes till my nose touches them. It's the same with roses. They don't have a scent either. Are the mangoes and the roses here afraid of sharing their presence?

I don't understand why everyone chews gum or uses mouthwash. I don't understand why everyone corrects my pronunciation as if they have the sole right over a language that has more exceptions than rules. A language that may or may not have been one of theirs just three generations prior.

I don't understand why everyone looks at me funny in my hijab, as if feeling sorry for me. I don't understand why when I bring my neighbours food I have cooked with love for hours, they tell me they can't eat it because they're "not a fan of Indian."

I don't understand why when I do tilawat-e-Quran, a recitation of the Quran in a melody, in my apartment one day, my neighbour calls the police, saying there is a terrorist next door, and the kind policeman from Egypt sitting in my living room, sipping cardamom chai I have made for him and his partner, tells me I would avoid a lot of trouble for myself if I recited my prayers privately, quietly. I ask him why it was okay for hospitals to say the Lord's Prayer on their intercom every morning for everyone to hear but I had to say my prayers quietly.

"I'm sorry, sister. Things are different here for Muslims, especially since 9/11," he says with a smile so profoundly sad I feel like the skies are splitting open with new darkness, with blacks so deep they suck me in.

I don't understand.

I don't understand why when I sing Punjabi folk songs in my apartment one day, just like I'd sing with my aunties while cooking, another neighbour calls the resident manager, saying it is hard for them to "focus with all these Pakis in the building with their voodoo songs," when there are louder parties with rock music just down the hall every single night.

I don't understand why when I wear my perfume that smells like the motia in my courtyard, my professor tells me it makes others sick because of their sensitivities to smells. "Could you wear something more neutral?" she says. I don't understand why my motia triggers sensitivities but Fruit Fusions and Rose Hips from Herbal Essences shampoos or citrusy scents from Garnier Fructis are boldly celebrated as the new trend.

I don't understand why when I wear my traditional clothes, no one sits next to me, or they turn their gaze away from me, or when I think they are about to compliment me, all I hear is "Wow. That is a lot of colour," as if my colours have offended them.

I don't understand why when I wear my bangles and my pa'zaib, a student in my chemistry class says it's too distracting for her and I should "maybe save my trinkets for special occasions."

I don't understand why everyone wears grim colours when there is so much sunshine and beauty in this land.

I don't understand why neurosurgeons and astrophysicists from my homeland work as taxi drivers instead of healing people and celebrating the mysteries of the universe.

I don't understand why there is only one little store in a city of almost a million people that sells halal meat and only a few stale spices from my homeland.

I don't understand why there is no Azaan to wake me up every day or make me pause to express gratitude four more times a day.

I don't understand why I can't hear my language anywhere I go, even from those I know are from my homeland.

I don't understand why people throw racist slurs at those with brown skin like mine on the downtown streets. To me, they look like my mama jaan's relatives from Kashmir, with their high cheekbones, deep-set eyes, and raven-black hair. I don't understand why no one sees their pain. I don't understand *why* they have so much pain. What happened to them?

I don't understand this foreign land. It doesn't speak to me. Perhaps I must get to know it first? But how?

As he held me at the airport, Baba jaani had said that as I entered the white man's world, I must pay attention, watch, observe, learn, and speak carefully. That I must never forget who I am.

"No matter where we go, puttar, we are birds that always know the path back to our nests. Your nest will always welcome you with open arms," he had said, with a tear-streaked face, as he kissed my forehead. "Rab Rakha, puttar. *May God protect you, little one.*" But I couldn't hear my God here. I couldn't hear myself here.

I couldn't be me here.

To find beauty in this darkness in this foreign land, I must quieten myself, I decide.

So, quieten myself, I do.

My Quran bothers them, so I recite it in whispers. My bangles bother them, so I wear them only at home. My spices bother them, so I never share my food. My food bothers them, so I keep them out of my kitchen and stay out of theirs. My colours bother them, so I stop wearing them. My perfumes bother them, so I start wearing theirs. My language bothers them, so I learn to speak like them. My clothes bother them, so I wear theirs. My presence bothers them, so I make myself invisible. My stories bother them, so I stop telling them.

My songs bother them, so I stop singing.

My voice bothers them, so I keep it to myself.

Pardes—a foreign land—is where I am. And I will learn to live here, I decide. Someday, I will meet my host, I decide.

I have my words, my magic. I have my laughter. I am guided by my ancestors. I have been prepared for this, I know. I will learn the rules, I decide. And learn them well, well enough to dare to bend them, break them, or leave them behind.

I Am Still Here

They're braided in my gajarah,
roses I used to believe in,
their petals soft, deep, cool,
a possibility of something beautiful,
perhaps?

Now they bleed,
their thorns piercing
deeper than my skin,
reminding me of the silent screams
behind closed doors,
where no one listens.

The roses in my gajarah wilt
with every racist slur,
every correction of my pronunciation,
every discomfort at my presence,
every mockery of my ways,
every assumption that I am stupid.
Because I am a brown woman,
that I must be poor,
oh so helpless, in need of rescuing,
in need of saving.
That I must be less than,
uncivilised, a savage, a barbarian,
a terrorist.

But I have been taught differently,
taught to love, taught to hold,
been taught by my aunties,
my grandmothers,
my ancestors.
Taught that hate has no place
in a garden blooming with life and laughter.
So, I hold it tightly,
even when it hurts,
even as it bleeds.
I am still here, still breathing,
even when my skin is a target
and my faith, my ways,
a reason to hate.

Yes, I have been taught differently,
So, I must believe in roses,
not for their petals
or their stunning deep reds,
but for their thorns,
for the way they survive
in a world that knows only
to pluck their roses away.

Zakham Sawaarna

Beautifying Wounds

Our apartment in Canada is small, the ceiling low and heavy. It feels suffocating, especially in this vast country where the skies stretch endlessly, and the air is so clean, so fresh, where the sunsets are stunning.

I throw myself into school, expecting school in Canada to also be a sanctuary. I take on cash jobs. My husband does too. We take courses at the university during the day, then rush to work. We clean toilets, make marketing calls in call centres, and pump gas. We drive people around in private taxis, and we care for the elderly. It feels strange to us that their children or grandchildren don't look after them or even visit them. My husband and I talk about this at home, quietly, then let it go. It's just the way of this place, we figure. We have been sent here to help nurture new trails for our young ones; we can't be too picky.

I'm starting to get used to my husband. He stands a couple of inches taller than me, broad shouldered but still carrying the easy looseness of youth, like a man who hasn't yet outgrown the boy he once was. His deep-set, dark-brown eyes sit steady, unreadable, holding something just out of reach, like a joke he hasn't decided whether to share. His skin is light, untouched by the sun. His smile, when it comes, is effortless, the kind that maybe once made girls laugh too easily, trust too quickly. His hair is thick and just unruly enough to make it seem like he doesn't care. He often runs his hand through it. There is an odd charm to him—something familiar, something practised, something that makes me want to believe he is harmless.

At home, I cook, and my husband cleans. Sometimes when I'm cooking, I think of Yawar and wonder how he is. And then quickly shake away the thought. I am married now. Mama jaan would remind me that I've had just over two years to forget him.

We fall into our daily routines, laughing sometimes, but mostly missing home. He makes friends easily; I don't. His friends come over often. We host them, and I'm always in the background. His friends tell me my food reminds them of home.

If ever a friend appreciates the food too much, that friend is never invited back.

And I pay for it later.

I don't speak to my parents much. Though my husband talks to his family regularly. I'm afraid to send letters to Mama jaan. What if she reads into my heart? What if she sees it? What if she feels the sadness in the ink on the paper? What if she writes back and my husband sees them?

He is protective, but not in a way that makes me feel safe. He says he doesn't like me walking alone to and from university or work because what if something happens? But it doesn't seem like it's safety he's worried about—it's control. He watches who I talk to, decides who is good for me, who I should avoid. He checks my computer, my tone, my laughter, my movements. He insists on having my class schedule so he can know where I will be at all times. "It is for your safety," he says. "It's because I care about you." He tells me he doesn't want anyone to take advantage of me, as if I'm stupid, but the only one making me shrink is him. If another man looks at me too long, he tenses beside me, his hands curling into fists, his jaw set in a way that makes my stomach twist. He tells me no one can take what is his.

His love is possessive, unpredictable, bitter, passive but frighteningly obsessive, unsharing, the kind of love wrapped in the darkness of envy and jealousy and wanting to keep all things for just yourself.

The kind of love that can only hurt.

The kind of love in a barren, parched land, where the sun never rises.

※

One night, I am laying out my clothes. I had been taking a series of courses in human rights. As part of one of the courses, I had been asked to attend public hearings for a human-rights tribunal about cases of human-rights violations with newcomers. I had absolutely loved the course, the instructor, the content, everything about it so far. It was the first course that spoke to the intersections of political conflict, land rights, and cultural protections, and what it meant to somehow wade through all that complexity to ensure all humans were valued in society. It was the first course that made me think about the relevance of my upbringing in resolving community conflicts. And I was so excited and so curious to see how a public process worked in this foreign land. Would people talk for days? Would they share food? Would they tell stories? Who would speak first? What would the decision-makers be like? Would they be the kind who are respected for their wisdom? Or the kind who are feared by their people? How were they selected to be decision-makers? How would decisions be made? Did I need to bring food to this hearing, like people always did when they came to our family's courtyard to work through conflicts?

I wanted to be there to witness it, to learn the ways of this land. I wanted to talk to people to understand.

I had explained all this to him. Several times.

"My professor told me who all will be there. Check out this list. Some very important and smart people!" I said excitedly. These were people I would likely need to speak to so I could stand a chance at getting a job in my field once I was done with school.

"You're paying far too much attention to this," he said, barely listening.

"Well, this *is* important! Plus, I've been practising my pronunciation for weeks now so no one can sense I've only been in Canada for two years," I say. "I can tell when I've said something like they're not used to hearing."

I throw out a few words to show him how I would enunciate each word. Rounding the edges of these words where I needed to, slowing others down, speeding up some.

"It always stings when people mock me. But, you know, every reaction teaches me what I need to know, I suppose," I add thoughtfully.

Every time I shared with him that someone had mocked me for a word I'd said differently, he always brushed it off. None of the racism, the barriers, the injustice of what we were navigating in this foreign land seemed to affect him.

None of that woke his possessiveness of me.

No.

What woke him up was me showing him what clothes I was planning on wearing to the hearing.

What woke him up was my conservative, classy dark-brown suit, with a black turtleneck, and a matching black hijab.

"It's too sexy," he says.

"That's your problem," I say playfully. "Plus, I'm simply not interested in speaking to people who can't respect me for my brain, for who I am."

He looks at me then with a fury so dark, my blood curdles and stops running in my veins, afraid of making the next turn, afraid of touching anything.

"They won't think of your brain if all they see is this." He stands up abruptly, flails his arms wildly over his body in a sickening gesture that makes my stomach drop.

"It is a pretty conservative suit, but I can pick something different if you prefer," I say weakly, knowing nothing is going to work.

I try to contend with him. I try to be brave.

We always speak with courage, Naano jaan used to say. *We never just accept, Laachiye, we wonder, we wonder some more, and then we ask.*

But speaking with courage with this man had not worked for me.

The black tunnel I always dreaded had already approached me. I had felt it crawling up my neck, coming in from behind me, enveloping me, a shiver, a cold sweat up my arms, taking my heart, consuming my lungs, screaming past my ears, leaving no room for another sound.

The tunnel. The dreaded tunnel.

The ringing in my ears consumes me. The beast had entered the room. A beast so hungry it did not know the pain it put its prey through.

As he hits me, slaps me, kicks me, I drift far away to my happy place. I float through the skies, watch the stars, touch the motia in my courtyard, hold the gulab in my fists.

Moonga Rani.

I visit the emerald queen and laugh with her. We sip delicious cardamom chai, as she shows me the beautiful dress she made. It's a deep-green velvet, the green of a forest so ancient the trees talk to each other all day long. A green so majestic, it didn't even need the shimmering gold silk threads that flowed along it like beautiful rivers flowing across the lands.

A dress her raja had said didn't do justice to her beauty, to her splendour, to her magic.

The next morning, standing in front of the mirror, I look at myself closely. Anyone seeing my face would know in a split second I had taken a beating.

Perhaps this is the moment. For me to break the first of many rules.

The hijab I had decided to wear years ago has to come off.

My bangs carefully placed over my bruised left cheek, and my swollen left eye carefully disguised with a whole lot of makeup, just in case, I am ready to head to the hearing. I had known he would torment me. But I am not ready to bend.

I am bruised, sure.

It hurts like hell, sure.

But I am not broken.

I am my grandmother.

I am me, a woman raised in love, in power.

The Grandmothers Knew

They knew they came from abundance,
from fields that stretched beyond sight,
hands that knew the weight of wheat,
from mountains that held guard,
unmovable, unshakeable.
They knew they came
from the scent of cardamom crushed between fingers,
carrying the patience of dough rising under a cloth
woven by the women before them.

They did not ask if they belonged,
did not wonder if they had enough.
They stood in the knowing,
the firm ground of their stories,
the loriyaan hummed to the little ones
who would one day carry their names.

They lit fires with dung cakes shaped by their own hands,
milked cows before the sun opened its eyes,
churned butter with arms strong from lifting more than burdens.
Weaving futures into rope, into baskets,
into the steady hands
that steered oxen through fields thick with promise.
Turned soil with fingers that braided the hair of warriors,
stitched futures into fabric dyed in the blood of pomegranates.

Their voices were not soft,
unyielding to the winds of weakness.
Their voices didn't say give me what he has,
begging in weakness,
from a drought, parched for more.

The grandmothers knew.
They knew their place
was at the head of the fire,
at the birth of revolutions,
at the firing of the tandoor that fed generations.
They did not shrink.
They did not defer.
They held the weight of history
in their spines, their knuckles, their knowing.
And when they spoke,
the earth leaned in.
The daughters listened,
the sons obeyed.
And scarcity became a lie
that would never be told again.

Ik Si Rani

There Once Was a Queen

High above the earth, across the seven skies, where the night sky stretched out in endless velvet darkness, there lived a queen, Moonga Rani. Her realm was a place of stars and shadows, constellations, and rivers of light and mystery that flowed across the heavens. Moonga Rani's magic was woven into the very fabric of the cosmos, allowing her to shape the twinkle of the stars, command the celestial winds by a simple movement of her fingers, making them rage with her, dance with her, play with her. Through her magic, she guided lost souls across the skies, showing them little freckles of light in the vast sea of darkness.

Once upon a time, a long time ago, many lives ago, her life had been filled with love. She had ruled alongside a kind and doting king, a king who lived by the chinar trees, in lush green valleys with crystal-clear waters. A king whose presence was like the gentle glow of the moon, steady and warm.

But then the stars had dimmed, and tragedy befell her when her king died in a battle he thought he could fight with love but had lost to the evil powers of envy and jealousy, leaving a gaping void in Moonga Rani's heart. Her palace, which stretched across the skies, once a place of beauty and harmony, a place where all came to find justice and fairness and compassion, and colour and joy and happiness, was now left in mourning.

The night sky had grown darker, as if grieving with her. But the true darkness came in the form of her new husband, who sought her love, not with love but with greed, with pride, with envy, with jealousy, with a desire to own every part of her.

This man was full of cruelty, his being cold and sharp like the edges of a broken star. His jealousy of her power fuelled his need to control her.

Moonga Rani's palace of eternal love and beauty had become a place of tears.

Her magic weakened with every harsh word, every blow that struck her gentle spirit, like a fading star. With each hurtful, unkind word, the stars dimmed, as though the heavens themselves could no longer bear witness to the darkness that had taken hold of her life.

There was no place to hide, she knew. She was failing herself. Failing her once beautiful king, who had loved her with every breath. She was failing her grandmothers, who had raised her in strength. She was failing her mustard fields, which had taught her the power of the land.

She was failing all the little girls who would look to her to find the meaning of love, the meaning of fighting for herself, the meaning of belonging to only herself. So, she searched for answers. Where she had always been able to find light was only darkness.

One night, she travelled to the edge of the cosmos, at the boundaries of her magic, where the winds howled and the rivers stretched in chaos, in anger, unruly, untamed. She reached out with all that she had left, her tears glimmering like falling meteors as they vanished into the void. She sang till her voice was a scream coming from deep within her, a scream so loud it made the winds stop, the rivers freeze.

It was there that a voice rose to meet her. A two-spirited being emerged from the mists of the cosmos, their form shifting like a shimmering aurora, a stunning coming together of a fierce woman and a gentle man.

"We have been waiting for you, my queen. I knew your king, the good one, that is," they said, with a voice both comforting and powerful, a voice soothing and inviting, like a lullaby echoing through her.

"You did?" Her tears were now rivers flowing along the edge of the cosmos.

"Yes, and he would not be happy knowing you are carrying this pain alone," they said in unison with other two-spirited beings who dwelled in the spaces between worlds, beings whose wisdom spanned the realms of light and darkness.

Together, they surrounded her and shared their power of insight with her.

"The night is more than darkness, our queen. It is a realm of light and shadow, of winds that can howl but also comfort, of rivers that can freeze but also heal. Sure, you can get absorbed in the chaos of a storm, you can retreat from a blazing fire, you can drown in an angry river. But you can also face the storm, channel it to wrap itself around you so you can walk through the blazing fire," they said, with care so deep Moonga Rani could feel it wrapped around her.

"Your calloused scars can become your shields, our queen. Find them, love them, show them they have a purpose. Show them they can protect you. And they will," they said.

That night, Moonga Rani returned to her palace with a new power. The power to wield her magic, to no longer conceal her pain but to transform it, to let it burn brightly as fuel for her power.

She would learn to channel her suffering into strength, to let her wounds become constellations that would someday tell her story.

Tavva

The Frying Pan

Over the year that follows, every harsh word he utters becomes my fuel. I tell myself I am creating a reservoir. What for, I'm not sure. I tell myself I must keep going. I feel like I'm walking taller, speaking louder, pushing back harder. Sometimes, it works. Other times, it unleashes a beating so intense, I wonder if the next breath I take will be my last.

One dreadful night, the answers to why I needed the reservoir come screaming across the skies.

After a long day of courses on campus and a tiring shift at a gas station, I come home to my husband telling me he invited his friends over for a gaming night.

"I'm so tired, and I still have a test to prepare for tomorrow," I plead.

"So? These are my friends," he says impatiently.

"Yes, I know they are your friends. It's just that . . ." I venture into territory I know is dangerous. "I've cooked for them twice already this week, and if we feed them again, between the two of us, we won't have money left to last the month. And it's not like we can feed them just lentils or potatoes. Meat is expensive. We can't afford to buy it again this month."

He looks up, and I wonder if what I'm saying is working.

Feeling brave, I add, "You know, maybe they can contribute, actually. I'll cook, but I can put together a short list you can send them—just a couple of things—for them to pick up. Between that and what we have, it might work."

"You want me to ask my friends to pick up groceries when *I* have invited them? As if I'm some poor beggar? Have you no shame?" His voice rises.

"Maybe you shouldn't have invited them if it's such a matter of pride for you. I don't know what kind of friends show up at their friends' homes empty-handed anyway. Maybe they'll learn a thing or two," I say bitterly.

I know I have gone too far.

He charges across the room like a wild beast whose den has just been violated.

It takes me a split second to realise what is happening and accept that I know this drill. I have lived it many times.

I can feel the sweat on my palms. I can smell my insides burn. Was something eating me from the inside? I tell myself I just need to breathe through this, as much as it makes my lungs want to jump out of my body so they never have to learn to breathe through this agony.

It will be over soon, I tell myself. *Every harsh word is your fuel,* I tell myself. Except I can't hear his words.

Every slap across your face increases your reservoir, I tell myself.

I collect four slaps. One after the other. I collect kicks.

"Do you not see what you do to me?" I think he is saying.

What a weird man, I tell myself.

"Your friends are leeches," I quietly say to him, pain coursing through me.

Leeches, I think. Leeches who suck blood and do so while preventing the blood from clotting. They're smart, those leeches. They know. They know where the incisions would go, the anticoagulant to push through their prey's system. His friends came with smiles, praises for him. The praises must be the anticoagulant.

Leeches. They were also used to treat poisonous blood. And he let them. He let them suck my blood.

Was I the poison? I wonder.

I do not mind the cooking. I *do* mind the extra shifts I had to pick up to be able to pay for the food. But it kept me away from this husband. It gave me space to do what I needed to do.

The kitchen was always my sanctuary. In my kitchen, I was transported to Naano jaan's kitchen, hear the sizzle of the fresh pakoray in the pan, the sweet, earthy scent of fresh cilantro and fennel seeds taking over, the chatter between Mama jaan and Khaala jaan as they visited Naano, old folk tunes in Reshma Ji's voice playing on her rickety cassette player.

Shehar bhamaar di kuriyon
Tussi nak wich nath na paiyo
Me bhul gaiyaan tussi bhul na jaeyo
Yaar naal baloch na layo
Hai o rabba naiyo lagda dil mera
Sajana baaj hoya hanera
Hai o rabba naiyo lagda dil mera

As we'd hum along, I'd ask, "Naano jaan, which spice is the happiest spice? Can I be that spice?"

"Happiness is in bringing together many spices, Laachiye," she would say, her warm smile filling me with all the colours I knew of.

Yup. Happiness had to be all the colours dancing together.

Standing in her kitchen, watching her throw in pinches of this and dashes of that, I always imagined each spice having its own magical power.

Ajwain, caram seeds, was a patient peacemaker, one that brought the rest of the spices together but still had its own voice.

Zeera, cumin, was a healer—warm and loving, like the dirt in the mustard fields.

Ilaaichi, cardamom, a mischievous, curious little one that masked the fierceness of laal mirch, hot red pepper. Now laal mirch was an angry one, an impatient fighter, not too bright despite its bright colour.

Dhaniya daana, coriander seeds, were little jesters, full of surprises, a little unexpected every time.

Haldi, turmeric, had the personality of spring, of new beginnings. Its bright yellow the colour of marigolds, the colour of flying kites across the sky on a warm monsoon evening, the colour of a setting sun.

Laung, clove, was an odd one, a mystery to be solved, perhaps the most misunderstood of them all, but was certainly generous because it came to the rescue when I had a toothache.

My spices always gave me strength. They were my reservoir.

Disappearing in the kitchen for hours gave me strength.

"Please just stop, hitting me is no way to express yourself." I dread the words as I see them coming out of my mouth.

The next several minutes are chapters Satan would write if he wrote about hell.

I don't scream.

Imli, tamarind, was a sour one, a little unhappy, a little unsettled, perhaps full of stories, the kind that give you goosebumps like a cold, wet winter morning did.

I know he is yelling. I hear nothing. Just the ringing in my ears.

Kesar, saffron, was a beautiful queen, generous, kind and loving, never overbearing, yet present. I wonder what a generous queen would say about this hell. Did Kesar know Moonga Rani?

He grabs my hair; he hits my head against the wall.

Sometime in the middle of the night, I wake up. I'm on the floor. Everything hurts so much. I walk myself to the bathroom and look at myself in the mirror.

Was this the face of a daughter raised in love? A daughter born in laughter.

A daughter raised in power.

Was this the face of a daughter I would raise?

I contort my face, trying to cry. No tears come. They rarely do.

I walk back into the kitchen. I grab the frying pan he had hit me with, still on the ground. It was a good weapon, this frying pan.

I could end all this in no time at all, I realise. I could smash his head into mush. There was an odd familiarity to that thought. Has this been one of my nightmares? Was I *in* a nightmare?

The first blow would knock him out, and the rest would just be noise. No one had come to my rescue in the years they had probably heard him hurting me. Why would they come now?

I walk into the room. He looks so comfortable. How could someone sleep after causing such pain? Was my pain his comfort? Could his pain now become my comfort?

I lift my arms, tighten my grip.

I take a breath.

Ffff. Pfff.

And then her words come. *Life is sacred. We do not end it, we earn it, we live it, we fight it, we honour it, Laachiye.*

Naano jaan. Please help me cry, I plead.

Jeena yahan,
marna yahan,
is ke siwaa,
aur jaana kahan.

We live here,
we die here,
where else can we go,
except here.

I could hear Naano jaan humming the words in my ears, soothing me, warming me, as if I had just woken up from a nightmare.

Saunf, fennel seed, was the most strategic of them all. Add a seed with the angry, impatient laal mirch, and the tongue wouldn't even know laal mirch was around. It would take five seconds before the tongue realises what happened.

Saunf knew how to play the long game.

That night, watching him sleep, protected by Naano jaan's words, and the frying pan by my side, I decided it was time to escape.

To My Evil Husband

In my next life,
I wish you are my son,
so I may raise you
with love as vast as the seven skies,
with care as deep as the oceans
touching the bowels of the earth.

So I may hold you to show you how,
sway you to show you how,
shower you with it all,
like snow glittering from the skies,
falling on you
one snowflake at a time,
becoming you,
the depths of you.
So I may love you for you,
love you for the world,
love you for her,
whom you are supposed to love.

In my next life,
I wish you are my son,
so I may raise you
to be seen.

For now, I must leave,
and you must grow.
You must heal,
your journey yours,
my journey mine.

Safar

The Journey

For months, I meticulously photocopy every document my husband and I had originally brought with us to Canada. One at a time. Every morning, I take one document with me to the human-rights tribunal office I intern at, photocopy it, and bring it back so he won't know it is missing. I have no idea if I'll ever need it, but I go through the ritual, as if it was sacred, as if my life depended on it. My birth certificate, my school records, my medical records, my phone bills, my grocery receipts, my transcripts, everything that seems to matter.

I give it care.

He had a key logger on my laptop at home and a remote logger on my account at the university, and he scrutinised every phone call I made and every call I received on the home phone. So, I send messages to my parents about my plans through my friends. While my parents insist that I must return home immediately, I refuse. I tell them I have invested too much to waste it away because of him. I tell them I want to finish my degree, so I have something to work with if I decide not to return to Canada.

When my boss tells me at the end of my internship that she would like me to stay on after I graduate, I thank her profusely and tell her I may decide to work with an organisation back home for a bit to see how things might be different there. On the day I am to leave Canada, I drop him off at work in my pyjamas, all my documents under my car seat, and leave for the airport.

I never hear from him again. It doesn't surprise me. No one likes admitting losing something they claim they cared for. Speaking to me would require facing his demons. At some level, perhaps he was relieved too?

No one enjoys being the devil, I tell myself.

I land in Lahore on a hot summer morning. Four long years have gone by since I left, and I have lived each day wondering if I'd even recognize my homeland. The answer comes flooding to me as the plane door opens—humid air flooding the cabin, carrying the unmistakable scent of my homeland, its spices, its mustard fields, its history. It's the smells of Lahore, the diesel, the dust; somewhere out there, I'm sure there's some gulab and cardamom, but I don't smell either of those, not yet. But I am wrapped in the comfort of knowing that I am finally back home.

All I smell is lightness, and a sense of freedom I am scared to celebrate.

For the first time in months, I let my tears flow. It's the only time I can let them flow. I know my baba jaani and mama jaan are going to be looking through my soul when they see me. And I can't let them see the damage.

Daughters don't return home, not in my family. I may be the first one, I'm not sure. But I know not many others will be there to welcome me home, and I appreciate that. I know my return won't be a celebration. At best, it will be an apologetic, empathetic acceptance.

So, I cry as I walk off the aeroplane and into the bus taking us to the terminal.

I cry as I get off the bus and walk into the terminal. I cry as I wait in line to see the passport-control officer.

I cry as I try not to cry walking through customs. I sob as my eyes land on my baba jaani and mama jaan. I weep as my baby brothers both hold me, telling me it's okay, and that I am now home.

I cry for days.

A short six months after my return to Lahore, I sign my divorce papers. Mama jaan tells me I am the first woman in our family, both on Baba jaani's side and hers, to ever be divorced.

My first year in Lahore is packed with activity. While my parents are starting to build a house in Lahore in anticipation of their eventual return back from Sharjah, I decide to live with my khaala jaani, who still lives in Naano jaan's home. I start working as a director of programming at a shelter called Naii Subha, or New Dawn, for at-risk youth. The shelter is in an old haveli, a palace, from the Mughal era that has been refurbished over the years to serve our needs.

Most of my clients are young adults, most between twelve and eighteen years old. Some joined gangs, some joined extremist groups, some left gangs but were then shunned by their families, their communities, and now have nowhere to go. Some suffered from addictions and hit rock bottom and sold their bodies on the streets. Some were shunned because they are gender fluid and there is no room for them in their conservative families. Some were supposed to wear suicide vests in the name of religion but couldn't pull the trigger when the time came and now can return to neither their families nor the organisations that recruited them. And some still want to wear vests and pull triggers.

Some don't know what they want.

Day after day, as I meet these young souls, I wonder what makes someone's pain so deep that they would rather hurt others, hurt themselves, than ask their pain what it needs.

How loud does someone's pain need to scream to be heard by others, by their own selves?

How lonely is that pain if it can't find anyone to speak to?

At Naii Subha, we try to create some space for that pain. Youth are welcome to stay at the shelter or leave if they wish. The gates are never locked. Sometimes, I wish we could have locked them, kept those who left safe. But I know better. I can't protect them; I know that too.

While they stay with us, youth are paired with counsellors for support, with a local religious and spiritual mentor to facilitate reinterpretation of extremist beliefs, with vocational centres for skills training and job placements. They also have access to at least two mentors who have transitioned back into society after spending time at our shelter. We bring in trainers to coach youth on how to have difficult taboo conversations in nonviolent ways. We bring in artists to see what might spark interest, what might engage them. We bring in martial-arts trainers who provide structure and an outlet for that anger bottled in every nook of their bodies. We bring in famous cricket and hockey and squash players to give motivational talks. We host sessions about humour and laughter so these young ones can reconnect with their young selves, find laughter in their lives. When they are ready, we bring in their families so they can build their capacity to be a part of the reintegration process.

We have movie nights, and tabla nights, where we sing and dance together.

We prepare them for a possible life after the shelter. We clean public spaces together. We plant trees. We go to markets together. We buy little gifts for each other. We learn together what it means to build your life again.

In a lot of ways, we are our own community at Naii Subha. And somewhere between the trauma all these youth carry, and my own trauma tucked deep inside, for no one to see, life settles in.

At home, no one asks me much about life in Canada. When I cry, they let me cry. When I am quiet, they let me be. When I am angry, they listen. They give me space, yes, but it doesn't feel like enough.

They don't ask to see my bruises, and I don't show them.

I don't know what I need. So, we just move on.

And many moons go by.

Several months after my return to Lahore, I find myself marching towards the parliament in the heart of our capital city, Islamabad.

Our voices rise together in chants that echo off the empty streets as over a hundred thousand of us move together. Our hearts pound in our chests, the weight of history and all the generations to come coursing through our beings. It is a hot summer afternoon; somehow the heat of the angry sun boils our insides even further.

The air is thick, but also hopeful. What it is hopeful with, I'm not sure.

I am there because I am finally free to scream at the top of my lungs. I am there because I want justice for all the young ones who come to Naii Subha every single day, bruised, beaten down, their lights dimmed by society's injustices and neglect.

I want to remind our authorities that we fought hard to gain independence from the British Raj and we couldn't just fall right back into being slaves to colonial systems. That they couldn't just impose rules that were not rooted in our ancestral ways, systems that didn't honour our grandmothers. I was there for my ancestors who had lost their lives fighting for that independence from the Raj.

I was there for our unborn children, who I couldn't imagine walking into a world full of chaos, of instability, of infighting, of us continuing to fight wars the British had created for us.

I was there for humanity so we could stop hurting each other.

I didn't know who I was demanding all this from, though. Or how in that moment, my shouting at the top of my lungs was going to achieve all, or some, or any of the things I was there for. Was I demanding them from the young, barely eighteen-year-old policeman in riot gear with more fear than authority in his eyes?

Or the young policeman beside him, ready to shoot tear gas at us?

Or from the streets of my homeland, which I was walking on as we approached the government building?

Or from those in those buildings? Could they even do anything about all the things I, Emahn, was demanding?

I don't know.

Did others marching alongside me know what they were marching for or if those we were demanding solutions from were even capable of solving things for us?

I don't know.

I just know I was furious. I was angry at life. I was angry at how men treated women: as property, as an object to possess, to own, as a thing to have, to rule over, to command, to use, to destroy as they saw fit, to rip apart from their mothers and their fathers and their aunties, and their laughter, and their voice.

I was angry at how I was left to rot in a foreign land where roses were beautiful, yes, but soulless, scentless. I was angry at how every time a man had hurt me, I had to find my *own* strength, find it from some magical place in the cosmos instead of some decent human being helping me, *any* decent human being helping me.

I was angry at all the bigotry, misogyny, and injustice in the world. I was angry at the hypocrisy of those in power, the disconnect between their actions and their words.

I was angry at the hypocrisy of our religions, our spirituality, our systems.

I was angry at how no one came to my aid when my husband beat me night after night.

I was angry at how no one at work asked me once if I needed help, despite seeing the poorly covered-up bruises on my face.

I was ashamed of how despite being born in love, despite being taught to love, that I had failed to be loved by a man.

I was ashamed of how I had failed to fight for *him*, for my Yawar. For the valleys of Kashmir. How I had failed to fight for *me*. Failed to fight for the chinar trees.

And then, in the middle of all that soul-scraping rage at the world, at the bottomless muck of shame at having failed my own self, came he.

In the middle of the batons unleashed on us, in the middle of the tear gas that filled the air, in the middle of me madly swinging my flagpole at the policemen, in the middle of sheer chaos, of angry screams, of powerful slogans, of shoving and stumbling, in the middle of me lying on the ground in a ball, a policeman beating the living hell out of me, came he.

"How dare you hit a woman!" he said, his voice deep and hoarse, and filled with such anger it felt like honey to my ears.

As I gasped for breath, my eyes watering uncontrollably with the tear gas, my lungs burning with each inhale, he charged at the policeman. The policeman redirected, the man put his hand out, and I took it.

We stumbled together, half running, half falling, making our way out of the crowd, down a narrow alley. I fell again, and he dropped to his knees beside me. Pulling a rag from his pocket, he pressed it into my face.

"Breathe through this," he said, his own breath coming in harsh gasps. I clutched the damp rag close to my nose and mouth, its dampness offering some relief from the burning in my throat.

My eyes stinging, tears streaming down my cheeks, I looked up at him.

"Thank you. I think you might have saved my life," I squeaked out.

"I was mostly trying to save the policeman from you"—he smiled—"but you're welcome. Can you walk? We should keep moving. It's not safe here," he said.

"Yeah," I said, grabbing his arm to get up. "My team will be meeting at the Alam Bookstore. Do you know where that is?"

"It's where I'm headed," he said.

"I'm Emahn," I said as we hobbled along narrow alleys.

"Shayan," he said. "Shayan Khan."

There's Comfort in Chaos

In the wreckage of others,
a closeness in darkness,
a knowing gnawing,
a familiarity that connects us,
wounds unhealed,
wounds undiscovered.

I wasn't looking for a healer,
I don't know if you're one.
But I'd like to walk by you,
see what binds us together,
see if we can carry each other.

Our pain could become our language,
a rhythm we know by heart.
We know how to hurt,
to live in darkness, in solitude,
in a universe with no one to trust.

But do we know joy?
Can we know joy?

Khelaah

A Void

Shayan is like a mesmerising fire, with radiant blues, and whites and vivid oranges and bold yellows, and unapologetic hints of red. He flickers and sways, and spirals, and moves with a hypnotic wildness.

Over the months that follow, I realise Shayan's anger at the world is like honey to me. It is beautiful, satisfying, and so desperately welcome. Where I couldn't, *didn't*, push, or question, he does. Every day. Where I am quiet and watch and observe, he is loud and bold and present and draws in others. He is fearless, and with him I feel protected. Like nothing in the world can dare hurt me.

Through Shayan, I learn what it means to have permission to feel pain. To have permission to hurt. To have permission to *feel* hurt. Deep, agonising hurt.

Shayan and I get married exactly six months from the day we first met, and a year and a half since I returned to Lahore. My family says nothing. They let me be.

Through Shayan, I uncover a world so different from mine, I forget who I am. For brief moments, I forget everything that had happened in my life, what had happened to me. I am grateful for those moments, and sometimes also worried. Some days, I feel like I'm floating outside the edges of everything I have known.

It is exhilarating and unsettling at the same time.

Shayan's world has no structure, no rules, no nezaam. Nothing can contain him. No system is fluid enough, no identity label enough. He floats across sexualities, dances between monogamy and polygamy, between being a friend and a lover to all around him, between knowing himself and questioning who he is.

One night, he paces the room restlessly, his bare feet soundless against the worn wooden floor of our bedroom, as if trying to grasp something just out of reach.

"Why do people need labels?" he asks, not really waiting for an answer. "Why do they need to know if I am this or that? If I belong here or there? Why does love have to come with a set of rules?"

I watch him from the bed, my legs folded beneath me. "Maybe it's not about rules. Maybe it's about knowing where you stand," I say softly.

He stops, turns to me, eyes ablaze. "Knowing where you stand? That's just another way of saying knowing where you're allowed to be. I don't want to be told where I can or cannot exist, Emahn. I just want to be."

"And do *you* know what that means?" I ask. "To just be?"

He exhales sharply, running a hand through his unruly hair. "Some days, I do. Some days, I think I have it all figured out. And then, the next moment"—he shakes his head, laughing bitterly—"the next moment, I don't even know who the fuck I am."

I reach for his hand, but he pulls away, pacing again.

"I don't want to be put in a box, Emahn. I don't want to wake up one day and realize I've become something predictable, something confined. I want to be free. Truly free."

I hesitate before speaking. "And what if, in trying to be everything, you end up belonging nowhere, Shayan?"

He stops. The question hanging between us.

"Then at least I know I wasn't caged," he whispers, tears welling up in his eyes.

I wonder what colour this freedom is that he desires.

Anarkali Bazaar feels unusually alive tonight. The air is thick with the scent of tavva-fried fish, every kind of spiced chaat I can imagine, sweet doodh patti, and many colours of sugary jalebiyan. I love these outings to the food street, which Shayan and I have gotten quickly accustomed to. The dhabas, stalls, spill out onto uneven centuries-old cobbled streets, their tin roofs strung with glowing fairy lights and old Pepsi signs that are faded but still proud. With hundreds of dhabas to choose from, we try something new each time and usually try a few things every time we visit.

Shayan and I stand by a street stall, devouring the gol guppay, tamarind water dripping between my fingers. He watches me with a smirk as I close my eyes, savoring the crispness, the explosion of spice and sourness against my tongue.

"You eat like you've never had these before, my dear wife," he teases, reaching for another.

"Because it feels like the first time every time," I reply, licking the remnants of chutney off my fingers.

He laughs, his face soft, unburdened.

Just then, a sharp voice cuts through the hum of the vendors and visitors of the bazaar.

"Oye, chup oye! Tun kaar chal, main teno dasnawan," a deep, coarse voice says. *"Shut up! Let's just get home, and I'll show you."*

We turn towards the commotion. A short, round man in a starched white shalwar kameez and black sandals, face flushed with fury, grips his wife's wrist tightly. She is small, wrapped in a faded green dupatta, eyes darting around as if searching for a way out.

"Main aithay tera nukar lagyaan?" his voice booms, louder than the vendors advertising their haleem and nihari and pakoray. *"Do I look like your servant to you?"*

The woman murmurs something, her voice too low to reach us. He yanks her arm. Hard. She stumbles, nearly falling. The crowd watches, but no one moves.

Except Shayan.

Pushing through the bystanders before I can grab his sleeve,

Shayan is on the guy. "Chhad hathh," he says, his voice low, dangerous. "*Let her hand go.*"

"Oye! Ai mera maamla eh. Teno ki siyaapa peya?" the man scoffs. "*This is my business. Why are you inconveniencing yourself?*"

Shayan doesn't reply. His jaw clenches, his eyes burn. The woman tries to tug her wrist free, but the man holds on.

And then Shayan swings. My stomach drops. My palms get sweaty.

His fist connects with the man's jaw with a sickening crunch. The man stumbles back, eyes wide with shock, hand flying to his face.

"Teri main." The man begins to swear, and lunges back at Shayan.

Gasps ripple through the bazaar. Someone yells. Someone else grabs Shayan by the shoulder, trying to pull him back, but he shoves them off. Others intervene now, pushing them apart. Everyone is shouting.

The woman covers her face with her green shawl, sobbing loudly as she disappears into the crowd with a handful of other women following her.

I watch in frozen horror as voices clash, as dust swirls in the commotion, some rickety song playing in the background as more people gather to watch the chaos. Shayan is breathing heavily, fists clenched, ready for another fight. But then, he sees me.

And just like that, it's over.

The ride home is suffocating. I leave my window open so I can breathe, but it doesn't seem to help much. Neither of us speaks. The city blurs past us—neon signs, shadowed alleyways, the distant sound of qawwali from a roadside café. Shayan's hands grip the steering wheel, knuckles raw, as if letting it go will throw us off a cliff. I don't reach for them. I don't reach for him.

At home, I crawl into bed. I don't ask if he's coming. I don't ask anything at all. I just listen.

The clink of a glass.

The pour. One drink. Then another. Then another. I close my eyes. Willing sleep to take me.

Suddenly, I hear a slam on my nightstand, and I jolt awake.

"What?" I say louder than I mean to.

The lamp wobbles. I flinch. Then his voice.

"Wake up!"

The room is still dark, the night barely shifting into dawn, but he is there, looming over me, his breath thick with whiskey, his presence vibrating with fury.

"Wake up, Emahn!" he roars again, this time grabbing the blanket and yanking it off me.

Cold air hits my skin. My body stiffens. Blood rushes to my face.

"What is wrong with you?" he spits, his voice slurring at the edges but sharp enough to cut through me. "How do you do it? How do you sleep while the world is burning, Your Royal Highness?"

I push myself up, my heart hammering, but I keep my voice steady. "Shayan, stop."

"No," he snaps, pacing the room, running a hand through his disheveled hair. "I don't get it. I don't get you. You walk through this world like it hasn't already torn you to shreds. Like you don't feel the same things I do. How, Emahn? How do you live with it? How do you laugh? How do you not sob every night? Or throw things around every night?"

His hand flies out suddenly, knocking over the glass of water on my nightstand. It crashes to the floor, water spreading across the rug like spilled blood. His rage radiates in fierce waves, bending the air and blurring the edges of reality, making it hard to see where his fire ends and the world begins. He is orange and crimson, spilling into an endless darkness, casting shadows that stretch and contrast far and wide, flickering as if they live.

"Stop this," I say again, slower, quieter this time.

He turns to me, his eyes wild, desperate. "I won't."

I watch the rise and fall of his chest, the tremor in his fingers.

"I can't. I can't erase my mother's screams from my mind. Night after night, as he hurt her. I saw my mother in that woman. I saw you in that woman. How do *you* not see it?" He drags his words out mockingly, as if dragging their clunk across the floor, scraping parts of it.

I exhale sharply, my shoulders sinking. "Your mother and I lived absolute hell, yes. But both of us also survived. Your mother raised you to care, Shayan. She turned her agony into something so much bigger than the hell. So much more important."

Something flickers across his face—betrayal, maybe, or

disappointment, or something else I can't understand. He shakes his head, laughing under his breath, bitter and broken.

"Wow. Some human-rights advocate you are. Go tell that to all the women in the world whose husbands are abusing them. Turn your agony into something bigger—that'll bring world peace," he mimics me, and I swallow hard, taking his harsh words in. "You'll never understand," he mutters. "Just go back to your sleep."

And then, just like that, he turns away, disappearing into the bathroom, the bottle still clutched in his hand.

I don't follow him. I know what comes next.

The sharp clink of the bottle hitting the counter.

The slow, deliberate slide of the medicine cabinet opening.

The faint rustle of fingers searching, finding.

The cold bite of metal against skin.

I tell myself he doesn't do it to die. He does it to feel. Because sometimes, pain is the only thing real enough to remind him he is alive. Tomorrow morning, I'll clean up after him. The bottles, the shards, the smell of whiskey, the hints of harms inflicted on himself.

I close my eyes, drawing my knees to my chest, the space between us stretching wide, heavy.

One night, Shayan and I visit a friend's house. Asim is not exactly Shayan's favourite person in the world, so he's already on edge. As we settle in with the pleasantries, I can sense this won't be smooth sailing for Shayan. The room is filled with people who enjoy debating revolution over expensive liquor, speaking for the oppressed but living in gated communities, shielded from the very struggles they seem to really romanticize.

As the night moves on, the debates get louder. At some point, Asim slurs, "Yaar, but at the end of the day, people just need to work harder. It's not like money is impossible to make."

Shayan, already several drinks in, stiffens. His fingers curl around his glass. The air in the room thickens. I know it's over. Edges of grey start floating around me. Bitter, angry, unforgiving.

"Work harder?" he repeats, his voice dangerously low.

Asim shrugs, swirling his whiskey. "I mean, yeah. People always blame the system, but look at us—we made something of ourselves."

The room goes quiet. Something snaps. I hear a coyote howl somewhere outside in the distance. My breathing gets shallow. I wish someone could suck the silence away and fill it with something kinder, something gentler.

"*We?*" Shayan barks, standing up so fast his chair scrapes against the floor. "You were born into money, Asim. Your father bought your first business. You've never starved, never stood in line for rationed flour, never had to worry about your house flooding in the monsoons. You don't get to sit here, drinking overpriced whiskey, talking about struggle like it's some Goddamn thought experiment."

For a few long seconds, no one moves. I hear shallow breaths.

"Relax, Shayan," someone says, laughing nervously. "It's just a discussion, man."

"It's not a fucking discussion to the people who live it!" His voice cracks, his chest heaving.

Asim rolls his eyes. "Here we go again. Always looking for a fight, man. Maybe if you weren't so angry all the time . . ."

And that's it. That's the last thing Shayan needs to hear.

He lunges.

The glass shatters first, hitting the floor in a burst of amber liquid and shards. Then, fists. A table crashes. People pull Shayan back, but his voice still cuts through the chaos, spitting words like venom, roaring so loudly I wonder if the entire neighbourhood can hear.

By the time I drag him out of there, his knuckles are bloodied, his breath ragged, his shirt torn. I tell him I'll drive and open the passenger door for him. He doesn't say a word the entire ride back, just stares out the window, jaw clenched, dark fury still radiating off him in waves.

When we get home, I turn the fan on as he sits on the edge of the bed, hunched over, elbows on his knees. His knuckles bloody, my dupatta wrapped around them. I bring some warm antiseptic water in a bowl and sit across from him on the bed.

"Shayan," I say softly, starting to unwrap the dupatta so I can bandage his hands. He doesn't move. "We need to talk."

A loud, dry chuckle escapes his lips. "No, we don't."

"We do."

He exhales sharply, shaking his head. "Emahn, please. Not tonight."

"If not tonight, then when?" My voice is steady, but inside, I am exhausted. His anger is not honey anymore. It has become bitter poison, and I don't want to keep taking spoonful after spoonful, night after night. He looks up at me now, eyes bloodshot.

"You think there's something to fix." He tilts his head, studying me with a mocking smile. "Like I'm some broken thing you can piece back together with love and tenderness and your little stories about your naani and your little things." His words cut me so deeply I feel like there's a river gushing angrily between the two parts of me.

"You don't have to mock me or my grandmother, Shayan. Show some respect. And no, I don't think you're broken," I say, even though some days, it feels like there is barely an inch of him that isn't bruised or pieced back together. "I think you're hurting. And I think you need help."

His jaw tightens. "And you think some therapist with a notebook and a checklist can make this all disappear?"

"Not disappear. But maybe help you carry it better."

He scoffs. "What are they going to tell me? Breathe? Go for a walk? Write down my feelings?" He laughs bitterly. "I know what I feel, Emahn. I feel rage. I feel disgust. I feel every ounce of injustice in this world burning inside of me, eating me alive, and I can't just sit there and—"

"And what?" I cut in. "Drink until it numbs you? Bleed it out and not have the decency to even clean up after yourself? Pick fights with strangers in the street? Pick fights with people who have supported you? Throw insults at me?"

His gaze flickers. His hands clench into fists. He shoves me. My mouth goes dry.

He gets off the bed, swings at the bowl of water with his fist, splashing it all over. His expression is contorted as if trying to sift through a million different emotions, and just as I hope with every little ounce of my body for him to say we can get help, he throws me deep into a well so dark I don't know if light has ever touched it.

"This is all you get, Emahn, you either accept me the way I am, or you're welcome to leave."

That winter, a year into our marriage, I find out I am pregnant. The day I do, something shifts in the universe. I stop watching Shayan. I do not want my child to see this darkness, I decide. I want my child to believe in something, in *anything*, when there is uncertainty. I want my child to know to find light in darkness. I want my child to cherish life, to bring hope to others.

I have tried to find the edges of his universe but can't see them. I don't know where to go in this vastness. My life *was* about the little things. The one drop of dew on the petal of a gulab. The power of a thorn that is so tiny you barely notice it. The little sequins in the sunflowers on the gold ribbon of my dress as the bad man had hurt me. The kiss of the first drop of the monsoon rain. And the millions of kisses from the skies as they showered on me. I don't know how to grasp his world. It's too big. Too vast.

Shayan is not just fire, I realise. Shayan is an inferno. An inferno that rages, a feral beast, with flames that tower and twist and churn, consuming everything they touch with a hunger that is insatiable.

And I am caught in this inferno's path, its dance, its dance of pain, its crackling and popping of every tree it consumes.

I had sought permission to hurt, yes, I had sought permission to be angry, yes. I had sought permission to be enraged at the world, but had I walked out of one hell only to enter another?

So, that night, as he drinks and sobs and wails and weeps, wanting someone to comfort him, hold him, I just sit there like a statue, like someone dead inside, like someone with nothing left to give, someone shameful, someone ugly, someone not enough for him, someone disconnected from his world.

That winter, I draw a line. Between me, our child in my belly, and his darkness.

I just sit there, and rock, and sing, running my hand over my belly, soothing my child.

Challa nau nau theve,
ve puttar mithray meve.
Ve Allah sabh nu deve.
O thiya sub nu devay.
Vay gall sun challeya,
kaanvaan ver maava thandiya chhaavan.

The ring spins and spins,
Sons are sweet, like dried fruit.
May God give one to every mother.
May daughters be born to all.
Oh listen, dear ring, dear crow,
mothers are the trees shading their children.

Two Hearts

Two hearts beating,
one within me, steady and comforting,
and then yours, heavy with pain, darkness,
blacks and greys and nothing in between.
A heart that wants to escape, but can't,
doesn't know how.

Your bottles rattle in the night,
your words of my inadequacy, your inability to feel pain
cutting through the silence.

As you weaponize your trauma, your pain, your anguish,
as you decide you want to stay there,
not walk, not try to get up,
I cradle a future I want to hold.

I wonder if this nikki duniya, this little life,
can heal what's broken in you,
or if this child
must compete with your insatiable desire to be angry,
to burn, to stay in hell,
a need I don't quite understand.

I dream of mornings without another empty bottle,
imagine you reaching for us instead.
But each day that goes by,
it's just us, this silly hope,
waiting for you to return,
or let us go.

But it's not you who brought us here.
We came freely, of our own will,
my own will,
to find someone who could love me,
but there isn't room for me.
So, I walk back to the fork in the road,
a path I wish I hadn't taken,
and I let you go.

Ik Si Rani

There Once Was a Queen

High above the earth, floating between the seven skies, where the night sky stretched out in endless soft, velvety darkness, Moonga Rani earned the title of the queen of adversity. She glowed in the night sky, her radiance woven from the darkness she had once endured. For many lives, she had taken every harsh word thrown at her and turned it into glittering, shimmering gemstones. Where others had withered and fallen away, Moonga Rani had turned every scar into a dazzling thread of scarlet blues, deep indigos, fiery reds that floated around, carrying whispers of sorrows, that circled around her like an indestructible aura, a boundless, unbreakable force.

She had been holding court for some lives again as she had done with her king, whom she had loved so deeply many lives ago. Moonga Rani was fair, kind, and compassionate. She was loved, revered, honoured, for her wisdom, for her boundless power and compassion.

One day, a young woman entered Moonga Rani's court, carrying a little secret within her. The kind of secret that fluttered quietly, like the faintest flicker of a new star, like the faint whisper of something sweet, something tender. It was never an easy journey for a new star to come to be in this universe, and this little star was floating in a darkness Moonga Rani recognized as she laid eyes on the young woman.

The young woman held her belly so tenderly, so protectively that it stirred something deep in Moonga Rani. She had been there once. Not anymore. As she watched the young woman, Moonga Rani's magic reached out to this unborn star, in beautiful shimmers of gold and silver braided with turquoise and greens. Something told Moonga Rani this was an ember to protect, an ember that could burn bright or, if she wasn't careful, float into the expanse of the universe.

The young woman wept and wept and wept some more. She explained how with every passing day, she feared more for the little star with the Darkness around it. Every time her husband gave up on life, Darkness would come, bringing gusts of winds, carrying a restless, helpless wail that made all the beings curl up and hope the winds would shift. Darkness would blow through the young woman's home like frozen edges of shattered starlight, cutting everything it touched.

No one could unhear, unsee, undo what Darkness did in its wake. And no matter how much strength the young woman mustered with every breath, with every lullaby she sang to the little star inside her, Darkness was too strong.

"Her little star wouldn't come to be," she wept.

Moonga Rani listened carefully. This one was difficult for her, and she knew she would have to seek counsel from her friends, her advisors, her confidants in the cosmos.

That night, Moonga Rani returned to the edge of the cosmos. To the edge of where there were no rules, the edge where the rivers of light flowed in torrents of gold and silver. To the edge where the path to the grandmothers was tucked away only for those who knew them.

Walking to the edge, she called out with all her strength, her voice rising into the night, the echoes carrying far beyond the boundaries of her realm, reaching deep into the spaces between the worlds. It was when her voice broke that she knew she had reached someone.

The two-spirited beings, her guides, appeared once more. Their beautiful forms shimmered and shifted, blending into the night as seamlessly as the lights and shadows that danced across the sky, making her smile.

"Hello, my friends," she whispered, blinking through the tears of joy that clouded her every time she visited them. *How could someone be sad in this beautiful cosmos?* she thought.

"We are here, my queen, the grandmothers have been waiting," they said, their voices harmonising as one, surrounding her with such love, care, and beauty that she forgot for a moment why she was even there. "You know the way; come along," they added, with a warmth that made the darkness around her melt away slowly, her feet feeling lighter. The velvet night with dancing stars and shimmering streaks opened around them then, like the petals of a marigold spiralling itself open to the universe, showing a path that stretched towards the heart of the cosmos, its most sacred place—the palace of the grandmothers.

Moonga Rani followed this path, walking alongside the two-spirited beings, to a place where the skies curved inward in a stunning spiral, weaving light and darkness together in a dance as old as time. There, between the seven skies, the air thick with the whispers of ancient stars, the winds singing songs forgotten by all but the oldest of beings, the most sacred of beings, she entered the palace and could already hear their laughter. They had always greeted her dressed in twinkling robes adorned with constellations, their silvery hair flowing freely around them like strands of shimmering stardust, weaving and curling in the weightless expanse around them. Their wrinkles were deep and ancient, carrying all the stories of the cosmos, their eyes holding the wisdom of the galaxies, their beings holding the knowledge of every star that was born and left to become stardust.

They had entered the palace together, Moonga Rani and the two-spirited beings.

"We have been waiting for you," one of the grandmothers spoke, her voice soft like a gentle breeze on a warm evening, calm and steady, wrapping Moonga Rani in a gentle melody of care and comfort.

They all gathered in a circle then, ready to listen to the matter on which Moonga Rani wished to seek counsel.

Moonga Rani explained to them the plight of the young woman. They listened intently, nodding, some closing their eyes, some rocking, some swaying with Moonga Rani's recounting.

"She seeks the colours of her pain in his. His pain is his pain. Hers is hers. It is not hers to heal what is not ready or willing to be healed," one of them said, her voice flowing deep into Moonga Rani, braiding itself with a knowing that had been hiding within her.

"She is not a medicine for his wounds, nor a cure for his darkness," another grandmother added softly. They all nodded.

"But she can heal him with love, and kindness, and compassion, and curiosity, could she not? Could she not channel his darkness into light?" one of the two-spirited beings asked.

"Not if his darkness is an endless void," another one responded, their voice shifting, becoming stronger.

Moonga Rani watched them all, the grandmothers and the two-spirited beings, in awe as they spoke in strength, in resilience, in power, in wisdom. In curiosity.

"She sees his pain because she knows pain," one of the grandmothers said. "She is searching for her pain in his darkness."

"Hmmm," they all then said in unison, as something settled for them all, as their braided voices echoed in the palace.

"One does not need to taste pain to be loved, to be seen," said another grandmother, her voice so gentle that Moonga Rani almost thought it was her own self whispering. "She can be her own medicine. See herself, honour herself."

"She must find her people, those who will help hold her up when she tires," another one chimed in, her voice steady and strong.

"She will need to teach her little star how to find its own power," said the youngest of the grandmothers.

And then, time stood still. They all looked at Moonga Rani, and she knew this was what she had waited for. She never left this palace without gifts for her people, but also gifts for herself. Gifts of wisdom.

"The answers she seeks are deep within her, tucked within nooks of doubt. She'll need to find those. Every time she finds one, she'll grow stronger, more answers weaving themselves into her power of intuition. She must find her power," the oldest of the grandmothers said. "Like you did through your darkness."

As Moonga Rani floated through the skies, away from the palace of the grandmothers, away from the heart of the cosmos, back through the place where the skies curved inward, back to her palace, holding their wisdom for the young woman, she felt gratitude vaster than she had ever felt before.

A sphere of Darkness hovered towards her then, materialising before her, pulsing, stretching, as if sensing her presence. It was not the wispy, fleeting kind of shadow she had blown away before. This one grew. It swirled, thick and undulating, a dense maelstrom of the deepest-black vapour, curling and uncurling like a thing alive, its tendrils licking at the sky like the arms of a restless beast. It stretched towards her, twisting and spiralling, reaching for her hungrily.

Moonga Rani stilled.

She had seen many forms of darkness in her many lives. Some gentle, lingering shadows that only needed acknowledgment before they drifted away. Others fought to stay.

The first tendril brushed against her ankle—cool, then suddenly biting. She gasped as it coiled around her foot, pulling. More tendrils shot forward, wrapping around her wrists, twisting up her arms, weaving through the scarlet blues and deep indigos of her own shimmering aura.

Her breath hitched. The darkness was seeping into her, climbing her body, pressing into her skin, curling between her fingers, twisting around her waist like a hundred slithering vines, thick and unrelenting, creeping into the spaces between her ribs, squeezing, forcing the air from her lungs.

She struggled.

She twisted, trying to shake it off, but it tightened, latching onto her like it had finally found something to claim. She reached for the sky, but the tendrils only pulled her deeper, the weight of them anchoring her, curling around her throat, pressing.

A sharp whisper slithered into her ears.

"You belong to me."

Her heart pounded. Darkness was alive, whispering, shifting, pressing against her with a force she had never known before. "You are made of me."

She clenched her teeth, pushing against them, trying to summon her strength, but the more she fought, the deeper they dug in.

The stars around her dimmed. She could feel herself slipping. For a moment, she almost let go. But then she remembered. She was Moonga Rani. She had walked through flames before. She had been scarred and remade. She had been crushed and reborn. And she had never belonged to Darkness.

Her hands curled into fists. Inhaling not just breath, but power—deep, full, from the core of the cosmos itself. She exhaled. A slow, steady breath.

Darkness shuddered.

She exhaled again, stronger this time. The tendrils twitched, recoiled, loosened. Every time she breathed, Darkness shivered.

With one final, long breath, this one filled with light, she parted her lips and blew at Darkness with every ounce of power the cosmos had given her.

Darkness dissolved, screaming a million screams as it unraveled, breaking into a thousand wisps, scattering into the vastness of the sky.

She pressed her palm to her chest, feeling the steady rhythm of her heartbeat. Darkness had tried to consume her. But it had forgotten that she was Moonga Rani.

And she had already learned how to survive the night.

Zoya

Life

The afternoon sun hangs low, casting long shadows across the courtyard at Naii Subha. The courtyard stretches wide, encircled by aged brick walls that I figure date back at least a couple of hundred years. It's a chilly afternoon, the air carrying a crispiness that bites gingerly at my skin. The boys are all bundled up in woollen sweaters, engrossed in a daily game of cricket. Their shouts and laughter echo across the open space, punctuated by the occasional sharp thwack of the ball meeting the bat. They go from words of encouragement to shaming each other for a missed catch in seconds.

Most afternoons, sitting on a bench near a motia bush, its small buds closed tightly, waiting for the cold season to pass, I watch the boys play. I love watching them happy, watching them be children, watching them reclaim small parts of their youth that were taken away from them. It is such a contrast to the angry men we find in our counselling sessions, recounting the injustices society has inflicted upon them.

I pull my shawl tighter around my shoulders, a slight chill seeping into the bench beneath me. I run my hand over my belly. I am seven months along and can feel the weight of my changing body. It has not been an easy pregnancy. I am having a daughter, and I have already picked a name for her—Zoya, meaning life.

The night I told Shayan, he had paced, hands shaking, breath uneven. I had watched him, waiting for him to say something—anything—but deep down, I already knew. For a full week after, he didn't say a word to me, and then one night, whiskey on his breath, with exhaustion so deep I thought it would drown me, he said, "How can you bring a child into *this* world?"

With tears in my eyes, I said softly, "Yes. I want to bring a child into this world, Shayan. This little one may be the medicine the world needs. I don't want to bring it into *this*." I had waved my hand, pointing to the void between us.

And that was it, wasn't it? Not into *this*.

The night he left us, he didn't slam the door. He just stood in the doorway for a long time, staring at us like he was trying to memorize something he knew he'd never see again. Then without a word, he turned and walked out.

I hadn't called after him. I hadn't moved. I just sat in the dark, rocking back and forth, my hand on my belly, telling my little one we were going to be okay.

My doctor has insisted several times that I need to stay home and rest. But I can't rest. My demons come charging out of the shadows if I try to slow down. So, I keep moving.

My thoughts are interrupted by a panicked Rafiqa, one of the caretakers at Naii Subha. We often joke that news of a new bird about to hatch comes to Rafiqa before the mother bird knows she is about to bring a chick into the world. Nothing gets past Rafiqa.

She approaches me and is out of breath. I smile and ask her to take a beat and tell me what is going on. Rafiqa's words tumble out in a garble that does not register at first. Hassan, one of the boys who had arrived at the shelter just weeks prior, has gone missing, she tells me. I remind her that we don't stop anyone from leaving.

She interrupts me and says that I am not listening to her.

"What don't I understand, Rafiqa jaan? What is wrong?" I say, trying not to get swept away in her panic.

"We were all noticing a shift in him, Baji. He said he is going back to the extremist organisation, that they have a mission for him finally. He is going to do something stupid, Baji. We need to stop him."

I'm worried now. And soon we are joined by one of Hassan's counsellors, and a few others. My breathing is now shallow, and I try to calm my frayed nerves.

We all migrate to an office away from the courtyard, so we don't worry others till we know what is going on. One of the counsellors recounts for us that Hassan had checked himself in after failing a suicide-bombing mission for an extremist organisation. He was afraid they were going to kill him and was ashamed that he had failed them. He had continued to refuse to speak to the religious counsellor, claiming the counsellor was the Shaitan—Satan—and would corrupt his mind and lead him astray from the path of truth. And last week, his friends had expressed some concern that Hassan had seemed distant, quieter, and increasingly frustrated.

We are all breathing heavily, we all talk over each other, and soon we realise, in going through our notes, that the last person to speak to Hassan was me. I am asked if I might have noticed anything unusual or if I had heard Hassan say anything about his plans. My mouth goes dry, and I think hard, but nothing unusual comes to mind. I look through my notes from that day, but nothing stands out. He was frustrated, yes. He hated his life, yes. He was angry at the world, yes. He had talked about wishing his father loved him, wishing his mother loved him. He was still grieving the loss of his family, who had been killed in a drone attack. He hated Amreeka—America—for everything it had done to his people. He hated that people thought he was an extremist. He asked me who an extremist even was. Nothing was out of the ordinary. He seemed rational. His behaviour made sense. His anger made sense.

He asked me what I would have done if someone had killed my entire family. And I had just said that I would be very angry too.

Had *that* pushed him over the edge? What had I missed? Had we talked about something else that made him decide he was going to return? Soon, my anxiety turns into debilitating fear. How could I have missed the signs? Why hadn't I done more? We had failed Hassan, and now a lot of people were about to get hurt.

"We have to find him" is all I can say.

"It doesn't work that way," someone says. "We have alerted the authorities, as is the protocol, and that is all we can do at this point."

We must find him. We must bring him back is all I can think. It's like my brain has lost all faculties to think beyond the one thing. It registers as the only possibility. We couldn't let him hurt himself, hurt others. Someone reminds us that people were always free to leave. But this seems different. Some agree with me that we should look for him, others don't.

It is pure chaos.

We search for him for the next several days. We violate our own boundaries of conduct. We know we are not supposed to go after a client, particularly one headed back into an extremist organisation. We know the authorities are searching for him, and are very disappointed at our failure to keep him in the shelter. Our model is clear; they arrive on their own, and they leave when they desire. We don't go looking for people. Except this time, the model is about to backfire on us, and there is nothing we can do to stop it.

We ask some of Hassan's friends in the shelter if they knew anything. We speak to anyone who may have heard anything, who may have seen Hassan last. We visit street vendors and alleys he used to frequent. We drive for hours each day, me pushing through my fatigue.

I barely sleep. All of us barely sleep. We are not sure what we are exactly hoping to find, but we keep looking. Hassan must be out there, somewhere, and I was going to find him, and talk sense into him. What makes me think that *I* can talk sense into someone who has blood on their mind, I don't know.

One afternoon, six days into us looking for Hassan, my phone rings. It is one of my contacts, a man who had encouraged Hassan to come to Naii Subha the first time. He says he had just seen Hassan with a group near an abandoned warehouse at the edge of the city. The hope filling me just seconds prior quickly turns to bitter dread, as I hear the man on the phone say his final words.

"He had a vest on, Baji. I understand he was headed to Barkat Market. We've alerted all the authorities. Everyone is trying to intercept at this point. There is nothing much we can do."

Hassan was about to destroy so many lives. How could I stop him?

With sweaty palms, a dry mouth, lungs that seem to have forgotten how to do their job, I leave Naii Subha without saying a word to anyone. I could talk him out of it, I tell myself. I had seen glimpses of his goodness, of the child beneath all the hurt and pain. If I could just look into his eyes, I could remind him that there was another way, that there was still a life ahead of him, a life worth trying to live for.

As I race to the market in my car, one hand firmly placed on the horn, hurling insults at anyone who tries to cut me off in traffic, my mind replays moments of my time with Hassan. My eyes well up with tears as I remember the day Hassan painted a mural in the common room; he had worked with a quiet intensity, his fingers stained with shades of blue and green, the smell of fresh paint thick in the air.

"Ms. Emahn, do you have a happy colour?" he had asked, his voice soft, almost reverent.

I had smiled. "I have a few, actually."

His face had lit up. "Tell me!"

I listed them—fuchsia, marigold, deep purples, the rich green of henna. He had mixed each colour with a deep frown, his brush dipping into his many pots of paint, carefully blending each shade till I murmured, "That's perfect, Hassan jaan!"

Days later, there it was—his mural, a stunning landscape of a valley nestled deep in the mountains, with wildflowers of the spring, celebrating all my happy colours.

I must find Hassan. He must live. But was this even my decision to make?

I have barely reached the market when the ground shakes beneath my feet and a deafening blast shatters the air. Smoke and screams fill the street as people run in every direction. I leave the car, my legs trembling beneath me. I cradle my belly, shielding my Zoya from the horror unfolding in front of me.

It is humid. The world has stopped breathing.

Nauseated, dizzy, sick to my stomach, I try to breathe through the metallic taste in my mouth.

A second blast goes off. I huddle close to the ground, holding my belly.

"It's okay, Zoya jaan. Everything will be okay." I am mostly talking to myself.

I stay there for what seems like an eternity. And soon, another blast goes off. More screams. New waves of chaos.

Five blasts in total. In a market filled with women and children. Filled with little ones getting bangles on their wrists for Eid. Filled with hopeful vendors finally able to make sales to sustain their families for times ahead. Filled with street vendors who barely make enough to make ends meet.

Filled with humans who value life more than Hassan did. Who value life more than everyone who had hurt Hassan. Who had failed Hassan.

They say the smell of death never leaves you. I wonder what colour death is. The colour of rubble, the colour of smoke? The colour of deep shadows that never leave you?

"Zoya?" I hold my belly. She was still with me. That is all that mattered.

The next several hours, I try to right what Hassan has wronged. I show Edhi ambulances who is still breathing and can be saved. I tell a stranger the pain will be over soon as I hold her. I tell her that her children would be so proud of her. This was a mother about to return to mother earth.

Zoya kicks again. Hard.

"Zoya jaan, sabar kar, puttar." My breathing labours. *"Please wait, my little one."* I try to soothe her. I know she can smell all this. Feel all this. Hear all this. If she had heard my lullabies, she could hear this. She could hear, feel, how humans were just awful, so capable of hurting each other.

I carry a lifeless child to his wailing mother. I carry his shoe to her.

It feels heavier than any shoe that tiny should be. I don't have words for her.

I don't have words for anyone. How a once-bustling street can turn into a chaotic tangle of overturned carts, shattered glass, debris, lost dreams, lost hopes is beyond what my brain can grasp. How can humans be so ugly to each other? How can someone be so hurt that their only way to be heard is to cause all this?

Zoya kicks again. This time, it feels more than a kick. She wants out. The pain is deep under. Deep inside.

"Zoya, puttar, not now," I plead as I dig, hands bleeding, through the rubble. I can see someone under there, trying to move. I must help them.

Zoya wouldn't listen. Naah. This stubborn little child. She was ready.

Pain shoots through my body. I drag myself to an Edhi ambulance.

"I think I'm in labour. She's not waiting." My hands are bloody, my clothes bloody, I sweat with pain I have never experienced before.

Naano jaan would often say the first sounds of a child wailing are the most beautiful sounds a mother can ever hear. I don't remember hearing a child cry.

I don't remember feeling a breath on me.

I remember me screaming.

I remember feeling death in my bones. In my spirit.

My daughter had decided this world was not a place for her.

In my frenzy to make sense of the chaos, to right someone else's wrong, I had lost my Zoya. In my gutting desperation to heal someone's pain, *anyone's* pain, I had lost the single most important thing in my life.

I had made the biggest mistake of my life.

Zoya, Puttar

I cradle your memory
like I would have cradled you,
drowning in the weight of your loss.

In the silence that holds me,
I see my motia trembling
its fragrance reaching out
as if to find you,
as if to gently soothe
the spaces you left behind.

The gulab withers,
its petals falling like words unsaid,
soft whispers that drift away on the wind.

The marigolds linger by the door,
their bright heads bowed,
grieving with me,
weeping with me,
in quiet solitude.

I touch the earth where you should have walked,
I feel the pulse of the universe, which keeps moving,
one foot in front of the other,
through loss, through grief, through darkness.

I remain here, Zoya jaan,
listening for the echo of your voice,
hoping I can hear your cry, just once,
so I can hold it forever in the melodies of my soul.

All I find is the soft rustle of leaves
and scents of flowers that fade too soon.

Now I am left gathering fragments,
the jasmines, the roses, the marigolds,
making a scattered gajarah for you,
as you float in the womb of the grandmothers.

You are my fire, my Zoya, puttar,
your memory, my reason to live.
I will always carry you,
through this life and my lives to come.

PART 3 — GENDA

Marigold

Genda

Marigold

They line a path I wish had never existed,
a stormy road of pain and resilience,
woven with those before us, those yet to come.

This genda, never chosen for its scent
but for its quiet power to protect,
draped over doorways, lining wedding paths,
bubbling alive like sunlight through clouds.

This genda, pregnant with blessings,
ancient songs, chants of joy,
the hum of laughter held in every bloom.

This genda, burning like flames in the fields,
its fragrance twined with prayer beads,
woven where the divine and human touch.

This genda, spirals curling inward,
delicate but unwavering,
holding light even as it wilts.

This genda, standing firm when my motia fades,
when the rains come, when seasons pass,
when I am tired but still here.

This genda, whispering in shadows,
telling those who listen,
Joy and pain can talk;
laughter rises even in despair.

This genda, unfading,
growing even in darkness,
reminding me, reminding you,
that life, like the genda,
endures. And blooms.

Jarrahn

Roots

A few months after losing my Zoya, I decide to return to Canada. I don't know if returning to a place that had cut me a million ways is the place I should go to. But I know I needed to run away, far away from any possibility of being cared for. Far away to the edge of the universe, where no one asks me about my daughter, where I can grieve without hurting others, stay in this place of numbness, this coldness, for the world around me.

My return to Canada is cathartic. It had taken months of convincing my family I was going to be okay on my own, that I was going to be safe. I reminded them that I had invested so much in my education, and I was not going to throw that away out of fear of my first husband, that I would not give him that power. My future was mine, and not something for him to stake a claim over. He had long ago moved to a different city far away from the one I was returning to. Plus, my homeland was not ready to have me back. She is a tough teacher. And I had more to learn to be able to survive. To be able to survive her.

Returning to Canada carries an odd fear and a sense of freedom at the same time. I'm not sure what the freedom is from. But I can go wherever I want; I can do whatever I want. I can call whomever I want, whenever I want. I can speak to whomever I want. I can talk to them about whatever I want. It's not like the last time I was here, I tell myself.

It scares me not knowing how to feel about returning to a place I had escaped from just almost four years prior.

Can I welcome the freedom I feel while also accepting the fear, the uncertainty, the heaviness?

For the first time in years, I feel lighter. My feet on the earth, heavy and slow and tentative, afraid of what the next step might bring, felt grounded. But I still carry a weight in me that stirs every time I see a bruise on someone, every time I hear a glass fall, a plate break, a door slam, a voice raised. I wonder if this land remembers. Do the winds that touch the corners of our being remember? I know the winds have touched me, carried my story, but have they told anyone? Does this land have the strength to hear how much more turmoil I am now carrying in my body?

My world seems a little muffled, a little wrung out, but also a little steady, a little less prickly.

This feeling scares me, but also comforts me. I don't know what to make of it.

Canada had not been an easy place to be. I had been othered, treated in ways I had not understood, told things I had not understood. It was always cold. Not just in the way winter stretched its long, pale fingers across the land, or how the wind howled through empty streets, but in the way it held its coldness in the spaces between people. In the way it looked at me, through me. A land vast enough to hold multitudes yet unwilling to hold me. I didn't need to belong here. Belonging was a thing this place did not offer freely, a thing I had long stopped reaching for. I only needed the quiet, the space to *be*—without expectation, without the weight of unspoken questions, without the slow, deliberate distance that told me I was something other.

Yes, Canada was always cold. And maybe that was fine. Cold would not ask anything of me. Because I had nothing to give.

But if I am to live in this foreign land again, it is time for me to understand my host, not to belong, but to earn my keep.

So I finally meet my host in these lands, the First Nations, the Métis, and the Inuit peoples of Turtle Island. It makes sense why their voices had not reached me back then. As I dive into the history of present-day Canada, the history of colonisation across this territory, it all makes sense. The British and French had both laid claim to these territories over a period of hundreds of years.

I learn that someone named John Cabot had landed on the shores of present-day Canada in 1497 and had claimed it for England. I imagine what it would be like for me to someday sit across from John Cabot after I "claimed" his home, his family, all his belongings, all his food for myself. Though I'm also not sure I would like whatever it is that John probably ate back then.

I imagine what John would say today about this claiming of someone else's land. Would he say he was just doing his job? Would he still feel pride for the accolades he received back then if he knew the havoc it caused after?

I had imagined having many similar conversations with a representative of the British Raj every time Miyan Ji, my great-grandfather, told us stories of British officers roaming our homelands, laying claim to our fields, our grain, our cattle, our waters, the air we breathed.

I learn that in Canada, the taking of lands had continued well into the 1800s, followed by assimilation policies and "Indian" residential school systems. From the late nineteenth century and well into the twentieth century, Canada had sponsored church-run schools to assimilate Indigenous children into Euro-Canadian ways of knowing, "removing the Indian out of them" and "civilising them." Their system had included a network of such schools, day schools, hospitals, sanitoriums, boarding schools, and other institutions that children were shuttled between.

Across Canada, these institutions had carried and still carried dark truths about physical and sexual abuse and, in some cases, medical experiments, nutrition experiments, and significant loss of cultural, familial, spiritual, and communal ties.

The last of the residential schools had closed in Canada only three years before I first arrived in the country. Most Canadians did not know about their dark history. Some people deny that history to this day.

The impacts of this legacy, compounded with other policies and systems, had gutted Indigenous people deeply, trauma spilling from one generation to the next, consuming entire families and communities.

I discover that the self-claimed superiority of the British Empire, the superiority of whiteness, of their faith systems, of their systems of "civility," which had consumed many generations in my homeland, had consumed generations here too.

In our homeland, the colonisers had vilified, brutalised, exoticised our brown skin. They had done the same here.

They had called our dances the ways of the devil, and our systems pagan. They had done the same here.

They had vilified our languages, our colours, our systems, our ways of being. They had done the same here.

They had called us lazy. They had done the same here.

They had stripped our lands of their rich resources. They had done the same here.

Miyan Ji would often tell us stories of gaining independence from the British Raj. He'd say the strongest way to fight back is to be. I never really understood that back then, but now, as I return to the human-rights tribunal office as an analyst, and work with testimonies of survivors of the residential school system, in seeing them talk about the ways they had survived and were reclaiming their ways of being, I finally understand what Miyan Ji had said all those years ago.

The strongest way to fight back is to be.

To be in our languages, in our customs, our ways of being. To be comfortable in our own skin. To know inherently in every cell of our bodies that we deserve to be treated with kindness, compassion, fairness, equality. To know inherently that we must treat others as we expect to be treated. To be is to be so aware of the roots you have, the roots you're always growing, the roots that reach beneath the surface, cell by cell, bit by bit, working through the dirt, the roots that intertwine with the roots of others.

To be is to find our relationships with the land, the wind, the waters, the little critters, the melodies of our ancient songs.

But what if we come from a way of being that is not connected to the land, the winds, the waters, the little critters, the melodies of ancient songs? What if our way to be is in laying claim, taking up, using, asserting our dominance?

I had learned that the descendants of those who had laid claim to Indigenous lands and those whose lands had been taken were all now trying to find ways to be, to exist, to live in these lands, together. The complexity of that is humbling.

Every day, I learn more about the impact of colonisation in Canada. I spend time in Indigenous communities across the country. I listen to newcomers who came to Canada decades before me, and to those who were "gifted" land after it was taken from Indigenous people, with limited knowledge of where that land had come from. Some had escaped their lands to survive, to find new beginnings, new hope, a sense of belonging in Canada. Many tell me how they tried to "become Canadian," giving up their own languages, cultures, and ways of being.

Day after day, I learn more about the intricately complicated history of these lands. A history that carries stories of grief, loss, uprooting, of new beginnings, of freedoms, of resilience. There is much I don't understand, but I must learn.

Each time I pull a thread, it unravels a world of unknowns, of stories silenced, stories unheard, stories untold.

So, I listen.

Seasons come and go. My life settles into a rhythm.

Every morning, I walk to the tribunal office. There, I work till my brain can take no more, saying yes to anything and everything I can possibly do to not let the darkness take over me. Somewhere in the darkness and pain of others, I don't have to think of mine. The stories I work with are not stories just at work; they become stories that are braided with mine. Stories that teach me, their pain comforting me.

So, while others talk about finding work-life balance, I work harder than those with lighter skin, cleaner "Canadian" accents. While others wait for opportunities, argue they are entitled to this, that, and the other, deserve this, that, and the other, I hungrily look for opportunities in the tightest of cracks, in the faintest of possibilities, in the scraps no one wants.

I work long hours, and then I walk back home, taking a different path each time. It becomes a ritual of its own, this walking. Sometimes, there is no particular destination, just a path to wherever the rhythm of my feet lead me. By the time I return to my place at night, my body is tired enough for sleep to hold me.

My house sits small and quiet by the river, tucked between the past and the present, downtown but just far enough to be left alone. The kind of place you could easily miss if you weren't looking, its weathered wooden porch sagging ever so slightly, windows wide and hungry for light. Inside, it's just enough for me. Tall ceilings, creaky floors, walls that don't quite hold warmth because of how old they are. The kitchen is small, cabinets worn at the edges, hinges that sigh every time I open them.

The river moves slowly behind the house, meandering through the town like a quiet heartbeat, greeting the cottonwoods, green ashes, maples, and elms that dot its path. Some nights, when I leave my window open, I hear the wind threading through their branches.

Downtown is just a few blocks away, so sometimes I hear the hum of late-night diners against the echo of a train moving through town.

The places I walk to change, the seasons change; some days I walk through sweltering summer heat, and other days I walk bundled in a parka with ice crystals forming on my eyelashes.

But no matter how much I walk, trying to move the grief around in my body so it doesn't just settle in and become a part of me, it stays. It's like a constant ringing, something I can touch if I want to but don't know how to care for just yet. It's staying because I have some unfinished business, I tell myself. Grief needs a process, it needs to be honoured like a guest, shown respect, its power acknowledged, before it can be let go, I tell myself.

It has been two years since I lost Zoya, but the gnawing feels both raw and ancient, as if I entered the world with it, as if it will continue into my next life. I haven't known what to do with the wound, or how to fill it with anything else. There is nothing else to fill it with.

I seek solace in my work, in the ability to move my feet, take myself places. Sometimes, I pause to look up at the skies, wondering if maybe this is the place where I should honour my Zoya, do a quiet ceremony beneath the trees, where the earth could cradle my sadness, and the sky could hold my love.

But the answer doesn't come.

So, I move on, walking across bustling squares and quiet parks. I watch the world move around me, people rushing past, cars streaming by, sounds rising and falling like the breaths of a distant sea. I wonder if this is where I might find a way to honour her, here amongst the living, amongst the bustling lights, where life surges forward even though for some, the world may be at a halt.

But the answer doesn't settle in my bones like it should.

So, I keep looking.

Do I need to just learn to live, to breathe in with the rhythm of the universe around me? How had they survived, my ancestors, I wonder? Under the weight of the British occupation, the power of resistance, the turmoil of having been ripped from parts of their lands, fragments of their beings, by lines drawn by those who had never even set foot in our lands.

Will I find it too, that strength? Perhaps somewhere in the winds that brush my face in these foreign lands, or in the stars scattered across the skies? If they could live, laugh, dream, dance the language of resilience, then perhaps, just perhaps, I can too.

Perhaps.

A Knock at My Door

A knock at my door,
a familiar knock.
I'm not expecting anyone,
but I open the door.

She stands there,
me,
waiting patiently, her feet steady,
her soft eyes,
a knowing smile.
A shape of strength I've never recognized.
How can you be there, when you are me?

She smiles knowingly.
"I am, and I can be.
I can be you, and I can be me.
I bring my friend Curiosity," she says.
"Curiosity knows Grief.
Grief needs love.
Curiosity is kind, brave, and warm,
and beautiful.

"Take her in your home,
in your heart, show her you care,
and she will show you how to be."

I let her in then,
me and her friend Curiosity.

"Curiosity, meet Grief.
Grief, meet Curiosity," I say.

Lubb

Search

I keep walking, day after day, following rivers that twist through valleys and fields, places where the world seems almost forgotten. I disappear for hours in the forests. In the deep greens and moss greens and fading greens, the greens of new leaves entering the world, and the browning greens of leaves returning home to mother earth. I wander amongst them, inhaling the scent of pines and cedars and warm earth, the crunch of the twigs beneath my feet as I walk. Every now and then, the rustling of the leaves seems to whisper something to me, but I can't hear the words. I hike up mountains, I touch the rocks beneath my feet, asking, wondering. I use my vacation days, my sick days, and any day that is a holiday to just walk. When people take their weekends to get together with their families, I spend them with the winds, the waters, the trees, any path that will accept me.

On one of my walks one evening, just as the sun begins to dip below the horizon, casting gentle streaks of fuchsias, blues, and oranges across the grasslands, I stop. I had left home at sunrise that morning, and it was almost time for the sun to set. I have walked by meadows, by willows, by fields of daisies. The simple, beautiful construction of daisies with the tiny yellow centres and white petals pulls me in, reminds me of the motia from my homeland.

The sky stretches endlessly above me, the colours bleeding together in a gentle, fading fire. The few scattered clouds each seem to carry a shimmer around them. The scene before my eyes is so vast, so painfully beautiful, it makes me wonder how many generations before me have seen the sun, the skies, the colours of these grasslands.

We used to sing Allama Iqbal's poem "Ya Rab" in school. It's a profound prayer that taps into his deep yearning for insight beyond what humans would see. An insight that is spiritual, mystical, magical; insight that comes from within, that touches all of divinity and beyond.

Mehroom-e-tamasha ko phir deeda-e-beena de,
dekha hai jo kuch mai ne auron ko bhi dikhla de.

In those two lines, Iqbal had pleaded to the universe to grant those who were deprived of sight, of attention, deprived from being seen a discerning eye, an eye that is insightful, an eye capable of deeper perception, of seeing things others didn't. Those who went unnoticed, unacknowledged, were the ones who saw what no one else could. He had pleaded to the universe to let those who couldn't see have a glimpse of what he had seen. There was an odd mix of arrogance and a claim to have seen beyond what others could, with a strand of acceptance of what it meant to be unseen yourself. As I watch the last of the streaks of fuchsia get absorbed into the blues of the night, I feel oddly connected to the lands around me, resisting but wondering.

It is as if these foreign lands have opened the door and wondered who was knocking.

I'm not ready to walk inside just yet. And neither is this land ready to let me in, I know that. But in that moment, there is a curiosity we have for each other. Could we find a way to speak to each other? To perhaps visit? To hear what memories this land carries? To hear what memories I carry that I have knocked on the door of this land with— with every step that I have taken?

I stand there, amidst the swaying grasses around me like a sea, and close my eyes.

I feel the cool air on my face, and for a moment, in the anonymity of this land that hasn't invited me in, I feel like I can speak in the presence of these winds, and they would hold my secrets.

And my tears finally flow.

"I'm trying to find the right way, Zoya jaan," I whisper, as though I'm confiding in the universe itself. "To honour you, to remember you. But I don't know if it's a place I need to find, or a ritual I need to perform, or a conversation I need to have. I don't even know what I'm looking for, puttar. You are with all our ancestors. Ask them. Tell me, puttar. Please tell me."

My words hang in the air, and I breathe. I breathe deeply.

Ffff. Pffff.

I let my body welcome the scent of these grasses around me. And for a long time, there is no answer—just the rustle of grasses, as if the grasses have received my words.

And then the answer comes.

It is there, in the field, surrounded by the winds, warm earth beneath my feet, with grief and curiosity, with a question so raw, so real, so willing to hear *any* answer the universe provides, that a feeling washes over me. It wraps around me, comes from a little voice within me, a sense of knowing that knocks at my heart, gently touches it, and then becomes the only rhythm my heart knows.

It's not a single ceremony or place that will honour her, but a way of living that carries my love for her forward. Each step I take, each place I visit, every breath with which I draw in the forests and cities and fields, is to be a conversation with the universe. Her memory can't be anchored to one ritual or one place. Her memory is in the way I touch the world, in the way I receive each moment, allowing myself to feel joy and sorrow, grief and love, anger and acceptance.

She is my fire, after all. My tiny little clay pot in the brick kiln on my rooftop. She is my orange and crimson in the marigolds, my radiant blues of the warm skies, my fuchsia in the spring flowers, my green of new beginnings, my golds that streak through it all. She came from an inferno of a father, a fire that couldn't be contained. And in this beautiful irony of life, she had burned me, she had burned *in* me, and now she was going to burn *with* me, fuel me for all my lives to come.

As I open my eyes, I have nothing else but laughter at the irony of it all.

Shayan, for all his chaos, had given me one of the most precious gifts I could have ever received in life, a gift of a fire so powerful, it will make me honour my daughter in the endless unfolding of life itself.

Hollowing Me

An empty stem, a shadowed field,
a crushed brick,
its pieces scattered into new bricks.

Will the monsoon still touch me?
Laugh with me,
comfort me, sing to me,
like Naano jaan to Mama jaan,
Mama jaan to me,
me to you?

You are my marigold, Zoya jaan,
one that can hold grief and grace,
like roots drinking deeply from the earth,
turning the darkness of the dirt
into a crown of fire and resilience,
even under a heavy sky.

So here I am,
in a field of seas,
holding you in pieces and in whole,
the memories of you floating with me.
The sunlight that kissed you once,
and the earth that holds you now.

You, my little marigold,
a memory nestled in me
a bright sorrow, a dark shadow,
soft as love.

I stay rooted, for you, for me,
for us life givers,
learning to bloom with the weight.

Ik Si Rani

There Once Was a Queen

High above the earth, in the endless expanse of the cosmos, where stardust swirled like rivers of light, Moonga Rani wandered. The velvet night wrapped around her like a cloak, as she moved through the silence of the seven skies, humming songs that went back many lives, her heart at peace.

One day, her journey led her to a creature she had never seen before, a being with beauty so vast, so radiant, it made her heart ache with pride and awe. *How could someone be so majestic, so stunningly beautiful, it stirred things inside you?* she wondered, as she carefully approached it.

The creature stood before her, its feathers alive with rich turquoise, sapphire blues, and golden streaks dancing like fire against the night. As it moved, its feathers caught and held the light, colours shifting like galaxies colliding, sending beams that radiated with the warmth of stars. Its tail trailed behind him, a river of stars, each feather a dazzling universe of colour and light, happiness and wonder, casting an almost hypnotic softness that pulsed with the intensity of burning stars.

Moonga Rani felt a pang of admiration; her breath caught, her heart fluttering open in quiet awe as she took in this vision before her.

It was as if the cosmos had poured every ounce of its beauty into this one being.

"Who is this beautiful magical being in our universe?" she asked the beings gathered in a circle around the beautiful creature, watching as it paraded before them, flaunting its shimmering display.

"His name is Zareen," they whispered, with a stir of unease, a faint sadness that trailed with dark wisps. His beauty was beyond what any of them had seen in the cosmos, but it carried a weight, a heaviness so thick it cast a shadow around him. They wanted to get close to him, show him how beautiful he was, ask him things, tell him stories, but they couldn't.

The shadows around him were a cage, a cage of pride he could parade in but never leave, they told Moonga Rani. It kept him trapped, away from others. He couldn't be touched, loved, held.

The creatures knew they must help him in some way, but they weren't sure how. Whispering softly, their voices like constellations merging into a single, radiant symphony, a delicate hum, shimmering like the dust of ancient stars, they said to Moonga Rani, "He is beautiful, but his pride grows with every feather he displays."

"It keeps making his cage stronger, his heart darker, with no room for others," murmured someone else.

Moonga Rani spoke then, feeling the deep stirrings of compassion and care.

"Beauty is a gift," she said gently, her voice dipped in kindness and wrapped in rivers of care. "We all carry it in our own way. But beauty with pride alone becomes hollow, untethered, alone, dark. Let us show him together another way, a kinder way, an even more beautiful way."

They all nodded, with an understanding that came from deep within, like a call from the most ancient corners of the cosmos. And the creatures of the cosmos weaved their gifts together—insight, wisdom, knowing, strength, compassion, and curiosity. The light of a thousand stars blended and pulsed, and Moonga Rani wrapped it all in a quiet enchantment, humming softly as she did, her own power bound by kindness and resilience.

Together, they reached out to Zareen with care, their woven power touching him lightly, transforming him softly.

Zareen's feathers glowed even more brightly, each colour pulsing ever so faintly with life. But as he lifted his head, he felt a weight in his feet. Looking down, he found them transformed, rough and knobby, coarse and mismatched, against his ethereal beauty.

Shock filled his eyes as he glared at the sight, his perfection shattered.

The dark cage of shadows that was containing him disappeared too, but he was too angry, too proud to notice.

Worried, Moonga Rani and the creatures surrounded Zareen, offering warmth, acceptance, and gentle guidance, trying to help him understand. But anger and confusion churned in him, storms gathering strength in his chest, consuming his brilliance with shadows that pulsed and twisted around him. His feathers flickered like embers, their turquoise and sapphire darkening with fury. With a furious shake of his wings, he erupted, sending a wave of fiery colour and searing light outwards, his feathers blazing with anger, scalding the stars around him, pushing Moonga Rani and the creatures away. Howling winds gathered in his wake, twisting and surging, carrying his rage into the vastness of the cosmos as he vanished into the depths, leaving only a storm of embers and colours trailing behind him, reds and blues searing against the blackness as they faded.

Moonga Rani and the creatures stood in the remnants of his fury, their hearts heavy with sadness, wrapped in the sorrow of his departure.

"He needs time. This is his journey," Moonga Rani whispered to all the creatures as they felt tiny little blankets of sorrow wrapping them in sadness.

Moonga Rani felt the sadness too but knew the cosmos had its way with all the creatures it carried. She knew the cosmos was a kind but firm teacher.

Zareen vanished for many lives, wandering alone in his anger, his feet a constant reminder of what he could not accept. But over time, something within him began to change. His pride no longer filled the silence around him, no longer caged him. Instead, his imperfection brought everyone closer to him. As he traveled through galaxies, he saw the creatures that gathered closer to him, not for his beauty alone but for the gentleness that slowly emerged within him. He saw how the creatures that gathered around him asked him things, asked him how he wove the stars of the cosmos in his feathers, where he found the stardust to speckle the gold shimmers in his tail. He saw how his heart opened with their curiosity. He saw how happiness filled him when he asked them about their gifts and how they had found them.

And it was in those moments that Zareen realised the gift the creatures and Moonga Rani had given him. It was the gift of humility. It was humility that had drawn these beings closer to him, he knew. Others could now see him—*really* see him—beyond his feathers.

With a softened heart, a tempered pride, he finally returned.

Moonga Rani welcomed him, her eyes warm with love. The creatures gathered around him, their presence a constellation of celebration, of acceptance, of joy.

Zareen breathed deeply and, with a heart filled with gratitude, plucked a single feather radiating with turquoise and gold, blues and greens, and a shimmer that held the stars from the cosmos that had honoured his journey.

"Take this," he said, his voice now soft and sincere, floating up to Moonga Rani. "A reminder to walk in humility, my queen."

Moonga Rani accepted the feather with a smile, holding it up to the night sky, where it shimmered, casting a gentle light that spread through the cosmos, a reminder for all who gaze upon it that beauty was only as powerful as the humility that grounded it, a reminder that rippled through the cosmos for eternity.

Basant

The Kite Festival

Seasons in Canada come and go. Life moves along in waves. Some waves are stronger than others. Some toss me around, shake me up, choke me even, and some just let me ride with them, float with them.

One afternoon, I am walking in the bush behind Elder Dawn. Dawn is barely five feet tall, her presence serene and gentle, with her long silver hair waterfalling down past her waist. Her face is a canvas of beautiful wrinkles, each line holding stories and wisdom she carries in her blood memory.

Following Dawn through the bush feels like stepping into another world, where every sound and every breath holds meaning. Her silver hair sways softly as she moves, brushing against branches and catching the sunlight that filters through the trees. She leads with a quiet purpose, her steps careful and deliberate, as if she's listening to the gentle pulse of the land itself. With her, I feel glimmers of being with my grandmothers back home.

She stops to point out a soft green bed of cedar leaves that are laid out under a large, sheltering tree.

"This," she says, her voice low and reverent, "is where the deer who are hurt come to heal. They know it is medicine from the Creator."

She kneels and brushes her fingers over the cedar. The energy of the cedar feels grounding, yet alive, moving around us with a calm presence.

"Cedar is the keeper of life," she says, "like a protector. It connects me to my kookum, my grandmother, just as it connects my kookum to her kookum."

This is maybe my dozenth time in this Anishinaabeg community. I have been visiting regularly to gather testimonies that the community has initiated to support various claims of human-rights violations in these schools.

Every time I come, I walk away with so many gifts in lessons, in teachings, in laughter, in curiosities, in things that dance in my head for days and weeks till I return. Every time I visit, I bring something I have made in my kitchen. We laugh about how the elders can't handle the spices I cook with, so I moderate them. And we laugh about how my system is far too fragile to handle moose meat.

Dawn stops again and turns to face me. "What are your people like?" she asks.

I am taken aback by her question. I have never been asked that question, and I have been in this country for nearly two decades now in all.

People always just assume. After all, all major news outlets have told the world about my people. Over and over again. About all the conflicts we have, about "our treatment" of women, about how we need to be saved, need to be rescued, need to be taught, advanced, civilised. Anyone who has eaten a samosa at an East Indian restaurant is an expert on my people. Anyone who has taken a week-long vacation to my homeland is an expert on my people. Anyone who has worn a Halloween costume with a sari and a teeka is an expert on my people. Anyone who has sent donations to some random humanitarian organisation probably four countries over is an expert on my people. We are labelled "the developing world." What could someone developing possibly teach someone who is developed?

Dawn's question feels so sincere, so curious, so kind that I tear up.

"That beautiful, eh?" She looks at me, through me.

"I'm sorry. It's just . . . no one has ever asked me this, and I've been here for two decades," I say.

"Hmmm. It's hard to ask about others when you come from a people still fighting to be seen," she says with kindness, with self-compassion, with a sense of knowing I understand. Frowning, she adds, "That's my excuse, at least. I don't know what white people's excuses are." She smirks, and I giggle at her words.

And before we know it, we're laughing at every word that comes out of our mouths.

"If you're born white, somehow you know everything, nothing new to learn, preprogrammed like those fancy TVs!" she slaps on.

"I feel ya, Dawn! They'll go eat butter chicken somewhere, and suddenly they know everything about my culture!" I offer, shaking my head as I laugh on.

"Is that what they eat in India, butter chicken?" she asks?

"Dawn, I'm not from India! I'm from Pakistan!" I snort, half shocked, half amused at the contradictions in this conversation.

"What, who knew?!" she says, a storm of giggles swirling beneath her steady gaze, ready to erupt.

"You would, if you'd have asked me!" I offer. "Well," I continue, "my people are like me. We love to laugh, though we joke that our kids are born with a scowl on their faces. I'm not sure why. We love to tell stories; we're born to eat. We love singing folk songs, we love our drums, we grow up with lots of teachings about family and reciprocity—we call it rakh rakho, len den . . . *how to visit, how to host*. Let's see, what else can I tell you?"

I am moving at a million words a minute, and I want to stop but I can't.

"Oh, we have large families, and we sort of live together, in large family systems, many of us in a home, often multiple generations. There's really no such thing as immediate family. We're all family. I didn't even realise growing up that a bunch of my uncles and aunties are just my parents' cousins, or sometimes not even that. They're just all from around our community. I am a Gujjar—people of the milk. . . ."

Suddenly, I stop talking and look at Dawn. With a voice that carries the kindness of a million seas, she says, "I have never seen you smile this big, my girl. You must really miss home."

Home. I miss home. Those three words just never do justice.

Being away from home is like walking with a missing limb and always knowing the ache won't go away, that you must just learn to live with it.

Missing home is like walking on the earth not knowing when it might split open and suck me in. It is learning to live with a heart that doesn't know where to sit in my body. Home was life itself—the place where colours bloomed, where my songs found their rhythm, where my tongue danced freely, unburdened, in the cadence of the language of my ancestors. It was where the air swelled with the echoes of celebrations—Eid-al-Fitr. Eid-al-Adha. Eid-Milad-un-Nabi. Yawn-e-Azaadi. Basant.

Oh, Basant.

The kite festival of flight, of spring, of a city coming alive in a riot of colour, was my favourite of them all. It brought the entire city to the rooftops, where kites danced with the wind, bound by the wild swirls of my happy colours—the yellow of the genda, the crimson of the gulab, the green of the motia leaves against a blazing blue sky, colours as vibrant as our folk songs. Sometimes, as the night would set in, Pa'ji, my older cousin, would fly a kite with a little lit candle nestled in it, which always felt magical as the kite floated up quietly. The battles of the kites were fierce but never cruel—every cut kite, every fallen warrior, was met with a victorious cry, the sky ringing with "Bo Kaata!" as if the very air carried our joy. The wind, our greatest ally, would lift our kites higher, lifting our spirits with them, painting Lahore with streaks of flight, with swirls of colour that belonged to no one and everyone all at once.

No festival was complete without food. As we'd be celebrating on the rooftops, our aunties would be frying fresh pakoray and bringing them up by the dozens, hot off the sizzling karahi. Nothing beats these deep-fried fritters made with besan and chickpea flour, loaded with potatoes, cilantro, coriander, cumin seeds, and my favourite of all—dried pomegranate seeds. The magic, though, lay in how warm they were. Break one open, and you'd still see wisps of steam rising.

Once in a while, we'd hear "Laddoo peethay" from a street vendor as he'd push his cart down the street, and we'd send one of our little cousins out to get enough for all on the rooftop. A short break from the kite flying would follow, with us gathering around the freshly acquired snacks. Eating these was always a two-hand affair; each laddoo, a deep-fried ball made of moong lentils, crispy on the outside, airy on the inside, had to be dunked in chutney made with imli and podeenah, tamarind and mint, and tossed in the mouth in one go. Every bite would entail a dribble of the chutney down the sides of our mouths, and the warmth of cumin, coriander, and green chilies on our tongues.

How do I explain the happiness in the eyes of Miyan Ji, who would often make his way up to the rooftop with Bebe Ji, both pretending to be angry about all the noise, only to find my daada jaani and daado jaan cheering all of us on? Bebe Ji, wrapped in her chaddar, her silver hair always neatly braided, would shake her head in mock disapproval, her thin, gold bangles clinking softly as she'd adjust the shawl around her shoulders. She was a woman of quiet authority, with hands that had kneaded endless rounds of dough, spun stories thick with wisdom, and carried generations in their kind touch. Often, after delivering a few grumbled warnings, she and Miyan Ji would decide they might as well just have some pakoray since they had made the long journey up to the highest rooftop. Seated on a manji hastily dragged over, she would break a crisp pakora in half and dip it in chutney, the corners of her mouth twitching into a knowing smile as she listened to the laughter of her children, grandchildren, and great-grandchildren.

I don't think I could ever really explain what it means to be torn apart from all things home.

Tears run down my cheeks as my mind returns from my Lahore rooftops, holding the doar, or spool, for Pa'ji, as he flies his kite, my eyes fixed on the skies, waiting to score another kite, ideally our neighbour's.

"I miss home a lot, Dawn. Sometimes, I look up at the moon, knowing this is the moon they can see from their rooftops too. And that gives me comfort, so there's that."

"You're always welcome to come here to find home," she says, holding my gaze.

Something about Dawn's words creaks open a tiny little window in me.

Dawn's words tether me, ground me, yet allow me, remind me that I can carry pieces of my rooftops with me, in me, as I fly in skies far away from home.

Doar

Spun with shades of silk,
kites soaring like spirits set free,
yellows and purples,
greens and reds,
pulsing with the beat of the drums,
echoing through us, with us,
across the rooftops.

The spirit of motia swirling,
little stars tucked in our hair,
dancing with marigold garlands,
happy oranges nodding in rhythm
to the laughter, the melodies,
the songs of my ancestors.

My Basant is happiness spun in colour,
life's brightest secrets set loose,
where hearts beat louder, bolder,
woven together in shades of spring,
in shades of joy, sparklers of happiness,
as our kites dip and dive and soar,
a thousand tiny suns,
tethered to us,
unbound in the skies.

Chaa

Chai

※

One morning, I walk into a café, taking in the soft lighting, warm wooden panels, earthy tones, large photos of coffee beans, and the rich aroma of coffee. I get in line and scroll through my phone as I wait. I check a few emails, like a few posts, laugh at a couple of adorable reels of dogs on walks refusing to walk and being carried by their owners instead, and before I know it, it's my turn to place my order. My usual is a tall blonde coffee with a splash of oat milk. Today, though, I feel like treating myself. My eyes land on "chai latte," and I wonder if this chai is anywhere close to the chai from the homeland. A young person named Katie greets me with a large smile.

"Morning! What can we get started for you today?"

"I'd love to try the chai latte. Do you just add the milk at the end, or is the chai cooked with the milk?" I ask. She gives me a puzzled look, and I catch myself. *Cooked*, I had said. She wouldn't know what it means to cook chai. They probably don't do that here.

"Ummm . . . we add steamed milk to the tea bags, yeah, if that's what you mean." She's trying. And I appreciate it.

"Sounds worth a try. I'll have a large one, please. Thank you."

My order placed, I join the small group of people waiting for their orders.

As I wait, my mind drifts to Lahore, to my courtyard, to Daada jaani. It's as if the memories have walked through the door to this place, picked me up, and taken me home just in time for story time.

Home to Lahori chaa.

One summer in Lahore, around the time I turn ten, Daada jaani walks through the entrance and through the courtyard. He seems a little agitated, with a frown on his forehead. Baba jaani greets him with a salaam.

"Salam-o-alaikum, Abba Ji, kaisa reya?" Baba jaani asks. *Salam, Abba Ji, how did it go?*

"Not good," Daada jaani responds curtly, the frown on his forehead deepening. "They didn't even ask me to sit for chaa," he adds. "It's like they've forgotten how to behave, forgotten all their traditions, their place in society. Who treats their bazurg, their elders, that way? Not even a cup of chai!" He is speaking fast and loudly, which is quite unlike him. His usually gentle voice is sharp, edgy, a little unsettled today.

"What's the big deal, Abba Ji? It's just chaa. Did they get a boatal, a cold drink, for you instead?"

"It's not just chaa, puttar," he says, in a deep, frustrated voice that suggests Baba jaani has stepped out of line. "Anyway, I need to rest these old bones." He dismisses him, and Baba jaani nods, getting the hint that Daada jaani wants to be left alone now.

As Daada jaani settles in on the manji by the motia in the courtyard, the late-afternoon sun shining warmly, I quietly go up to him and very softly offer to massage his head.

He smiles a very tired smile and says, "I hope this won't be a ten-rupee one, puttar. I'd like to request a fifty-rupee one today. Special ala. *The special one.*"

Grinning, I say, "Naah, naah, today it'll be a hundred-rupee one, and super-duper extra special!"

"Well, who can say no to that." He laughs. He laughs so easily, and so brightly, everything seems more beautiful. I summon my baby cousin Anaya and ask her to fetch some mustard oil and gather some others so we can give Daada jaani a massage. She does, and soon we're a little team of magicians, huddled around Daada jaani's manji.

I dip my fingers in warm mustard oil and start massaging his head. Anaya massages his left foot. Little Zoobi gets his right foot. Hammad works on his left hand, and little Ali gets going on his right hand. Daada jaani lets out a hearty laugh.

"Oh, waaaa ji waaah, super-duper double extra special!" I give all my baby cousins a nod and a grin of approval, and they all beam with pride.

As we work, in the background, Daado jaan tells us she'll get a pot of chai going.

Massaging his temples, I move my fingers in gentle, circular motions, feeling the tension in Daada jaani's forehead slowly melting away beneath my little fingertips. He takes a deep breath and smiles a smile of contentment. That makes me happy. It always worries me when Daada jaani is worried. And why wouldn't it? He's my daada jaani, after all. His worry is my worry. Just like my worry is his worry. I realise, though, that I don't even know why he's worried today.

"Daada jaani, ik gal puchaan?" I ask. *"May I ask you something?"*

His smile widens. "I was waiting for this, puttar. Go on."

"What worries you today, Daada jaani?" I ask softly. "I can feel it right here." I place my hand across his forehead a little too excitedly, and it lets out a little *plat*. Daada jaani doesn't seem to mind. I hope I didn't hurt him.

He takes a deep breath in, and suddenly there is a calm in the air, as if it, too, is settling in to listen to his words.

Daada jaani explains that he visited the future in-laws of one of my aunties to negotiate a smaller amount of jahaiz. Jahaiz, or dowry, is a cultural practice where the bride's family gives money, goods, or property to the groom's family as part of the marriage arrangements. Traditionally, dowries were intended to provide financial security for the bride and to help the newly married couple establish their household. However, in many societies, the practise has evolved in ways that can be a strain on the bride's family, and in some cases, dowry demands can lead to harassment or violence against women.

In my family, all my unmarried aunties had petiyan—chests—stored in the house, filled with items collected over the years: cutlery sets, radios, makeup kits, clothes, sheets, blankets, silverware, imitation jewelry, watches. Many of these things were either sent by relatives working in the Middle East or purchased locally with money sent back home. Those chests were quiet witnesses to a tradition both deeply entrenched and profoundly challenging.

As I listen to Daada jaani, I wonder if Mama jaan has a peti for me, too, somewhere. If she does, I sure hope it is packed with books.

"They know we can't afford so much jahaiz; I had told them this the first time we met them. So, when I went to speak to them, they knew that was why I was there. They didn't even ask me if I would stay for chaa. It was so disrespectful," he says, shaking his head. I try but still don't quite understand and know it would not be appropriate to interrupt him, so I start fidgeting. As if sensing the question brewing in my head, he adds, "It told me they don't want to listen, puttar. Worse yet, they didn't even want me to stay long enough that their hearts might open to hear what I had to say.

"Puttar, when we invite someone to stay for chaa, we invite them to be with us, stay with us, share what is rich, pure, and beautiful. Chaa doesn't just emerge from the fields. It is prepared with care, with intention, with love, it takes time. Inviting someone to stay for chaa means we fuss over them. We send someone to the market to pick up rusk to serve with the chaa. We tell the shopkeeper we are hosting so they give us the best of what they have. We add laachi and gurr to the chaa, we serve our milk that we work so hard for, and our spices, and our effort. All become a part of the conversation, puttar."

I frown, really thinking about this. I am in awe that one cup of chaa can mean so much.

"Inviting someone for chaa means we are ready to listen to them. Doesn't matter the outcome," he concludes. "By sharing chaa, we share our love. That is what shows that we care."

Daado jaan joins us then, with steaming cups of chaa and a big pile of rusks for all to dunk should we decide to do that, and dunk we do.

As I dunk my rusk in and slurp the luxuriously creamy, sweet, milky cardamom chaa, I understand, its fragrance wrapping me softly, its warmth hugging me. Daada jaani's words settle in. It's not just chaa, it's a spell. A spell that, when cast, brings people together.

"Merbaani, Daado jaan," I say, feeling every word of gratitude towards her. *"Thank you."* She has laboured, she has loved, she has respected, and she has fed our souls with this gift of chaa.

"Jeeyondi ray, puttar," she says, smiling proudly. *"Live well!"*

A few months later, I watched as trucks were loaded with jahaiz for my phupho's new home. A twenty-one-inch TV, a fridge, an oven, baskets upon baskets of things ready to be delivered to her future husband's place. I wonder if Daada jaani had returned to try and reduce how much dowry he could afford. I wonder if her future in-laws had agreed to listen to his words.

I wonder if they had served chaa.

Our Ancestors' Stories

Their stories come in words,
in the quiet folding of their hands,
in the silver rivers that run across their skins,
etched deep in all the years they've carried.

Laughter spilling like an old song,
each note dipped in the wisdom of many lives,
melodies rising with the wind,
twirling like kites against a sky still warm with memory.

Stories unfurling in the creases of their eyes,
where grief and joy have held each other lovingly,
where love has never faltered.

Their words never rush; they arrive slow, steady,
like monsoon rains kissing parched earth,
like the lull of a song hummed against a child's warm cheek.
Our little hearts gather around them,
their voices wrapping us,
each syllable cradled in the hush of time.

As time murmurs around us,
as their voices, deep and knowing,
build trails between yesterday and today,
carrying us home with every whispered tale.

Chacha

The Uncle

One sunny summer afternoon, I am sitting around a dinner table with Jocelyn. Jocelyn is in her sixties now, having survived a painfully unforgiving life on the streets as a sex worker. Having transitioned out from the trade in her forties just under two decades ago, she has dedicated her life to supporting other women and two-spirit peoples in transitioning out and finding financial independence, recovery, and healing. She is now working with a group of Indigenous folks, building a healing village for women and two-spirit folks who have experienced sexual violence and human trafficking. Today, Jocelyn tells me about one of her pimps, Alfred, who could always find her, no matter how far away she ran.

"They're scrawny assholes, but somehow have such a big presence in the minds of young twelve-year-olds," she says. "I look back at the living carcass he is and wonder why on earth I was scared of the idiot." She laughs so loudly it startles me.

Jocelyn rocks back and forth as she talks. Her deep, raspy voice is beautiful yet raw, tough edges to it, some words sharper, more authoritative, others tender, almost submissive. Her voice reminds me of rocks on the ocean shore that are somewhere along their journey of transformation from rocks to pebbles.

"He was just *awful*. So warped in his head that I would go steal something and hit someone just so I could get locked up for a few days," she says. "That bastard would still come find me. He knew the police and did them favours. Often, I was the favour."

She says this without the slightest quiver in her voice, and I am in awe of her strength. She must have told this part of the story many times, I figure. It's as if the air in the room has heard it before.

"Sometimes, I think I just did things for people so maybe I could feel loved, so I could feel that stupid warmth of love everyone talks about. I just wanted to be loved. How pathetic is that?" Her words come in short bursts as her lungs try to pull in air. I place my hand on hers, trying to breathe deeply, urging her to breathe along.

Minutes pass.

"For me, healing means finding a way to feel love. To love the land so the land can love us back, honour our sisters and others so they can honour us back, just love life so life can love us back. Straightforward enough?" She is laughing and crying as she says this.

As I watch Jocelyn starting to rock again, I wonder if her body is rocking with the weight of her words. Or if it is relief, a gentle celebration as each word makes its way from a deep corner somewhere in her body all the way to her lips to be finally told. For years, these words must have stayed tucked away, hidden in some corner of a muscle, a corner no one could access, a corner sacred to her, a corner no one could steal from. Her words must have been her closest friends.

Like mine.

"Jocelyn? How did the pimp find you in the first place?" I ask softly.

"He was my uncle."

Suddenly, a memory rises to the surface.

Twelve. I was twelve years old.

Every night, I would try to keep my eyes open. It wasn't easy. The darkness engulfing me as I would try to find something visually stimulating that could keep me awake. Even in darkness, sometimes there is light. But not then. I couldn't turn the lights back on, knowing they would wake up my little brothers, who would both be peacefully snoring away in the bunk bed across from me. I slept on a mattress on the floor.

I used to sleep in a bed, but since the bad man hurt me four years prior, I slept on the mattress wrapped in a plastic cover with a sheet on top. It wasn't the most comfortable, and would softly crunch every time I moved, but it was easier for Mama jaan and me to clean in the morning. We would just need to wash the sheet and wipe the plastic with soap and water.

We had done it for four years. She and I.

We never said a word to each other as we cleaned each morning. I often wondered why Mama jaan hadn't said a word to me about the bad man. Never asked me how I was feeling or thinking. But then again, she didn't have to. Every morning, she knew. She saw it. She relived it. She cleaned with me. We picked up the pieces of me, of us, together.

In silence.

Sometimes, silence screams louder than words. In silence, we hear things unsaid, things unfelt, things unseen. Silence is power.

Some mornings, I would wonder if when she held me for the very first time, looked at me the first time, if she knew I would be so much work. She tells me often I came into this world with a big smile and a lot of hair, that I smiled before I cried. Did she know then that I would also bring grief?

Many mornings, I made silent pledges to never cause Mama jaan more grief. I'm not sure how, but I pledged, nonetheless.

For four years after the bad man hurt me, I had been taken to several hakeem uncles, to doctors, to specialists, but nothing seemed to work. While the doctors prescribed medication, the traditional healers made jars upon jars of special medicine rolled up in balls. My parents called these hakeemi laddoo, medicine balls made by healers. They're medicine, and medicines are typically bitter, but these were delicious. Every time I'd pop one in my mouth, I'd welcome the flavours with gratitude: roasted mustard seeds that seemed to have kept their warmth, their earthy essence a quiet reminder of the soil and fields they came from. Carefully pitted dates and honey from a local bee farmer joined them, all rolled up into a hopeful bite.

I'd take two hakeemi laddoo every night before bed. I'd even limit my water intake after seven at night. Yet, every morning, I'd wake up in a puddle of sweat, horror, and nightmares. In my nightmares, the bad man would hurt me again. And if he wasn't hurting me, he'd try to hurt my little brothers. Or my little cousins. Night after night, I would smell him, hear him, and as soon as he'd start hurting me, I'd get paralyzed. Night after night, I would try to move. Move something. An arm, a leg, a finger. Nothing. Nothing would move. I'd try to scream, but no sound would come. And just when I'd be sure he was about to kill me, I'd wake up in a warm puddle.

My parents didn't understand why the laddoo didn't work.

They would've never worked. I knew that. They wouldn't work, they could not work, because they were supposed to help me heal from the bad man.

But what about the uncle, my chacha, who no one knew about?

He was sent to live with us in the Gulf by Daada jaani, to help support the family back home financially. There were still many unmarried daughters who needed dowries or money for school uniforms, or books and supplies. Money was needed for Umrah or Hajj as our elders aged and wanted to complete their religious obligations. The family home needed maintenance as her bones aged and the structure deteriorated. Money was needed to support funerals, new births, weddings, and more in the community. Technological advancements in the country were straining traditional milk suppliers, and it was getting expensive to keep up. Money was needed for us to care for our elders at home as they had cared for us when we were little. As seasons went by, more and more men from the family were sent overseas to try and earn enough to sustain all our collective obligations.

My chacha was one such man.

And he was my living nightmare.

The uncle had been coming into my room every few nights since I turned eleven. He would enter my room, thinking I was asleep. He would stand by my bed, watch me sleep, and touch himself. If I were awake, I would make some noise, turn and twist, and pretend that I was waking up. And when I did that, he would leave, and I would lie awake, dreading sleep.

Sleep is where I would see the bad man. Awake is where I would see my chacha. Sometimes, as I lay awake dreading sleep, I would wonder if Chacha did this to my baby cousins. My little Anaya? In that moment, I would feel rage so consuming, so beastly, that sleep would scurry away. But rage was not the solution. At least not a good one. Naano jaan had taught me that.

Of course the hakeemi laddoo wouldn't work. Unless a laddoo carries the power to protect children from bad men, they can't possibly work.

A year later, shortly after my thirteenth birthday, I woke up one night and saw my shirt undone. He had touched me. And I had slept through it. As the realisation filled me with dark, deep, agonising horror, the train came. The sweat. The blue door. The seventh floor. My maroon dress. The beautiful gold ribbon. The bad man. The sharp pain. An instant uneasiness in my stomach followed. My insides were on fire, repulsing, my ears ringing, a churn in my stomach like I had swallowed a truth, a beast I should have denied, pushed away.

I threw up.

Naano jaan's gentle voice as she would rock me. *Koi gal nai, puttar. Koi gal nai.* It's okay, little one. It's okay.

That morning, I stayed home from school. I mustered the courage to talk to Mama jaan. My pledge to never cause her more grief morphing into a painful mix of failure and disappointment. I told her what Chacha had been doing, about how I didn't think the laddoo would work, about how I needed her help to make him stop. I told her I would have talked to Naano jaan about it, but she was gone, and I didn't know what to do. I told her I could only talk to Naano jaan in my dreams, and I was afraid of sleeping. And I didn't know who to ask. Or if Naano jaan could even hear me anymore.

"Please help me. Please do something, Mama jaan," I had pleaded, all the courage and hope I had in me packed into that plea.

She had just looked at me, with an emptiness that I didn't think could exist. Her eyes were glassy, void, dull, lifeless.

I know I had exhausted her. Had I also killed the life in her?

"I don't know what to say, Laachiye. I don't know what to do," she had said so faintly, I almost thought I had imagined it.

And then she got up and left.

And I was alone.

Ffff. Pfff.

The thing about being the granddaughter of a powerful matriarch is one forgets their mother is human. Their mother is complex. Beautiful yet imperfect. A fighter who maybe needs rest sometimes. A fighter who in their own fights may have forgotten to rock their child, to hold them, soothe them.

That day, aged thirteen, I learned what it meant to fend for yourself, to never ask, to draw in even tighter if I felt I should open myself to love, to trust no one, to never let a soul close.

Kaali laachi, black cardamom. Naano jaan had always called me Laachi. And then everyone had called me Laachi. Laachi was playful, bursting with life and surprises. A seed of laachi meant a celebration of life.

Was I still Laachi?

Naano jaan would say kaali laachi was her least favourite spice. Added when a dish had burned ever so slightly but could still be salvaged, kaali laachi was used to mask that burnt flavour, smoothing out the burnt edges into a smoky depth, a slight breeziness, a bold earthiness, a layered complexity, an odd confusion so the person eating couldn't figure out what flavour to hang on to.

Kaali laachi was only added if one had neglected the cooking pot, had forgotten to attend to it, be with it, celebrate it.

Had I become kaali laachi?

That night, I confronted my uncle. I didn't need courage to do it. I needed courage to ask for help. And that help had been denied. So, here I was, alone, with my own strength.

I didn't wait for him to deny anything. I didn't wait for him to acknowledge anything. I told him I knew what he had been doing, that he sickened me. I told him if he ever entered my room again, I would destroy every relation he had in this world—Baba jaani, Daada jaani, every cousin, every brother, every shopkeeper, every sister, every daughter.

"You do understand what I'm saying?" I asked him, my voice strong and stripped of all innocence.

He nodded and said, "I thought you liked it."

He thought I liked it.

Howling winds. A low moan that starts as the wind tries to make its way through narrow alleyways, rushing past trees, so angry, so horrified, so unsure of the direction it will take next, a life of its own, a fury so fuelled by pain and helplessness, it doesn't care what stands in its path. It doesn't care who caused the pain, who received it.

Did I scream the scream of a howling wind?

I don't remember.

He never entered my room again. I never spoke a word to him again. I refused to acknowledge his existence as he lived in our house for one more year after that.

I didn't even notice him.

Years later, on the day he got married, he asked if we could speak. As sick as it made me to look at him, I watched his face as he spoke.

He said he had always loved me. That I was the most beautiful person he had ever known. That I was the only person who knew how to love another human no matter who they were, or how much darkness they carried. That he could never love someone as deeply as he loved me. That I was the only person he wished he could love.

Sigh.

This was not an apology.

I didn't know what it was. An explanation? A rationalisation? A sickening justification to himself? Here I thought he was going to beg for forgiveness so he could enter the next journey of his life in peace. No. This was a very muddled, very confused, very sickening nonapology.

I turned around and left. Any words I would have said would have hung in the air for him to touch.

So, I kept my words to myself. They were mine to keep.

I never saw him again.

Where Is Your Apology?

I am owed some words.
They do not come, they do not rise.
Unbirthed, unclaimed,
while the fire you sparked rages in me,
its flames clawing up, roaring to be heard.

Do you know the shape of my rage?
Coiling and burning,
a blaze fed by your silence,
searing its way through innocence lost,
twisting like smoke
in the deepest nooks of my heart,
turning memories to ash,
memories I can't unsee, unfeel, forget.

Tell me, do you feel the anguish,
does it rise in you too,
press like it does on me?
Why is it so hard to speak it,
to admit, to say?

What are you hiding from,
what darkness in you keeps your lips shut,
keeps you free,
while I am held in this rage?

Maybe you never learned
that fire cannot stay hidden,
that wounds smoulder
in the souls of those they've marked.

I am still here,
born again in the embers,
facing your silence with flames that never go quiet,
a demand you cannot ignore.

Where is your apology?
Where is the reckoning you owe me,
words to water the scorched earth you left?

Speak, speak! Or feel my fire grow,
because in your silence, I burn alone,
waiting for the words
that should have come lives ago.

Maafi

Forgiveness

"You see, some of us can forgive. Others can't. Some want to. Others don't," says Fred. We're sitting by the water, just across the road from the roundhouse. We've just ended a day of deliberations, and Fred had asked me to join him by the water to go over something. I can tell this is difficult for him. I don't say a word. Just nod with a gentle *mmhmm* every now and then. It's not my place.

"For some it's the outcome of conditioning, of colonisation, of being forced to adopt another religion that has all these different views of forgiveness and grace and redemption and confessions," he continues, his voice picking up thorns of frustration. "What were we confessing about? We were kids! They said we were broken. We weren't broken before we got there. The nuns and the priests broke us."

He shakes his head as if saying no to a memory wanting to creep in with its darkness.

"For some it's the outcome of their own healing journey. The outcome of ceremonies. With their drums, their shaking tents, sweat lodges, on the land, on the water, reminding us of how we belong to the land and not the other way around. It's different for all of us, you see. And we must honour each other. If we don't . . ." His voice breaks ever so slightly, and I look up. He has tears in his eyes now, and I don't know what to say, or do. So, I just nod.

"We have our grandchildren and their children to answer to, just like I answer to my grandmother, who was made to beg for food in our own lands."

He goes silent.

Seconds pass, and then minutes pass, as we just look at the water. We can hear the birds chirping, the critters singing. The wind seems to be thinking with us; a gentle *whoosh* as it dances around the trees, around the shore, reminding us it is listening, seeing, hearing, carrying our words.

I imagine how cold the water might be. Lake water is not like the water in the Gulf. I could float in the salty water of the Arabian Gulf, be in and out of the water at the same time as the water would guide me, bounce me, rock me.

I wonder if life can work that way. Can we be right and wrong at the same time? Certain and uncertain? Curious and knowing?

"I'm listening, Fred. I'm here," I offer quietly, and then ask, "Hey, Fred? What does forgiveness look like to you?"

He laughs a mocking laugh. "Me? I can't forgive. Give us our land back. Return our economies back to us that were destroyed, making us beg when it was our right to receive sustenance from our lands. They did that to my grandparents, you see?"

"Mmhmm," I offer. He has shared this story with me before, and yet it is so raw, so painful, so present each time.

Some stories are like that. Their colours never fade.

"So, what do you think? How do we write about this?" he asks, looking at me with a smile that I know he smiles when he knows the answer already but won't say it. He wants me to come to it myself.

Sigh. That's what Daada jaani used to do, I am reminded. Ah, these elders! So stubborn. If Fred knows the answer, why wouldn't he just tell me what to do?

Because that's not how we learn, Laachiye, I hear Naano jaan's voice in my head.

"I'll give that some thought, Fred," I say, feeling the weight of the question already. I have no idea what the answer is, or how I will get there. But Fred is like my daada jaani in this foreign land, and I must be brave, just like we used to be on the rooftop when Daada jaani would ask us questions about what Layla should do.

I must think, I must trust, I must listen, must ask.

"Sounds good," he says, a little quicker than I thought he would, and gets up to go. "Call me when you have the answer."

I get up, pack my things, and drive back to the city.

Just three years prior, Canadians had received a painfully harsh reminder of the dark legacy of the residential school system when 215 unmarked graves were uncovered in Kamloops, British Columbia. The graves reminded Canadians and the churches of the children that were still missing, children who never returned home, children Canada and the churches still needed to return to their grieving families, their mothers, their grandmothers, their lands. Shortly after the news came, I received a phone call from Fred. I was asked to make my way to the community to meet the elders the next morning. Having barely slept, with my own nightmares, which often entailed digging for children, looking for my Zoya in the rubble, I drove out, wondering what I could possibly do to support.

That day, as we sat in the roundhouse around a drum, my heart had grown heavier by the hour as I listened to the elders recount their memories of where the children were. By the end of the day, we had built out a plan for recording the survivors' testimonies with the human-rights tribunal that would support searching for unmarked graves around the school grounds in the community. These were children the elders had seen being buried, heard of being buried, and, in some sickeningly horrifying instances, been forced by the nuns and priests to help bury. The elders knew where these children were and were ready to summon the strength to share. Whether or not I was ready to hold their words was irrelevant. I had been asked by those I honoured like I honour my ancestors.

Would I have said no had Naano jaan asked? Of course not.

The three years that followed were a basket of everything horrific, uncovering stories gut-wrenchingly unjust, and matched in power by the drums, the ceremonies, the songs, the dances, the sheer raw power in human resilience. The elders gathered every few days to remember, to share, and to hold space for each other. They pored over thousands of archival records that were still being uncovered, old photos of them as children brought in from museums, personal archives, temporarily loaned by churches, a collage of miscellaneous collections all over the country. Basically, anything and everything we could get our hands on to patch together their truth, understand what happened in these schools, where the children who died or went missing were, where they were buried, and what it all meant for the journey ahead.

Every time they gathered, the elders called on and reminded us of the power of the land. The power of the water. The skies. The people. The power of sacred ties to mother earth. Our job in the process as the human-rights tribunal was to bear witness, to document, to pull it all together however they wanted us to. This was their story, and our job was to hold space for them to tell it.

Now, Fred had asked me to figure out how the journey could be written about in a manner that all non-Indigenous Canadians would understand, would hear the voices as those of their own skin, own language, own culture, own creed, own knowledge systems. How the story could be told so non-Indigenous Canadians could feel the cold darkness of this legacy as if experienced by their own, while also celebrating the strength of the survivors, as if celebrating their own ancestors. It was important that non-Indigenous Canadians understood how complicated forgiveness was, how complicated trauma was, and why survivors simply couldn't, as a collective, "just get over it," given that a couple of national apologies had been made. The first came in 2008 by then–Prime Minister Stephen Harper, and the second came from the pope in 2023 on his visit to Canada. That's two apologies fifteen years apart.

But was that enough? *Is* that enough? Does apologising mean all is forgiven? Who does the responsibility of apologising lie with? Who forgives?

How does one forgive?

Forgiveness. Maafi. The word "maafi" has its roots in the Arabic "ma'afa," meaning pardon or forgiveness. The term has been adopted into nine South Asian languages, including Urdu, Hindi, Punjabi, Farsi, Pashto, Bengali, Gujarati, Kashmiri, and Sindhi. So maafi is forgiveness in four of the languages I live with. I *should* know what forgiveness is.

I don't.

To me, maafi was like trying to look inside a kencha, a marble, trying to figure out what colours were playing hide-and-seek inside. The harder you tried to find them, the more colours you saw, your impatient eye dancing from one colour to the other as if they were playing some game on you. The second you thought you knew the colour to be green, you saw a streak of yellow. Oh, wait, perhaps it was a teal. No. Not teal. Maybe a blue? Wait, where did that white come from? And now all the colours seem to converge.

Sigh. I had a complicated relationship with maafi.

As I crawled into bed that night, I felt like I was dragging bags of flour behind me. Fred's question weighed heavily. How do we write about forgiveness? I didn't sleep well, my brain restless, my heart so heavy.

Just before the crack of dawn, two solid nightmares having plagued my night, I slip my kayak into the muddy river I live on the shores of. The river is quiet this time of day. I tell myself it's because the river does not want to wake up the little ones who have been tucked in with lullabies rocking them. The kind Mama jaan used to sing to me as my eyes resisted sleep, worried about the nightmares that would come if my eyes closed.

Lalla lalla lori
Doodh di katori
Doodh che patasha
Maano karey tamasha

My life jacket on, I start paddling against the current. It'll make the journey back easier. Rewarding. As the paddle slices through the water in gentle hushes and soft splashes, my kayak glides, embracing the stunning hues of gold, pink, and purple of the skies being woken up by the sun, the light playfully dancing off the river, as if trying to figure out what adventure it was headed into for the day. My kayak hugs the shoreline as it journeys the river, greeting the cottonwoods, the willows, the green ashes, the silver maples, the elms, the oaks. I start to feel lighter, start to feel like I can breathe.

As if I spoke too soon, I feel a sudden gust of wind in the silence, like an uninvited guest. My heart races. As if I woke her up too early, the river has something to humble me with. I feel its pull, deep into its belly. Like a child being summoned.

Are You What We Need, Forgiveness?

To make us human,
to end our wars?
Or are you just another path,
a permission, a place of no consequence
for those who I wish will burn
in the deepest depths of hell.

I need forgiveness that doesn't soften
the edges of what's sharp,
that doesn't make him free,
or demand my silence in return.

Tell me, Forgiveness,
are you a power, or just a relief?
Do you lift me higher than this ache,
or simply ask me to bear it with grace?
Is this the strength they speak of,
to hold both rage and mercy
in the same clenched hand?
Or must I choose between them,
between justice and peace,
between healing and harm?

Why are you, Forgiveness?
If I let this go into the open sky,
will that teach the world a way
to keep its hands gentle?
To know hurt and still not give it?
If one of us must be the bigger person,
will that stop the wound from spreading?

If I let you in, Forgiveness,
will we grow closer to a world
in which we stop breaking each other,
and start becoming whole?

Keechar

Muddy Water

I am eleven years old, coming home from playing a game of cricket with Baba jaani, my chacha, and my mamoo jaan, Mama jaan's brother, whom I deeply adored. As they haul their kit bags out of the car, I am trying to build a case for a chocolate stop at Agha Uncle's store. The Lion is my favourite chocolate, but I know Mama jaan's favourite is Cadbury, and Baba jaani would do anything for Mama jaan, so I claim I want a Cadbury and can get Mama jaan one while I'm at it. As I grin a pleading grin, of course.

"Please, naaaa, Baba jaani. Sirf ik chocolate. *Just one chocolate, please.*"

"Ja, Simran, jee la apni zindagi. *Go, Simran, go live your life.*" Using a movie dialogue from *Dilwale Dulhania Le Jayenge* that had become a household staple between fathers and daughters these days.

Grinning the grin of victory now, I turn to run to Agha Uncle's shop, when I see him.

The bad man.

Blacks, greys, metal in my mouth. The train. The beast. The train. Sweat. The blue door. The Lacnor milk. My beautiful maroon birthday dress. The sharp pain for days. The beautiful golden ribbon. The plastic on my mattress I had to sleep on for the last three years.

I don't have words. I can't remember any. Words have a bizarre way of floating away from us sometimes.

Baba jaani and my uncles notice. They know. They see it in my eyes.

The next several minutes are complete chaos. I see it. I don't hear it. They all seem to be moving slowly. Arms are flying. Punches are thrown. My uncles are beating up the bad man.

Blood.

More shouting. More yelling.

More men gather.

A few women huddle around me. I don't know these women. One of them hugs me close. She tries to turn my head to make me look away. I don't. I can't. I need to see this.

I have wet myself. Yet the woman holds me, running her hand through my hair. More women gather.

What are the men saying?

Some men are trying to hold my uncles back from the bad man. The bad man is wearing all white. White shirt, white pants, white shoes. He must be coming from a party, I think. Or going to one.

Not anymore.

Qari Saab, the imam from the local mosque, has entered the chaos. He is talking to my father. They all seem to be yelling. Hands flailing. The ringing in my ears needs to stop. I look at my hands. They're shaking, I think. It's hard to see. There are tears getting in the way.

I must start counting.

Touching the tip of my thumb to each of the three segments on my fingers, if I start now, I can get to thirty. Thirty in total. When I get to thirty, I'll be able to hear.

First my left hand. Then the right hand.

I take a breath. My lungs are on fire. Half a breath comes. Will this do? It must. Maybe one more try? I can do this.

The air is thick. Naano jaan said when the air is thick, we gulp it instead. Like my favourite googly-eyed black fish in my aquarium I had told her about. She had laughed and we had pretended to be googly-eyed, fat-cheeked fish.

Fish can swim. I wish I could swim. I'd swim so far away. I would meet turtles and dolphins and be friends with them.

I take in a gulp of air. *Huhp.*

Then another. *Huhp.*

I move a shaking thumb to segment one.

One.

Thumb to segment two. *Two.*

Three.

Nine more fingers to go. If only these hands would stop shaking. I try to look at them. Why are the tears getting in the way? Not now, tears. Please wait. I'll make time for you, I know you are worried for me, I tell them. I will make time for you, I promise.

Four. Four. Five. Six.

Seven. Eight. Nine.

Nine.

I hear her voice. Naano jaan's voice. *Laachiye, chal, puttar.* Go on, little one.

Ten. Eleven.

Eleven. I am eleven years old.

Twelve.

Huhp. Huhp.

Ffff. Pfff.

Thirteen. Fourteen. Fifteen.

I clench my left fist. A little hug to my hand. Thank you, hand. Thank you so much, fingers. *I love you.*

I move to my right hand.

Ffff. Deep breath in. A little sound creeps in. Is it the jingle of someone's bangles?

Pfff.

Sixteen. Seventeen. Eighteen.

Ffff. Pfff.

Nineteen. Twenty. Twenty-one.

Twenty-two. Twenty-three. Twenty-four.

Ffff.

It *is* the jingle of her bangles. A little rustle of her crimson sari.

Pfff.

Twenty-five. Twenty-six. Twenty-seven.

The woman's voice. "It's okay, Emahn, my beautiful dear Emahn. We are here with you. You're so brave. It's okay. He can't hurt you anymore."

Ffff.

Twenty-eight. Twenty-nine.

But he had hurt me already.

Pfff. Thirty.

Qari Saab's voice to my baba jaani: "Saabir, my brother, you must forgive him."

Baba jaani looks at me. I shake my head. I plead with my eyes. With my hands, which are still shaking. In my clothes, drenched with sweat, fear, and horror. Does horror have a smell? A colour? Would it be black? But I like black, especially with gold.

I plead without words. *Don't let him go, Baba jaani. Please, Baba jaani.*

Baba jaani is sobbing. I feel his sobs in my body. I want to hug him. Tell him "Everything will be okay, Baba jaani." I want to kiss his forehead, tell him it's not his fault. That I love him so much. That he is the best baba jaani in the whole world. That everything will be okay.

Baba jaani speaks in a voice that is so loud, yet so weak. *So* weak.

"We forgive you. Up to you to settle your accounts with your God, whoever, whatever they may be. Up to you to settle your conscience, your life that has passed, your life today, your life ahead, your descendants, your daughters. Yes, may your God give you daughters so you may learn."

Who is Baba jaani saying this to? This is not my baba. My baba is strong. My baba wins cricket tournaments. My baba settles other people's conflicts. My baba makes sure decisions are fair.

My baba makes sure daughters are protected.

My baba does not take other people's right to forgive. Not his daughter's. This is not my baba.

Ffff. Pfff.

But he is. And he just did. They all just did.

Baba jaani looks at Qari Saab, his face streaked with tears, his hands joined in front of his chest, as if thanking the qari. He looks at my uncles. They nod and join their hands too. He looks at all the men in the circle.

They all nod.

In that moment, as my power, my right to forgive, is taken away from me, I crumble.

Horror was in the elevator. Horror was in the actions of the bad man. Horror was in the pain my body carried. Horror *is* in the pain that my body still carries.

Horror was in the maafi, the forgiveness that did *not* come from me.

As days, weeks, seasons, and years went on, I went back to that day outside Agha Uncle's store many times, feeling the unfairness of it, the weight of it, the pain of it. That pain became my friend; I embraced it, sometimes wrestled with it, wanted it to go away, but eventually just settled in with it.

The kayak. I am in the middle of the river. The shore is a ways away. I turn around.

The water of this river is so muddy, yet it keeps flowing, meandering around every bend along its path, gently taking a little bit more of mother earth's shores as it moves, as if gathering keepsakes, little memories, little testimonies, little stories. Getting muddier as it moves.

Forgiveness is a muddy river, I decide.

Dialling his number that morning, I hope I have the right answer, or close to it, for Fred. It's the only answer I can come up with.

"We need to honour them all, Fred, like you said. Every single survivor gets to decide if they want to forgive. Not that they must, or should, or would, or could because of someone else, someone else's faith. We must *say* all that, in all its muddiness and complexity, and contradictions. It doesn't matter if it's perfect or the same story about forgiveness. Where harm is unique, forgiveness must also be unique. It's not fair to forgive on someone else's behalf. Forgiveness is a sacred bond between the person harmed and the person who caused it. It's between humans, not their Gods. That's too convenient. So, we must talk about it all. It's not one narrative. It's rich. It's full. It's complicated. We must embrace the messiness."

I realize I am rambling. I stop.

"Sounds good. Get to work, then."

I can tell through the phone that he is smiling.

Over the days that follow my conversation with Fred about forgiveness, my brain keeps drifting to Baba jaani's words. Every time it does, my breathing gets shallower, my heart feels heavier, my jaw tightens, I feel like I'm dragging the sacks of flour again. Blacks, greys, a slow ring of the train as it lurks right behind me, waiting to crawl up the tunnel if I don't pay attention. I am restless and withdrawn.

I want to be alone.

I want to disappear.

I travel up and down the elevator.

Why had Baba jaani forgiven on my behalf? It wasn't his place. It was no one else's place but mine.

But had he? Had he forgiven the bad man? Why had we never talked about it since? Was he not equipped with the skills to process this? Had our society not equipped him? Was the conversation too painful to survive? Did he not love me? Was I not lovable?

Of course he did. Of course I was. Of course I am.

Could all these things be true at the same time?

The muddy river, I remind myself. It only gets muddier with time.

Rumi had said, "Out beyond the ideas of wrongdoing and rightdoing, there is a field. I'll meet you there."

I want to play in Rumi's field.

Had Baba forgiven on my behalf or had he forgiven for the impact on *him*?

He was now someone who'd failed to protect his daughter the one time. A man with a "tainted" daughter, according to his society. A father who would have to work harder to find her a suitor. The owner of a home marked by a deep scar on its door. A mediator whose credibility would be questioned whenever an outcome displeased someone. A member of his community expected to carry his shame visibly, to walk with his head bowed.

And yet he had walked with pride, holding his head high that *I* was, that *I* am his daughter. Every. Single. Day.

And I walk this planet with a painfully relentless drive to prove I'm worthy of his pride.

What an absolute mess.

And here I thought I was done.

Life sure is humbling. Just when you think a chapter has flown by, Curiosity knocks on the door again, a soft hello, a melody of a song you thought you had forgotten, perhaps a line in a poem, or sometimes a difficult question from a friend: *Don't we all make it about us?*

Yes. I suppose we do.

Sigh.

Some days, I hate letting Curiosity in through my door.

As years go on, I hear God gave my chacha many daughters.

I wonder why. Weren't daughters sacred? Sacred blooms, braided together with all that is gentle, fierce, and alive? Like a motia, their presence soft yet grounding, steady, their quiet presence lingering long after they're gone? Like a gulab, blooming in layers, their love and loyalty unfolding petal by petal, packed with will and determination, protecting what needs to be protected? Like a genda, joyful and fierce, bold, unapologetic?

Wouldn't bad men destroy the spirit that is a daughter? Would a man like my chacha even understand this? See this? See all that his daughters hold?

Daada jaani would often say that to honour a daughter is to celebrate her, lift her up in all her complexity, to protect her when that is what she seeks. It is in honouring one's daughter, in seeing all her sacredness, that we find our own humanity flickering a little brighter, a little truer.

One time, Guddi Baji had said it was men who need to be taught lessons in life who are gifted daughters. I never understood that. I think of my baby cousin Anaya, and all my other baby cousins, with their innocence, their playfulness, their mischief. For anyone like my baby cousins to be born to bad men doesn't seem fair at all.

Yes, we daughters can be good teachers by just being who we are, but what if we were tired of being teachers and needed a break? Worse yet, what if men who needed to learn, didn't? What if they hurt us?

What if Chacha hurt his own daughters?

With that thought, I'm filled with an overwhelming need to protect his daughters from him. Or perhaps he didn't hurt them but lived in fear that someone else might. Sometimes, that dark and painfully bitter thought of him living in fear till his final breaths come, till he returns to the earth, comforts me like an old, heavy blanket.

Would that be justice? Or is that what nonforgiveness looks like?

Sometimes, I imagine what it would be like to visit him on his deathbed. Would I remind him of the horror I'd lived through? Would I scream and tell him I deserved his apology? That I was just a child. Would I tell him of the pain I'd carried in my body for decades? Would I tell him I wanted to send anonymous letters to his house to remind him of what he had done so he could live in fear of what I would do next?

Or would I be able to feel compassion for his frail, dying bones? Would I feel empathy for the restlessness he, too, must have carried, for having harmed me? Would I curse him to keep returning to the earth many more lives till he could undo the harm he had done? Would I remember in that moment, when I want nothing but pain for him, how I was raised to love, to pour unconditionally, to live as a reminder of the beauty of humanity, the simplicity of a child, the complexity of understanding it all?

Would I remember kindness?

Would I remember that perhaps he harmed me because he, too, had been harmed in some way, by someone? Perhaps he didn't know what love was. Perhaps he was never shown.

Perhaps.

Maafi. Forgiveness.

I do not forgive him. May he never return to fix the harm he did.

May he be forgotten. By me. By all.

A Conversation with Forgiveness

Who are you, Forgiveness?
I have tried to be curious,
to wonder, be patient.
But I ask you with what burns inside me,
the rage of a storm,
curling, agonising, inside me,
its winds churning questions,
thick and fierce, blacks and greys,
its lightning flashing anger,
white and raw.

Who are you, Forgiveness?
Are you soft, something I can hold?
Are you *in* me, somewhere I can't find?
Have we met before, perhaps?
Would it make me small to feel you,
or strong to give you away?

Would the child in me understand you,
what it means to let hurt walk free,
to hold pain like a fragile feather
and blow it into the winds,
watching it scatter, losing shape,
until it's only air, only sky?

Who are you, Forgiveness?
Would inviting you mean letting go
of this warmth I know so well,
this spark, this anger that has protected me,
its fire a light in my darkest times?

Who are you, Forgiveness?
Would you reshape my scars,
make them softer, something new?
Or would you only hide the ache beneath,
like roots twisting in the soil,
deep and unseen, but still there,
whispering at night, a secret I carry?

Who are you, Forgiveness?
Maybe, just maybe,
you're not a single answer,
but the strength to keep asking,
the strength to hold
my fury and my compassion as one,
my love and my kindness as one,
my hurt and my courage as one,
my voice and my being as one,
and know that all are mine,
that all have built me whole,
bit by bit.

Tishnagi

The Pain of Longing

One evening, I attend a dance performance in Canada by a local dance group with a friend. We've been planning an event where we want to bring together performers from different cultural backgrounds to create a collaborative performance, symbolising the power of music and dance in fostering peace.

As I sit there in the audience, taking notes, one dancer draws me in like no one else that evening.

Embodying the elegance of a gently flowing river, she moves effortlessly across the stage, her red dupatta following her like a shadow, the gentle chime of her pa'zaib echoing whispers of resilience unseen, unknown. As if she hears me, her feet strike the ground with rhythmic perfection, the echo of the pa'zaib harmonising with the beat of the dholki, reminding me that her strength, her resilience, is not a myth, but very alive, very present, breathing, taking it all in. She slides her hands up in movements that seem to flow through me as I watch each of her fingers swaying in perfect harmony with the melody. She is the river, I decide. Flowing, breathing, playfully turning corners, twirling every time something comes in her path—but not without a splash.

She wants the rocks to know that they are in her path as she turns away from them with a frown, carrying on with her journey.

The beat of the dholki pulses through the air, my heart beating with it, and before I know it, I am in the courtyard in Lahore. I can feel the floor under my feet, the bottom of my feet, cool with henna despite the warm air around me, the pa'zaib on my ankles, the gold ribbon with sequins on my stunning sea-green and gold ghagra playfully touching my calves as I sway. I know how to draw attention to these ankles. A gentle lift of the ghagra, a gentle strike of the foot after the dholki stops, as if skipping the perfect harmony between me and the beat. That *chhunn* of the pa'zaib, followed by the click of my tongue and a subtle frown, my finger now touching my pa'zaib, disciplining it for having missed the harmony, will draw their eyes, their hearts, their desires. And just as they watch, drawn in, slowly, powerfully, magically, I'll turn my gaze up, find their eyes.

My breath catches, and without the slightest warning, I'm back in the auditorium, sitting in front of the stage, watching the dancer in her ghagra, my heart racing, my mouth dry, the walls caving in. I can see the dancer, but I can't hear much anymore. Did the dholki stop? I turn to see my friend looking at me, wondering if I'm okay.

I need to get out of here is the only thought churning in my head.

"This was awesome. I'm going to head out. Take notes for the rest of the performances? We'll need a shortlist." I hope I said those words right.

I rush out, make my way through the crowd, leave the building, head into the parking lot, fumble with my keys, and then remember I don't need keys to unlock my car, it is unlocked already.

I sit in my car for the next little while. It's running. I don't remember starting it.

I'm unsettled. Where had I gone? What were these memories?

As if they hear me summoning them, they come flooding through the gates. The courtyard. The summer heat. The ghagra. My ghagra.

My pa'zaib.

My dances.

My movements.

My voice.

My eyes.

My stories.

The boliyan in the gidda—the couplets in one of the folk dances—all the aunties loved. We would unpack any new impromptu ones for days.

"Remember the one about him wanting to hold you in the wheat field, and you saying no?" We laugh at the silliness of it all.

And then someone else would chime in, "Remember the one about the well water turning into the monsoon rain with your clothes clinging to your body?" The aunties laughing, us girls giggling.

"Remember the one about him braiding jasmine in your hair?"

"Oh hoooo." We would tease each other and laugh.

"Remember the one about overhearing the neighbours fighting and running to tell your mum only to run into the dhobi uncle's hot son on the way?" Big laughter erupts.

So much laughter.

"I was watching him watching you as you danced, Laachiye," someone had piped in. "I thought he was for sure going to die." Giggles.

"He's going to end up sending his parents to ask for your hand, Laachiye."

Tsk. Nope. No one gets this hand.

There it was.

My hand *had* been given away.

I was fifteen the day I did not say yes. My silence was yes enough.

I had been ripped away from my aunties, my cousins, my dances, my language, my colours, my songs, my voice, my pa'zaib, my playfulness . . . and thrown into a country so foreign, so drab, so unknown, so unsure about its existence, so black and white, so unaware of its own arrogance.

And I was always alone in this land. No one to speak my language to.

And there it was.

There it is.

I have never grieved being a child bride.

The loss of my courtyards. The loss of my rooftops. The loss of my gajaray.

Tishnagi—the soul-crushing weight, pain, agony one feels in longing. Agony that comes from deep within. The ache, the helplessness of longing.

The longing for home.
The longing to return home.
Have I learned enough lessons from this foreign land?
Can I return home?

I gather the courage to attend an Eid prayer at a mosque here in Canada. I know it won't be anything like Eid back home, but it'll be something. And maybe it's time.

For the last two decades, I've been reclaiming small pockets of space for people who look like me, for my colours, my songs, my language, the pieces of myself that I left behind. Where I used to be the only person of colour at leadership tables, the only woman of colour, there are now others too.

It's still nowhere near enough, but it's something. Where once there was just one little store in a city of nearly a million that sold halal meat and a few spices from my homeland, there are now several more.

There's still no Azaan to remind me to pause, but I see more of us nodding our heads in salaam, our hands on our hearts, as we pass each other on the streets. I find myself smiling when I hear my language here and there, slipping through pockets of this place. Invitations to follow Christ are still commonplace on billboards, while an invitation to a mosque still invites suspicion, or an intelligence agent's knock on the door.

With more of us here, there are also more racist slurs. Strangers still tell me to go back to where I came from. Some days, I want to scream, to tell them I never wanted to be here, I never chose it. That I come from a world so rich, a world cradled in ritual, wrapped in song, layered in raw, ancient beauty.

So, I do what I can. I keep calling for compassion, for love, for a little space in each other's hearts to listen, to empathise, to tolerate, to accept. I work to bring people together so they can see each other's humanity. One morning, I find a letter in my mailbox, threatening me to stop doing that or regret the day I was born.

I moved from that neighbourhood weeks later.

Another afternoon, two years after Donald Trump first gets

elected in America and gives permission to those seeding hate in Canada to feel free to hate openly, a young white guy in a truck tries to run me over while screaming, *"You Paki bitch."* I spend an hour after that gathering myself and wondering if it's time for me to just return home after all.

Would I have wanted to raise Zoya in this land?

I keep running, while trying to claim my place in this foreign land. I keep hiding, while trying to be seen. I keep staying in the background, while wanting my voice to matter.

This morning, though, I decided to reclaim Eid.

As I stand in front of the mirror, I take a deep breath, the final touches of my outfit coming into focus. I'm wearing black and gold bangles on my wrists, stacked delicately; first a thick, gold, intricately engraved bangle, then twelve black ones, the black of a raven, then another thick gold, twelve more blacks, and then another gold. The combination of the engraved gold and plain black adds a beautiful coming together of complexity and simplicity to this ensemble that goes perfectly with my black lehnga with gold embroidery, adorned with little mirrors that dance in the light.

I adjust my dupatta, my henna-stained fingers lifting and then dropping the dupatta just an inch off my forehead, that sweet spot that frames my face and shows off my jhumkay. My bangles tinkle softly through the adjustment, their sound a gentle, playful melody that adds to the celebration of Eid.

Bangles have adorned our wrists for thousands of years. The simpler ancient ones were made with terracotta, shells, copper, and bronze. These ancient ones worn by our ancestors set the stage for the far more intricate ones that emerged by the time we placed them on our wrists, as continuing symbols of tradition, femininity, and, sometimes, status.

My favourite ones were always kacch di chooriyan, glass bangles. Crafted from coloured glass, heated and shaped into thin circular bands, glass bangles required skilled artisans to make. Fragile yet beautiful, their simplicity had a gentle pureness to them. Every Eid in Lahore, we'd huddle up in a rickshaw and head out to Anarkali Bazaar to find bangles to match our Eid outfits.

Colours of happiness. Every colour imaginable. Colours that seem to catch the light so they can dance together, play together, laugh together. Thousands upon thousands of blues, reds, mustard yellows, greens, fuchsias, oranges.

Hundreds of hues—hundreds of reds.

Laal—the boldest of reds, intense, passionate.

Rani—the red of the queens, with a hint of pink, a hint of sophistication, tentativeness, care.

Maroon—the red with hints of brown, a mature red, refined, wise, cultured.

Gulabi—the red of roses, playful, youthful, joyful, the red of celebrations.

Rust—the red with orange, a red of warmth, of earthiness, the red of autumn, the turn of a season, a symbol of change.

Mehrun—a complex red that is almost brown, a symbol of dignity, gravitas, tradition.

Crimson—the red with hints of blues, vivid, mysterious. Intricate, curious.

Pomegranate—the red of richness, opulence, abundance.

And Anarkali Bazaar had all these reds and then some, in unimaginable numbers of hues and textures.

And I loved them all.

Walking through the winding alleys of bangle shops on either side, the chatter, the haggling, the clinking sound of bangles slipped onto wrists, the hum of eager hearts celebrating their finds perfectly matching their outfits, their joy filling the electric air. Every Eid, my soul would dance with the dance of the bangles.

Eid in Canada had always been different. I remember my first Eid. Working at a call centre, I had approached Madeline, my boss, to have a day off to celebrate. There was no bangle market to go to, or cousins to laugh with, or street vendors to haggle with. There were no rooftops to dance on, eidi to collect from our elders and pass on to our little cousins. There was no laughter, no love to celebrate.

But it was Eid. And I had to honour it. So, I had carefully rehearsed what I would say. It was not a holiday in Canada, so I had to explain why I needed the day off. It wasn't a holiday most Canadians knew about either, so I had to educate while I attempted my ask.

"Hey, Madeline, I was wondering if I could have a day off next week on either Monday or Tuesday. It's Eid, it's a Muslim celebration. There are two each year, and we usually spend the day starting with an Eid prayer and then visiting friends and eating together and celebrating. It's based on the lunar calendar, so it could fall either on Monday or Tuesday, depending on the sighting of the moon." Despite rehearsing them, I had rushed through my words, my heart racing, a bitter taste in my mouth.

"Oh, interesting! I've never heard of it. Is this the day brown people wear that stuff on their hands?" she had said. I had winced. I knew what she meant. I had nodded.

"Yeah, that's henna. Comes from a plant; the depth of the colour varies depending on how long—"

She interrupted me. "Yeah, that shit stinks. I had a colleague one time who'd show up with it sometimes. Eeesh." She made a face, curdling my insides into a mix of anger, frustration, and disrespect.

"No. It's not a holiday here, so unfortunately, not much I can do," she said and walked away.

I had stood there. Insulted. Disrespected. My traditions had been thrown out without the slightest consideration, conversation, or space.

I had worked that Eid, calling people for donations for community-development initiatives in my newly minted Canadian accent I was still perfecting. With henna on my hands. And bangles on my wrists.

If I ever have employees, they would get to celebrate their holidays, their traditions, their people, I had decided that day. If Canada doesn't, too bad. We from other lands would, I had decided.

Sigh.

Today, as I walk into the mosque for Eid prayers, I know my employees are celebrating their holidays however they wish. They didn't have to beg, be insulted, be rejected, be told they don't belong. They belonged as much as they wanted to.

At the mosque, I am greeted with bright outfits, big grins, candy-stained teeth, little ones in traditional outfits—giggling in their lehngay, kurtay, and sherwaniyan. Some complain about how their outfits itch and how the little mirrors or sequins hurt them, and how they're too hot, or how they can't run in them. Some want more candy; others are bored and want to go home. Yet others complain about how loud it is.

Their mothers patiently work with each one.

I laugh at the chaos of it all and hope someday, these little ones will know what these outfits represent. What their golds, silvers, mirrors, colours speak of.

As we finish the Eid prayer, I hold my hands together, palms up in prayer. I pray for my homeland. I pray for the little ones to always remember where we come from. I pray to someday return to my markets, to my colours, to my people, to my songs, my celebrations.

Later that evening, as I am taking them off my wrists, a black bangle breaks. I close my eyes, and offer gratitude to it, for having been with me. Sharing its fragility, its beauty, its playfulness with me. Though delicate and easily broken, these bangles carry unspoken strength that outshines their fragility.

They carry stories, these bangles. My stories, the stories of my homeland. The stories of our women. Of their strength, their beauty, their resilience to receive, to weave into something beautiful whatever the world throws at them.

They Circle My Wrists

Their glass frames a fragile promise,
burnt oranges of marigolds,
blues of starry summer nights,
silky blacks of the ink on my takhti,
the hues of a land I left
but that lives right here,
circling my skin.

Each bangle holds stories,
of rituals and whispered blessings,
of fingers laced with henna,
of hair adorned with motia,
a world wrapped in blankets of cardamom.

In their soft clinks,
I hear the laughter of my aunties,
the lullabies of my mother,
the wisdom of my grandmother,
the giggles of my cousins,
their voices held in the winds
that once touched fields I can smell,
if I close my eyes.

Does this foreign land have space
for such beauty, such fragility?
Is there room for ways of being,
woven with silks and quiet resilience,
or only for one note, one colour, one beat?

Can it hold their gentle ways,
or is it only open to the bold, the loud, the privileged?
Can it see our resilience as power,
or is it only open to power as rebellion?

I wonder if this place will ever know
the language these bangles speak,
or if I alone must carry their rhythm, their weight,
like a quiet, endless plea to return.
A plea in story, a plea of power,
a plea of beauty in survival,
a plea that is unapologetically mine.

Pellah Roza

The First Fast

It's getting warmer as more and more people pile into the large room. I can feel my heart beating. *I hear you, heart, I know you're excited. I know you're worried. I hear you. I got you.*

This is a big night. And I want it to go well. Though I also don't really know what that means. Will I be able to tell?

I am launching my nonprofit tonight, with a mission to make peace possible through grassroots community initiatives. And to mark the launch, we are doing just that. I have made a feast for 120 people, though if my grandparents have taught me well, there is probably enough food for a couple of hundred people. I want everyone to have their fill and take leftovers home.

We're in our office in an old building that at one point used to be a warehouse. As is typical for heritage buildings in old cities in Canada, they feature tall ceilings, exposed brick, and a whole lot of character.

The brick always gives this room, with exposed ducts along the ceiling and old, beaten-down hardwood floors, a rustic charm that invites awe from visitors to our office.

These bricks, or I suppose any bricks, have always held a special spot in my heart. They take me to the rooftops of Lahore, to the brick kiln Daada jaani used to gather us kids around.

For a moment, my fingers lazily running over one of the bricks, I let my mind wander to the rooftop, to the brick kiln that we would gather around for story time. I wonder if these bricks also carry stories like our bricks used to.

These bricks are different, I know. They're somewhere between a pale ivory to a light beige, with tiny little specks of a lighter brown here and there. They somehow present as more polished, more proper, more refined. I wonder whether if I asked these bricks, would they tell me they also *feel* more polished, more proper, more refined, more civilised, like the people of this land feel when they compare themselves to people from my land? To those of us from the "developing nations"?

I wonder if these bricks have ever heard of my bricks. My bricks with their rich, vibrant deep crimson, which would sometimes be a deep maroon depending on which part of Punjab the clay to make them was harvested from. The bricks of my homeland, which are known to carry prints of the past.

As the story goes, sometime between the tenth and twelfth centuries in Lahore, long before the grandeur of the Mughal Empire graced the region, the city's builders worked with what they had: small, irregular bricks, each handcrafted from clay harvested from the iron-rich, deep-red soils of the land. Each brick was crafted with care and in varying sizes and shapes. These ancient bricks were typically seven to eight inches long, four to five inches wide, and one to two inches thick. The structures built with them were robust yet simple, their imperfections and masterfully puzzled-together bricks masked with thick layers of mortar. Many of these early buildings still stand proud and bold in the Androon Shehar Lahore, the markets in the inner city of Lahore, endearingly unashamed of their quaint asymmetries and mismatched lines.

As centuries flew by, with the arrival of the Mughals to the region came a passion for grand and intricate architecture. The Mughals were known for their majestic forts, elegant palaces, and gardens, and had a bit of a different vision for their buildings. And they required materials that would match their grand ideas. Our quaint mismatched bricks would no longer do. So, brickmaking transformed. Our new bricks were longer, nine to eleven inches in length, about the same width as the old ones at four to six inches, and much wider, going up to three inches. The uniformity allowed for finer, more precise construction, the coming together of more intricate patterns and detailed craftsmanship that became the hallmark of Mughal courtyards.

Then came the British. They loved our bricks, perhaps a little too much, but our bricks needed to be produced more efficiently, in a factory, by people in uniforms, and all bricks had to look the same. Brickmaking transformed again. Our bricks got shorter, wider, and thicker. These made them easier to handle and more suited to the construction methods and architectural styles favoured by the British. Our bricks also met new materials, such as reinforced concrete, and together they became the foundation of an evolving, transforming, adapting, ever-responding landscape.

Today, walking through the narrow streets of the Androon Lahore, you can see the prints of the eras, the prints of the Lahori brickmakers, and if you listen closely, you can hear the stories of these brickmakers through the centuries, their hands moulding the deep-red clay between their fingers. If you watch carefully, you can see buildings that were once a Mughal palace next to one proudly built by the British as the headquarters of the East India Company, each building carrying our sacred bricks, which have quietly listened, watched, and carried our stories.

I look at the pale white bricks in the room we're in and decide these bricks, too, must have a story to tell. Who were the visitors to their land? How had their ancestors been moulded over the years? Were they shaped, and reshaped? What buildings did they become walls in? What stories did they bear witness to? Did they witness love, celebration, beauty, or grief, hardship, and injustice? Did they witness humans honouring each other or finding reasons to hate each other?

They must have seen it all, heard it all, I decide. The happiness, the sorrow, the joy, the confusion, the uncertainty, the curiosity, the delight, the wonder, the complexity of what it means to be human.

As people pile in, someone directs them to the chairs set up for guests.

We have five tall stools in the front, one for me, one for my Israeli Canadian friend Sheryl, one for my Palestinian Canadian friend

Ahmad, one for my Anishinaabe friend Tori Littlechild, and one for Liz, our Scottish Canadian facilitator.

Liz invites all to settle in and invites Tori to start us off in a good way.

Clearing his throat, he says, "I was told there would be food. Nobody told me we had to fast."

His joke sinks in, and the room erupts into laughter. Everyone seems to relax a bit.

"Tobacco"—Tori holds a pouch out of the bundle I have gifted him for being there for this important day—"is one of the four sacred medicines gifted to us by the Creator. I was given this bundle by my sister today to start things off in a good way." He looks at me with a slight nod, and my heart smiles. I place my hand on my heart and nod in gratitude. He turns to the audience and continues. "The Creator gave us tobacco, alongside sweetgrass, sage, and cedar. We honour tobacco, we hold it up as it carries our prayers to the spirits of our ancestors, and to the heart of mother earth, where it has been harvested from in a good way. When we offer tobacco, we are not just giving a piece of a plant; we are giving a part of our spirit, our respect, and our gratitude. So, with that, I welcome you here to our lands, our Indigenous lands, our Turtle Island, and invite you to open your minds, your hearts, your eyes to what we have to share, what my sister has to share, to what we have to say. Miigwetch."

"Chi-Miigwetch, Tori. *Thank you very much*," I say, feeling all the gratitude in the world coming together as I thank him for starting us off in a good way.

Liz then invites Sheryl to go next. Sheryl is a peace activist from the Jewish community in the city. I had met her months ago at an event, her powerful stories settling in me. She reminds me so much of Guddi Baji with her quiet wisdom, and reflections that are earnest and so full of hope.

Sheryl shares a story about her grandmother, Yaffa, and an evening in Jerusalem when they sat on a stone bench overlooking the Old City, the golden light of the setting sun casting long shadows over the ancient walls. The quiet hum of life in the city had filled the air as Sheryl had rested her head on Yaffa's shoulder and asked her for a story.

Yaffa had smiled, though her eyes held a heaviness. She spoke of their ancestors who had walked that land, prayed there, and celebrated there. Jerusalem wasn't just a city, she had explained—it was the heart of their people, a place of belonging.

But there were times, Yaffa had told her, when their people were forced to leave. Driven out from Egypt, Spain, Russia, and Poland simply because they were Jewish. Her gaze had drifted to the Western Wall then. These stones carry our prayers, our tears, and our longing, she had said. Each one holds a story.

She had told Sheryl about her childhood in a village in Europe, shadowed by fear. How her mother had taught her to bake challah and kugel, each recipe becoming a memory, a piece of home.

Their people have been hurt, Yaffa had said, but they had held on to their faith, their stories, and the hope of returning to a place "where we could be safe, where we could be seen."

Sheryl had asked Yaffa how they could keep their story alive, and Yaffa had said, "By sharing it, even when it feels like we're still fighting to be understood."

As Sheryl wraps up her story, an applause runs through the room. Sheryl's story is a beautiful reminder of how we never walk alone—we continue the journeys of our ancestors and carve the paths for our little ones so they can live their dreams, their hopes.

Thanking Sheryl, Liz then invites Ahmad to go next.

I have had the honour of listening to Ahmad many times. He reminds me of my brothers back in the homeland, and I am so grateful for his presence. Ahmad adjusts his keffiyeh and begins.

Ahmad's story is about his grandfather, Jiddo, and the olive trees of their village in Palestine. Ahmad must have been six or seven, sitting with Jiddo on a worn stone wall at the edge of their family's grove. Ahmad had asked Jiddo to tell him a story about where they came from. Jiddo had smiled, but there was a heaviness in his eyes, a shadow that hinted at memories too painful to hold lightly. He touched the soil, letting it slip through his fingers, as if trying to hold on to something lost.

Jiddo told him about a time, many years ago, when their family had lived in another village, one nestled deeper in the hills. It was a place of life and beauty, with olive trees as far as the eye could see—trees their ancestors had tended to for generations. He told Ahmad that those trees were more than just trees; they were history, strength, resilience, and roots.

Ahmad had started to see the trees differently that day. Their twisted trunks, sturdy branches, and silvery leaves seemed alive, as if they, too, carried the weight of Jiddo's story.

When Ahmad had asked what happened to that village, why they had left, Jiddo spoke of the nakba, the catastrophe. Soldiers had come, and in an instant, everything had changed. The olive trees, the fields, their homes—everything they loved—were left behind.

When Ahmad asked him if they would ever go back, Jiddo had replied, "Inshallah. *Allah willing.*" But that even if they didn't, their roots ran deep, deeper than the oldest olive tree. As long as they remembered, as long as they carried their stories, they would still be home.

In that moment, Ahmad realized the olive trees weren't just trees. They were family, history, and belonging, deeply rooted in a land he had never seen but felt in every part of him.

A short silence follows as we let Ahmad's story settle in our bones.

"Shukran, Ahmad." I place my hand on my heart and nod in gratitude, acknowledging him, his story, his courage to keep walking despite the heaviness of each step.

It is now my turn. Since it's Ramadan, the month of fasting for Muslims around the world, I share a story about my pellah roza, my first fast.

Fasting for us is a sacred ritual, custom, requirement, duty. Fasting teaches us self-discipline, self-control, a little bit of compassion, empathy, appreciation for what we have, and an opportunity to express our gratitude.

I am ten years old. It is my first fast, and it's a hot summer day. I am hungry, and restless, and picking fights with my brothers.

I go up to my father and say, "Baba jaani, this is really hard. I can't do it."

To my surprise, he looks up from the newspaper and says, smiling, "You don't have to."

Of course I have to. I can't just not do it. What does he mean?

"Did I ever tell you about a chirri roza, a bird fast?" he asks, wrapping up the newspaper and turning to me.

"Nai, Baba jaani," I say, instantly enchanted by whatever this fast is. Baba jaani has a way with stories.

"Well, a chirri roza is the kind of roza especially for children. You fast till you see a little bird, and as soon as you spot a little bird, you can break your fast. And if you don't see a little bird, you break it when the sun goes to bed. Would you like to go find a bird?"

Would I ever. "Yes!" I shriek with joy, running to put my slippers on.

Soon, we are walking around, looking for birds. In hindsight, there was no way we would have found a bird. It was forty degrees Celsius in the middle of the afternoon. These birds were likely snoozing far away from the heat. But we keep looking.

Our first stop along the journey is at a mithai, a sweets shop. Baba jaani asks Halwaai Uncle to make eight little boxes of miscellaneous sweets. Uncle wraps them in a beautiful deep-burgundy wrapping paper with a stunning dull-gold ribbon with a bow on top.

Baba jaani puts these in two bags and asks me to carry one.

"Who is the mithai for, Baba jaani?" I ask him as we leave the store.

"You'll see, puttar," he says with a smile.

We walk down the street and arrive at our next stop—Agha Uncle's grocery store. We pop in, and I ask Uncle how Afra jaan is doing.

"Good, telling me how to live my life now!" He laughs. I love how easily Agha Uncle laughs. Baba jaani tells Agha Uncle that the reason for our visit today is that I am fasting my first fast and wanted to celebrate that with Agha Uncle. Baba jaani asks me to give a box of sweets from my bag to him.

Taking the box, Agha Uncle looks at me with a huge smile and, placing his hand gently on my head, says, "Oh, mubarak, Emahn jaan! I will enjoy these with much pleasure. You are a brave child. It's hard for little children to fast. Wow!"

I beam with pride. He is right. It *is* hard for us children. I had not put anything in my mouth from the kitchen in hours. Hours! I had patiently watched Mama jaan cook and prepare and had not sampled anything, not tasted anything, not even tried to sneak anything quietly while no one was watching.

"Tashakur, Agha Uncle!" I glow.

Then we walk over to the barbershop of nai uncle, the barber uncle. We do the same thing. We share a beautiful burgundy box, I get congratulated. Then to the dhobi, the laundry uncle's shop. Then to doctor uncle's clinic. Then to kasaai, the butcher uncle's chicken shop.

By the time we are done, it's two hours to sundown.

Baba jaani suddenly stops. "Look, puttar! Chirri!"

I looked up, and sure enough. There's a tiny little chickadee perched on a tree. She must have just learned how to fly. I wonder how brave the little bird had to be to learn how to fly.

"Chirri roza, puttar! You can break your fast now!" said Baba jaani.

I pause, give it some thought, and while my tummy is rumbling in agony, my heart is full. Plus, we have told so many uncles how brave I am, and I want to stay brave. And it wasn't *that* difficult, was it?

I look up at Baba jaani and shake my head slowly.

"Nai, Baba jaani. I'll break my fast when the sun goes to sleep."

"As you wish, puttar ji." He smiles and puts his hand on my head. "You're a brave one, Laachiye." His voice cracks ever so subtly, and his eyes fill with tears.

"I know!" I laugh.

Hand in hand, me hopping, Baba jaani and I head home.

"There, that was my first fast."

I get a beautiful applause from the audience, which I receive in gratitude.

"Today, I break my fast with you all around me, around us," I say, as I gesture to Ahmad, to Sheryl, to Tori, to Liz.

And with that, we invite people to break the fast with us as they hear the Azaan. We play the Azaan on the speaker. For me, it is the first time I have heard the Azaan play out loud since I have arrived in this foreign land, in front of people not from my faith, not from my home, not from my language, not from my lands.

As the first "Allahu Akbar" emerges, a beautiful hush falls over the guests. The muezzin's voice is strong yet gentle, rising and falling in a pattern that is both familiar and comforting.

The room embraces the solemn beauty of the Azaan. The words seem to float in the air, making their way around, touching each person ever so tentatively, curiously, cautiously. With his voice, I float between home and these foreign lands I walk on. Between knowing and not knowing. Between curiosity and certainty. Between belonging and not belonging.

As the final words—"la illaaha ill'Allah"—fade, the room remains quiet for a moment, holding on to the peace and solemnity brought by the call to prayer.

"It's okay to breathe," I whisper loudly, an invitation to all who seem to have held their breath to honour the sacred call. Laughter erupts.

We break our fast.

We eat together. We trade stories from our homes, from our courtyards, our rooftops, our kitchens, our playgrounds, our fields, our stone benches, our ancient walls, our ancestors.

Later that night, after everyone has left, I take a moment to honour these white bricks.

They're certainly not my red bricks, but these white bricks have now borne witness to, heard, the stories of the hosts of these foreign lands—an Anishinaabe storyteller, a Palestinian Muslim brother, an Israeli Jewish sister, a crazy-haired Punjabi Kashmiri girl—and have felt the melody of the Azaan.

Perhaps, just perhaps, like the red bricks from my homeland, these white bricks, too, can hold stories.

My Gajarah

On my wrists rests my motia,
its scent a quiet murmur,
pulling me back to my soils.
Petals white as dawn, soft as my fields,
holding me steady, reminding me
of my lands, where the roots run deep,
the air thick with stories and memories
and songs that hum my name in every note.

On my wrist rests my gulab,
each shade, each petal,
a language of love
I learn the hard way,
love that shelters and stings,
love that binds, love that sets free,
love that aches in every cell of my bones,
love that carves tenderness
I didn't know I longed for.

On my wrist rests my genda,
hues of gold and orange,
roots clinging to the earth like a memory
for those who've known fire
and still choose to rise,
season after season, scarred,
bruised, yet standing tall.

On my wrist rests my gajarah,
my motia, my gulab,
my genda
held in a thread that pulls them together,
as I walk through lands not mine,
with roots not mine, ways not mine,
that unfold before me, that undo me.

In each step, this place humbles me,
reminds me to be more human,
to carry pieces of many worlds,
to know that in these imperfect lands,
I find fragments of my own,
fragile, fierce, and fully alive.

Epilogue

There once was a rani who was struck by grief at the loss of her daughter, at the loss of her home, her people, her land, her songs, her winds, her motia, her gulab, her genda.

One night, she is woken up by Ayah, a grandmother.

"Come," says Ayah, transforming into a child, surrounded by lights, the playful sort at a carnival.

Rani follows her, carefully, cautiously. *Who is this child?* she wonders.

There is a playful spirit to this child. Is this her daughter? Can it *be* her daughter? Rani shakes the thought.

It can't be. Her daughter is long gone.

Yet something about this playful spirit draws her. Rani follows it through the carnival, and before she knows it, she is standing at the foot of a mountain. Standing firm in the mountain are grandmothers as old as time. A dozen of them. Wearing stunning blacks, reds, and golds, they are singing the songs of Rani's ancestors. The blacks they wear have the depth of many nights. Their reds hold the mystery of many lives. Their golds carry the warmth of seven moons.

"Do you sing?" Ayah asks Rani.

"I do, but I'm always worried it'll break when I hit the higher notes," Rani says quietly.

"My silly girl, it is when the voice breaks that it touches the divine, so sing. Sing like you're reaching the divine."

"I will try," says Rani softly. "I want to meet the other grandmothers. I miss mine so much. She was my wisdom."

Suddenly, all the grandmothers stop singing and look at each other, and then at Rani, confused.

"Come with us," they say, their melodies weaving into one.

They gather around Rani, as they together float, Rani in their midst, as if being carried by them. Humming the songs of Rani's ancestors, they first take Rani to the depths of the oceans, picking little stars that sit along the dark ocean floor, collecting them as they go.

As they move up from the oceans towards the skies, their blacks turn to blues to silver. Their reds turn to oranges to fuchsia to fire. Their golds turn to sparkling stardust that follows them, swirling and trailing behind them.

Rani realises the grandmothers are growing in number as they move. Each star they had picked from the ocean bed transforms into another grandmother.

Who are they? Rani wonders.

As they float up to the skies, they pick up more stars along the way, each transforming into another grandmother. Some trailing stardust playfully becomes little flowers in their silvery hair.

Before Rani knows it, she is surrounded by hundreds of grandmothers. They stretch across the cosmos, as far as Rani's eyes can see. Together, they float into the most ancient part of the cosmos, the heart of it. Sparkling, shimmering, with stardust at their feet, they enter the brilliant palace together.

And then they stop. And silence takes over. Silence so deep Rani wonders if she has lost the ability to hear, silence so dark Rani wonders if she has lost her sight.

Ayah walks up to Rani and takes her hand.

"Come, we have to show you something," she says, with a gentleness so soft it floats through every little nook, every hidden corner of Rani's being.

Ayah leads Rani to a wall. There is something on the wall covered in a twinkling white sheet.

"Go on, look. Look closely," Ayah says.

With hands that tremble, Rani slowly removes the sheet.

And there on the wall is a mirror. Rani's breath catches.

The woman in the mirror is stunning. Her hair flows like the galaxies of the cosmos, stardust held in every strand. She has a million wrinkles on her face, around her eyes, each wrinkle a lifetime of stories, of lessons, of beauty like Rani has never seen before.

Rani realises she has stopped breathing.

"But that's me," she says, her voice trembling. "It can't be."

"It is. It *is* you. You are a grandmother," they sing together.

Rani looks at Ayah, and Ayah nods with a warmth that courses through Rani.

Tears run down Rani's wrinkles, weaving themselves with every beautiful line that holds tales from her lives across the cosmos.

Something stirs deep within her then, a curiosity wrapped in worry. *But I couldn't even birth my daughter; how can I be a grandmother?* Rani wonders.

And then, as if the cosmos splits open to reveal the most powerful of its magic, she steps forward.

Zoya.

Zoya's curls flow like a young river learning how to dance to the rhythm of the mountains she plays with. Her eyes are the brown that comes together when all the colours blend and hold each other in love. Her eyes sparkle and twinkle and shine as if holding the most mischievous of secrets.

Her smile is the smile of a million stars being born.

"Zoya jaan, why didn't you stay? I'm not sure I even held you," cries Rani.

"Oh, Ma, you've always held me; you carried me for *me*," she says softly, holding Rani's gaze.

And there, deep in the cosmos, Rani holds her Zoya for what feels like an eternity, their tears becoming winding rivers that flow down to the heart of mother earth, reaching deep within its soils, quenching the thirst of parched roots, bringing to blooms resting seeds.

And then it is time for Rani to return.

As they stand at the entrance to the cosmos, with her hand placed on her belly, Rani asks fearfully, "But I can't have children. What if I can never give birth again?"

With a wisdom that stretches within everything birthed in the vastness of the cosmos, they reply, "You live across lives, across skies, across lands, across the cosmos. You have carried us, birthed some of us through your womb, some through your heart, some through your words, some through your mind, and many more await in your soul.

"You are a giver of life, in all its beautiful forms," they say.

And so, with a heart filled with the love of a million lives, a soul as ancient as the cosmos itself, Rani floats across the skies, singing songs with a voice that crackles, with a voice that touches the divine, songs as ancient as time, protecting daughters and mothers, and sisters, and little ones learning to sing.

For all the lives to come.

Acknowledgments

This novel is a culmination of heart work, and gosh, such hard work. And no hard work is ever solo work. None of this would have been possible without the incredible people I get to share this universe with.

To my husband, Donovan, my best friend, my greatest cheerleader, my partner in all things life and beyond—thank you for the gift of space to grieve and grow, Chanda. For the care to soften, the love to thrive, and the safety to simply be. Thank you for trying to understand me and maintaining that mystery is your vibe! It's so very gracious of you. Thank you for holding me with patience and kindness, for walking alongside me, and for always finding reasons to laugh together. Thank you for bringing Julia, Keziah, and Sam into our lives. You three kids and your beautiful partners are my soul, my ground, and my skies. I love you all so very much.

Thank you to my lovely Pops Clint and Ma Pearl and sista Heidi for being my little village in this foreign land.

To my beautiful and absolutely kickass parents, Sadiq and Munazza—thank you for your relentless drive to support me, no matter what, and for always cheering me on with an unwavering belief in me. I'd always ask for you to be my parents—in every life.

To my outrageously handsome and hilarious brothers, Waqas and Naqash—thank you for the laughter during the darkest of times, which carried me through life's storms. Thank you for standing by me, like the mountains of the homeland. Let's always keep the shah'per double spirit alive! May I always reserve the right to call you both khottay.

To my book coach, Scott Martin—thank you for your patience and compassion, for throwing yourself so beautifully at this, for holding space for difficult conversations, for powerful journeys, for guiding me skillfully through the many trauma learnings we unpacked together. Thank you, Martin and Jill, for welcoming me to your beautiful farm, your home, and your beautiful family. Thank you for bringing so many beautiful souls together—Nicole, Chris, Tony, and Luz—as we all braided our healing journeys.

To my sounding board, Meaghan Morrish, thank you for sharing your beautiful mind and for holding space for me to share and celebrate the beauty of my world.

To my dearest Naina jaan, Ehan jaan, Maazo jaan, Qeeno jaan, and Insha jaan—thank you for the gentleness with which you call me Fufu. You soften me every day with the love you pour into my life. Always honour the mothers who have brought you into this world—Ana jaan, Maham jaan, Kaneez jaan—and the mothers who guide you as you journey through life.

To my very dear friends, Jennie, Leanna, Gabrielle, and Mahnoor—thank you for being my circle of joy. May we always find reasons to laugh together. Life would be quite bland without you.

To my publisher, Girl Friday Books! Thank you for bringing together such a brilliant team of folks who knew how to hold these words in care, while also bringing them to the world in a beautiful way. Thank you, Christina, Kristin, and Katie for your patience with me as I learned so many cool things through this process. Thank you, Diana, for pouring love and kindness into the developmental edit process—you have been such an amazing teacher! Thank you, Reshma and team, for holding space and actively finding ways to honour my languages—I had no idea the editing process could feel so meaningful and be fun!

To my crew, team Full Swing, team Strategic Charm, Courtney, and Carly, thank you for walking this adventurous path with me. A special shoutout to team ExCons at Narratives for jumping into action with your creative brilliance every time I sent a smoke signal!

To all the Elders in Canada who have guided me over the years with wisdom so vast it feels like I am entering my first day of school every time I sit with you—thank you for showing me the power of listening, learning, and leaning into humility. Thank you for welcoming me in these lands to learn how to walk alongside you.

To my ancestors—thank you for showing me the endless faces of life, for showing me how to honour the chhoti chhoti khushiyan—the little little joys. Thank you for your resilience, for your stories, for the power of curiosity, for the power of humility—for all your teachings etched into my being. Thank you for always watching over me. You are my roots and my branches, the storm and the calm, and everything in between.

To my readers—thank you for journeying with me. If you find even one small thread of beauty in these pages to weave into your own lives—do so boldly, find your voice, your courage, find *you*, beautiful, complicated, unapologetic you. Reclaim yourself, hold yourself, celebrate yourself—and know that I walk with you, humming songs from my homeland as we walk together.

Author's Note

I have spent my life working in spaces where voices have been erased, histories distorted, and pain dismissed. Where systems that claim to empower often fail, burdened despite their claims of intersectionality by their own racial and gender biases. Where survival is instinctual, but healing is a choice—a courageous, defiant choice.

As a global peace negotiator, an environmental planner, an intergenerational survivor of the partition of India and Pakistan, and a newcomer in Canada, my work and life have taken me into spaces of deep listening—where trauma awareness and trauma learning lie at the heart of how we engage with others professionally and personally, how we conduct ourselves, and what approaches we use to bring people together.

This book, *Gajarah*, is my offering to those who have been told they do not belong. To those who have carried their homelands within them when the land beneath their feet was taken away. To those who have been severed from their stories and are now weaving them back together. It is for the daughters who have learned too soon the weight of responsibility. For the matriarchs who have held entire worlds together with their hands. For the allies carefully looking for ways to walk that do no further harm.

In my work, I have sought to decolonise not just research, policies, and systems but our very ways of knowing, being, and imagining a future where peace is not simply the absence of conflict but a profound ability in societies to have difficult conversations. I have walked alongside communities who have born the weight of colonisation, war, forced displacement, and systemic oppression, and I have witnessed the power of storytelling in reclaiming dignity, identity, and justice. To quote Rumi, "Out beyond the ideas of wrongdoing and rightdoing, there is a field. I'll meet you there." I imagine a future where we can all meet in the field, where peace is not an endpoint but a practice of interweaving our stories and cultivating the field together.

If this book has found you, if it has touched something unnamed within you, I invite you to carry the conversation forward. To sit in the discomfort of history—not with shame, guilt, or burden—but with a curiosity to understand, to imagine beyond what we have been told, and to challenge meaningfully the structures we have inherited.
With a fistful of love, a pinch of rage, and a pot full of reverence,
Somia Sadiq

Song Notes

The lyrics referenced from "Hai O Rabba Naiyo Lagda Dil Mera" were originally performed by Reshma, a legendary Pakistani folk singer known for her hauntingly soulful voice. This song was composed by Ghulam Qadri and Ustad Nathoo Khan. It is included here as a cultural and emotional touchstone under the principle of fair dealing, in tribute to the generational memory and resonance Reshma ji's music continues to carry across borders and time.

The quoted lyrics "Jeena yahan, marna yahan . . ." are from the song "Jeena Yahan Marna Yahan" (1970), with lyrics by Shailendra, music by Shankar-Jaikishan, performed by Mukesh, from the film *Mera Naam Joker*. Used here under the principle of fair dealing for literary and artistic transformation.

The lines "Challa nau nau theve . . ." are drawn from Punjabi folk traditions, passed down orally through generations. They are included here as a tribute to the collective cultural memory and wisdom of Punjabi women, whose poetry and songs continue to live in our hearts and homes.

The lines "Mehroom-e-tamasha ko phir deeda-e-beena de, Dekha hai jo kuch maine, auron ko bhi dikhla de" are attributed to Dr. Allama Muhammad Iqbal (1877–1938), a renowned philosopher-poet of South

Asia. These verses are included here for educational and reflective purposes, in homage to Iqbal's enduring legacy of spiritual awakening and visionary thought.

The lines "Lalla lalla lori, doodh ki katori, doodh main patasha, maano karey tamasha" are part of a widely known South Asian lullaby, passed down through oral tradition across generations. As with many folk rhymes, the exact origin and authorship are unknown. These lines are shared here as an homage to the collective cultural memory of caregivers, grandmothers, and mothers whose songs continue to cradle generations into comfort and rest.

Author Q&A

Please tell us a little about yourself and your book.

I'm a peace negotiator by day, a writer by heart, and someone who firmly believes that cardamom chai, jasmine, and storytelling can basically heal most things! *Gajarah* is my debut novel—a poetic intergenerational story about grief, memory, and the little kid inside us all who just wants to be seen, be adored, and maybe dance in the rain. It's about healing—not the neat stick-to-a-schedule kind, but the messy, sloppy, magical kind. At its core, *Gajarah* is a love letter to anyone who's ever longed for home—even if they couldn't quite name what home means to them.

What was the inspiration or spark behind writing *Gajarah*?

I wrote *Gajarah* because I needed to find language for what lives in the in-between—between cultures, between homelands, between generations. To me, memory is an act of resistance, and storytelling is a beautiful form of return. This book is stitched from my own journey as a daughter of migration, a witness to trauma and resilience, and a woman who walks alongside others in their search for home, healing, and wholeness.

What do you hope readers take away from *Gajarah* after they've read the last page?

That healing is not linear—it begins to unfold the moment we turn towards the little kid within us with tenderness, adoration, and care. When we stop trying to fix that kid, silence them, and instead sit beside them, braid their hair, let them dance, cry, laugh, and be, we start feeling the magic of healing. Because when that kid feels safe, seen, and celebrated, they don't just soften, they start to love us back. And in that sacred exchange, we remember who we were before the world told us to forget. *Gajarah* invites readers into that space of return: to memory, to body, to voice, and to the inner child who always knew the way home. Through *Gajarah*, I hope to invite my readers to own their healing journey.

How long did it take you to write *Gajarah*?

In a lot of ways, *Gajarah* has been in my being for a very long time. Writing it in earnest took about a year.

How did you develop the characters?

The characters in *Gajarah* came to me more like visitors than inventions. They arrived with their own rhythms, wounds, and wisdom—and my job was to listen. Some were inspired by people I've met in life: elders who carry entire histories in their silence, aunties with fierce hearts and even fiercer eyebrows, and little girls who feel everything all at once! So I didn't so much "create" them as I remembered them. They emerged through story work, memory, and moments where parts of *me* met them on the page.

What has been the most rewarding experience of publishing your debut novel?

Receiving messages from my readers that say they feel seen, that *Gajarah* has equipped them with language to understand themselves and the world around them!

What are some of your favorite books?

I love Alka Joshi's The Jaipur Trilogy and Arundhati Roy's *The God of Small Things*. I am also a huge fan of Nikita Gill's radiant blend of poetry and poetic prose, which is a beautiful braid of empowerment and softness. *Braiding Sweetgrass* by Robin Wall Kimmerer is another book that sings to me with its love and reverence for mother nature and her gifts.

Did you always want to be an author?

I have been writing since a very young age—poems, short stories, reflections, little notes to myself of lessons I've picked up along the way. So in a way, perhaps. Yes, I suppose I've always wanted to be an author!

Do you have any advice for people who want to be writers?

Start small. Start journaling. Start recording little voice notes. Write about what you see, what you feel, write about what else might be happening that you don't see. A few lines. Honour your own creative process and give yourself permission to accept that your process is unique to you. Being kind to yourself is the most important thing you can do for yourself as a writer.

Can you share what you're working on now?

I am so deeply appreciative of engaging in the incredible conversations that *Gajarah* has sparked, and I am also working on my next book, *Baaliyan*!

Will you come to my book club?

I get this request a lot. I would love to speak at your book club. If you are interested in having me at your book club (in person or virtually), please contact me through the form on my website: www.somiasadiq.com.

Gajarah Book Club Discussion Questions

THE NOT-SO-DANGEROUS QUESTIONS

1. Which elder in the story felt familiar to you? Did they remind you of someone you love (or miss)?
2. Which flower or natural symbol in the book are you most drawn to, and why? (Jasmine, marigold, cedar, stars, etc.)
3. What is your relationship with colours like? What feelings do they evoke for you?
4. If you could spend a day with Emahn, what would you ask her? What do you think she might say?
5. What three words would you use to describe how you felt after reading Gajarah? No wrong answers—just say what comes up.

THE DEFINITELY DANGEROUS QUESTIONS

1. What does home mean to you? Have you ever felt far away from it?
2. How has grief shaped who you are today? Is there a story, spoken or unspoken, that still lives inside you?
3. How did Emahn's relationship with forgiveness sit with you? What is your relationship with forgiveness like?

4. What does resilience look like in your family's story? Is there a part of that story you're still trying to understand or make peace with?
5. When was the last time you felt like you truly belonged—to a place, a person, a moment? What did that feel like in your body?

FINAL QUESTION: AN INVITATION

If you could whisper one thing to the little child in you—the one still carrying questions, wonder, and bruises—what would you say? And what do you think they've been waiting to hear?

About the Author

© Chantelle Dione Enns

Somia Sadiq is an award-winning entrepreneur, global peace negotiator, and visionary leader in conflict transformation strategies. As the founder of Narratives, an award-winning planning firm; of Kahanee, a nonprofit amplifying storytelling for peacebuilding; and of Ravayat, a nonprofit amplifying ancestral conflict resolution and dialogue systems in Pakistan, she pioneers trauma-informed, strength-based approaches to leadership, governance, and social change.

With ancestral roots in post-colonial Punjab and Kashmir, Somia brings a relentless drive to decolonise our ways of thinking, knowing, and being. She is a tenacious boundary pusher, advancing peacebuilding and reconciliation efforts across the globe. A dedicated space maker, she actively works to create pathways for more women of colour to assume leadership roles in decision-making spaces, challenging systemic barriers with courage and conviction.

With over two decades of experience in community relations, impact assessment, and decolonised planning, Somia has worked with governments, Indigenous Nations, and organisations globally to bridge divides and foster meaningful, systemic transformation. A highly sought-after keynote speaker, she blends business acumen with cultural wisdom, storytelling, and humour to inspire action in leadership, policy, and peacebuilding spaces.

Recognized for her groundbreaking contributions, Somia was inducted into the College of Fellows of the Canadian Institute of Planners, the highest honour for a professional planner in Canada. She has been featured on major podcasts and media platforms, sharing insights on identity-based conflict resolution, trauma-informed leadership, and the power of narratives in shaping societies.

Somia believes stories have the power to advance diplomacy, break barriers, and promote healing. *Gajarah*, her debut novel, is a testament to that belief and is a lyrical and evocative exploration of resilience, identity, and ancestral wisdom. Through her leadership, speaking engagements, and writing, she continues to challenge the status quo, championing transformative change with an entrepreneurial spirit and an unwavering commitment to justice, reconciliation, and the power of human connection.